A GREAT MAN

WORKS BY ARNOLD BENNETT

NOVELS

A Man from the North
Anna of the Five Towns
Leonora
A Great Man
Sacred and Profane Love
Whom God hath Joined
Buried Alive
The Old Wives' Tale
The Glimpse
Lilian
Mr. Prohack

Helen with the High Hand
The Price of Love
Clayhanger
Hilda Lessways
These Twain
The Roll Call
The Card
The Regent
The Lion's Share
The Pretty Lady
Riceyman Steps

FANTASIAS

The Grand Babylon Hotel
The Gates of Wrath
Teresa of Watling Street

The Loot of Cities
Hugo
The Ghost

The City of Pleasure

SHORT STORIES

Tales of the Five Towns
Elsie and the Child

The Grim Smile of the Five Towns
The Matador of the Five Towns

BELLES-LETTRES

Journalism for Women
Fame and Fiction
How to Become an Author
The Truth about an Author
Mental Efficiency
How to Live on Twenty-four
    Hours a Day
The Human Machine
Things that have Interested Me

Literary Taste
The Feast of St. Friend
Married Life
The Author's Craft
Liberty
Over There
Books and Persons
Self and Self-Management
How to Make the Best of Life

Things that have Interested Me (Second Series)

DRAMA

Polite Farces
Cupid and Common Sense
What the Public Wants
The Honeymoon
The Love Match

The Great Adventure
The Title
Judith
Sacred and Profane Love
Body and Soul

Don Juan

MISCELLANEOUS

Their United State
Paris Nights

Our Women
The Log of the "Velsa"

(In Collaboration with Eden Phillpotts)

The Sinews of War: A Romance
The Statue: A Romance

(In Collaboration with Edward Knoblock)

Milestones
London Life

A GREAT MAN

A FROLIC

BY

ARNOLD BENNETT

METHUEN & CO. LTD.
36 ESSEX STREET W.C.
LONDON

This Book was Originally Published by Messrs. Chatto & Windus
First Published (Fifth Edition, Cr. 8vo), by Methuen & Co. Ltd. 1915
Sixth Edition 1915
Seventh and Eighth Editions 1917
Ninth Edition (Fcap. 8vo, Cheap Form) 1919
Tenth Edition (Crown 8vo, Cheap Form) 1924
Eleventh Edition (Fcap. 8vo) 1925

TO

MY DEAR FRIEND

FREDERICK MARRIOTT

AND TO

THE IMPERISHABLE MEMORY

OF

OLD TIMES

▼

Debt? *Is it not the duty of the State, as well as of the individual, to pay its debts?* In order to support the argument with which I began this communication, perhaps you will permit me, sir, to briefly outline the history of the National Debt, our national shame. In 1688 the National Debt was little more than six hundred thousand pounds. . . ."

After briefly outlining the history of the National Debt, Mr. Knight began a new paragraph thus:

"In the immortal words of Shakspere, wh——"

But at this point he was interrupted. A young and pleasant woman in a white apron pushed open the door

"Henry," she called from the doorway.

"Well?"

"You'd better go now."

"Very well, Annie; I'll go instantly."

He dropped the pen, reduced the gas to a speck of blue, and in half a minute was hurrying along Oxford Street. The hour was ten o'clock, and the month was July; the evening favoured romance. He turned into Bury Street, and knocked like fate at a front-door with a brass tablet on it, No. 8 of the street.

"No, sir. He isn't in at the moment, sir," said the maid who answered Mr. Knight's imperious summons.

"Not in!" exclaimed Mr. Knight.

"No, sir. He was called away half an hour ago or hardly, and may be out till very late."

"Called away!" exclaimed Mr. Knight. He was astounded, shocked, pained. "But I warned him three months ago!"

"Did you, sir? Is it anything very urgent, sir?"

"It's——" Mr. Knight hesitated, blushing. The girl looked so young and innocent.

"Because if it is, master left word that anyone was to go to Dr. Christopher's, 22 Argyll Street."

"You will be sure to tell your master that I came," said Mr. Knight frigidly, departing.

At 22 Argyll Street he was informed that Dr. Christopher had likewise been called away, and had left a recommendation that urgent cases, if any, should apply to Dr. Quain Short, 15 Bury Street. His anger was naturally increased by the absence of this second doctor, but it was far more increased by the fact that Dr. Quain Short happened to live in Bury Street. At that moment the enigma of the universe was wrapped up for him in the question, Why should he have been compelled to walk all the way from Bury Street to Argyll Street merely in order to walk all the way back again? And he became a trinity consisting of Disgusted, Indignant, and One Who would Like to Know, the middle term predominating. When he discovered that No. 15 Bury Street was exactly opposite No. 8 Bury Street, his feelings were such as break bell-wires.

"Dr. Quain Short is at the Alhambra Theatre this evening with the family," a middle-aged and formidable housekeeper announced in reply to Mr. Knight's query. "In case of urgency he is to be fetched. His box is No. 3."

"The Alhambra Theatre! Where is that?" gasped Mr. Knight.

It should be explained that he held the stage in abhorrence, and, further, that the Alhambra had then only been opened for a very brief period.

"Two out, and the third at the theatre!" Mr. Knight mused grimly, hastening through Seven Dials. "At the theatre, of all places!"

A letter to the *Times* about the medical pro-

fession was just shaping itself in his mind as he
arrived at the Alhambra and saw that a piece
entitled *King Carrot* filled the bill.

"*King Karrot!*" he muttered scornfully, em-
phasizing the dangerously explosive consonants in
a manner which expressed with complete adequacy,
not only his indignation against the entire medical
profession, but his utter and profound contempt for
the fatuities of the modern stage.

The politeness of the officials and the prompt
appearance of Dr. Quain Short did something to
mollify the draper's manager of ten years' standing,
though he was not pleased when the doctor insisted
on going first to his surgery for certain requisites.
It was half-past eleven when he returned home;
Dr. Quain Short was supposed to be hard behind.

"How long you've been!" said a voice on the
second flight of stairs. "It's all over. A boy.
And dear Susan is doing splendidly. Mrs Puddiphatt says she never saw such a——"

From the attic floor came the sound of a child
crying shrilly and lustily:

"Aunt Annie! Aunt Annie! Aunt *Annie!*"

"Run up and quieten him!" Mr. Knight commanded. "It's like him to begin making a noise
just now. I'll take a look at Susan—and my first-
born."

CHAPTER II

TOM

IN the attic a child of seven years was sitting up in a cot placed by the side of his dear Aunt Annie's bed. He had an extremely intelligent, inquisitorial, and agnostical face, and a fair, curled head of hair, which he scratched with one hand as Aunt Annie entered the room and held the candle on high in order to survey him.

"Well?" inquired Aunt Annie firmly.

"Well?" said Tom Knight, determined not to commit himself, and waiting warily for a chance, like a duellist.

"What's all this noise for? I told you I specially wanted you to go to sleep at once to-night."

"Yes," said Tom, staring at the counterpane and picking imaginary bits off it. "And you might have known I shouldn't go to sleep after *that*!"

"And here it's nearly midnight!" Aunt Annie proceeded. "What do you want?"

"You—you've left the comb in my hair," said Tom. He nearly cried.

Every night Aunt Annie curled Tom's hair.

"Is it such a tiny boy that it couldn't take it out itself?" Aunt Annie said kindly, going to the

6

cot and extracting the comb. "Now try to sleep." She kissed him.

"And I've heard burglars," Tom continued, without moving.

"Oh no, you've not," Aunt Annie pronounced sharply. "You can't hear burglars every night, you know."

"I heard running about, and doors shutting and things."

"That was Uncle Henry and me. Will you promise to be a good boy if I tell you a secret?"

"I shan't *promise*," Tom replied. "But if it's a good secret I'll try—hard."

"Well, you've got a cousin, a little boy, ever so little! There! What do you think of that?"

"I knew someone had got into the house!" was Tom's dispassionate remark. "What's his name?"

"He hasn't any name yet, but he will have soon."

"Did he come up the stairs?" Tom asked.

Aunt Annie laughed. "No," she said.

"Then, he must have come through the window or down the chimney; and he wouldn't come down the chimney 'cause of the soot. So he came through the window. Whose little boy is he? Yours?"

"No. Aunt Susan's."

"I suppose she knows he's come?"

"Oh yes. She knows. And she's very glad. Now go to sleep. And I'll tell Aunt Susan you'll be a good boy."

"You'd better not," Tom warned her. "I don't feel sure. And I say, auntie, will there come any more little boys to-night?"

"I don't think so, dear." Aunt Annie smiled. She was half-way through the door, and spoke into the passage.

" But are you sure?" Tom persisted.

" Yes, I'm sure. Go to sleep."

" Doesn't Aunt Susan want another one?"

" No, she doesn't. Go to sleep, I say."

" 'Cause, when I came, another little boy came just afterwards, and he died, that little boy did. And mamma, too. Father told me."

" Yes, yes," said Aunt Annie, closing the door. " Bee-by."

" I didn't promise," Tom murmured to his conscience. " But it's a good secret," he added brazenly. He climbed over the edge of the cot, and let himself down gently till his feet touched the floor. He found his clothes, which Aunt Annie invariably placed on a chair in a certain changeless order, and he put some of them on, somehow. Then he softly opened the door and crept down the stairs to the second floor. He was an adventurous and incalculable child, and he desired to see the baby.

Persons who called on Mr. Henry Knight in his private capacity rang at the side door to the right of the shop, and were instructed by the shop caretaker to mount two flights of stairs, having mounted which they would perceive in front of them a door, where they were to ring again. This door was usually closed, but to-night Tom found it ajar. He peeped out and downwards, and thought of the vast showroom below and the wonderful regions of the street. Then he drew in his head, and concealed himself behind the plush portière. From his hiding-place he could watch the door of Uncle Henry's and Aunt Susan's bedroom, and he could also, whenever he felt inclined, glance down the stairway.

He waited, with the patience and the fatalism of infancy, for something to happen.

After an interval of time not mathematically to

be computed, Tom heard a step on the stairs and looked forth. A tall gentleman wearing a high hat and carrying a black bag was ascending. In a flash Tom recollected a talk with his dead father, in which that glorious and gay parent had explained to him that he, Tom, had been brought to his mother's room by the doctor in a black bag.

Tom pulled open the door at the head of the stairs, went outside, and drew the door to behind him.

"Are you the doctor?" he demanded, staring intently at the bag to see whether anything wriggled within.

"Yes, my man," said the doctor. It was Quain Short, wrenched from the Alhambra.

"Well, they don't want another one. They've got one," Tom asserted, still observing the bag.

"You're sure?"

"Yes. Aunt Annie said particularly that they didn't want another one."

"Who is it that has come? Do you know his name? Christopher—is that it?"

"I don't know his name. But he's come, and he's in the bedroom now, with Aunt Susan."

"How annoying?" said Dr. Quain Short under his breath, and he went.

Tom re-entered, and took up his old position behind the portière.

Presently he heard another step on the stair, and issued out again to reconnoitre. And, lo! another tall gentleman wearing another high hat and carrying another black bag was ascending.

"This makes three," Tom said.

"What's that, my little man?" asked the gentleman, smiling. It was Dr. Christopher.

"This makes three. And they only want one.

The first one came ever such a long time ago.
And I can tell you Aunt Susan was very glad when
he did come.

"Dear, dear!" exclaimed Dr. Christopher.
"Then I'm too late, my little man. I was afraid
I might be. Everything all right, eh?"

Tom nodded, and Dr. Christopher departed.

And then, after a further pause, up came another
tall gentleman, high hat, and black bag.

"This is four," said Tom.

"What's that, Tommy?" asked Mr. Henry
Knight's regular physician and surgeon. "What
are you doing there?"

"One came hours since," Tom said. "And they
don't want any more." Then he gazed at the bag,
which was larger and glossier than its predecessors.
"Have you brought a *very* nice one?" he inquired.

"They don't really want another, but perhaps
if it's *very*——"

It was this momentary uncertainty on Tom's part
that possibly saved my hero's life. For the parents
were quite inexperienced, and Mrs. Puddiphatt was
an accoucheuse of the sixties, and the newborn
child was near to dying in the bedroom without
anybody being aware of the fact.

"A very nice what?" the doctor questioned
gruffly.

"Baby. In that bag," Tom stammered.

"Out of the way, my bold buccaneer," said the
doctor, striding across the mat into the corridor.

At two o'clock the next morning, Tom being
asleep, and all going well with wife and child, Mr.
Henry Knight returned at length to his sitting-
room, and resumed the composition of the letter to
the editor of the *Standard*. The work existed as an
artistic whole in his head, and he could not persuade

himself to seek rest until he had got it down in black and white; for, though he wrote letters instead of sonnets, he was nevertheless a sort of a poet by temperament. You behold him calm now, master once more of his emotions, and not that agitated, pompous, and slightly ridiculous person who lately stamped over Oxford Street and stormed the Alhambra Theatre. And in order to help the excellent father of my hero back into your esteem, let me point out that the imminence and the actuality of fatherhood constitute a somewhat disturbing experience, which does not occur to a man every day.

Mr. Knight dipped pen in ink, and continued:

" . . . who I hold to be not only the greatest poet, but also the greatest moral teacher that England has ever produced:

" 'To thine own self be true,
And it must follow, as the night the day,
Thou canst not then be false to any man.'

" In conclusion, sir, I ask, without fear of contradiction, are we or are we not, in this matter of the National Debt, to be true to our national selves?
" Yours obediently,
"A CONSCIENTIOUS TAXPAYER."

The signature troubled him. His pen hovered threateningly over it, and finally he struck it out and wrote instead: "Paterfamilias." He felt that this pseudonym was perhaps a little inapposite, but some impulse stronger than himself forced him to employ it.

CHAPTER III

HIS CHRISTENING

"BUT haven't I told you that I was just writing the very name when Annie came in to warn me?"

Mr. Knight addressed the question, kindly and mildly, yet with a hint of annoyance, to his young wife, who was nursing their son with all the experience of three months' practice. It was Sunday morning, and they had finished breakfast in the sitting-room. Within an hour or two the heir was to be taken to the Great Queen Street Wesleyan Methodist Chapel for the solemn rite of baptism.

"Yes, lovey," said Mrs. Knight. "You've told me, time and again. But oh, Henry! Your name's just Henry Knight, and I want his to be just Henry Knight, too! I want him to be called after you."

And the mother, buxom, simple, and adoring, glanced appealingly with bright eyes at the man who for her epitomised the majesty and perfections of his sex.

"He will be Henry Knight," the father persisted, rather coldly.

But Mrs. Knight shook her head.

Then Aunt Annie came into the room, pushing

Tom before her. Tom was magnificently uncomfortable in his best clothes.

"What's the matter, Sue?" Aunt Annie demanded, as soon as she had noticed her sister's face. And in a moment, in the fraction of a second, and solely by reason of Aunt Annie's question, the situation became serious. It jumped up, as domestic situations sometimes do, suddenly to the temperature at which thunderstorms are probable. It grew close, heavy, and perilous.

Mrs. Knight shook her head again. "Nothing," she managed to reply.

"Susan wants——" Mr. Knight began suavely to explain.

"He keeps on saying he would like him to be called——" Mrs. Knight burst out.

"No I don't—no I don't!" Mr. Knight interrupted. "Not if you don't wish it."

A silence followed. Mr. Knight drummed lightly and nervously on the tablecloth. Mrs. Knight sniffed, threw back her head so that the tears should not fall out of her eyes, and gently patted the baby's back with her right hand. Aunt Annie hesitated whether to speak or not to speak.

Tom remarked in a loud voice:

"If I were you, I should call him Tom, like me. Then, as soon as he can talk, I could say, 'How do, Cousin Tom?' and he could say back, 'How do, Cousin Tom?'"

"But we should always be getting mixed up between you, you silly boy!" said Aunt Annie, smiling, and trying to be bright and sunny.

"No, you wouldn't," Tom replied. "Because I should be Big Tom, and of course he'd only be Little Tom. And I don't think I'm a silly boy, either."

"Will you be silent, sir!" Mr. Knight ordered in a voice of wrath. And, by way of indicating that the cord of tension had at last snapped, he boxed Tom's left ear, which happened to be the nearest.

Mrs. Knight lost control of her tears, and they escaped. She offered the baby to Aunt Annie.

"Take him. He's asleep. Put him in the cradle," she sobbed.

"Yes, dear," said Aunt Annie intimately, in a tone to show how well she knew that poor women must always cling together in seasons of stress and times of oppression.

Mrs. Knight hurried out of the room. Mr. Knight cherished an injury. He felt aggrieved because Susan could not see that, though six months ago she had been entitled to her whims and fancies, she was so no longer. He felt, in fact, that Susan was taking an unfair advantage of him. The logic of the thing was spread out plainly and irrefutably in his mind. And then, quite swiftly, the logic of the thing vanished, and Mr. Knight rose and hastened after his wife.

"You deserved it, you know," said Aunt Annie to Tom.

"Did I?" The child seemed to speculate.

They both stared at the baby, who lay peacefully in his cradle, for several minutes.

"Annie, come here for a minute." Mr. Knight was calling from another room.

"Yes, Henry. Now, Tom, don't touch the cradle. And if baby begins to cry, run and tell me."

"Yes, auntie."

And Aunt Annie went. She neglected to close the door behind her; Tom closed it noiselessly.

Never before had he been left alone with the baby. He examined with minute care such parts of the living organism as were visible, and then, after courageously fighting temptation and suffering defeat, he touched the baby's broad, flat nose. He scarcely touched it, yet the baby stirred and mewed faintly. Tom began to rock the cradle, at first gently, then with nervous violence. The faint mew became a regular and sustained cry.

He glanced at the door, and decided that he would make a further effort to lull the ridiculous agitation of this strange and mysterious being. Bending down, he seized the baby in both hands, and tried to nurse it as his two aunts nursed it. The infant's weight was considerable; it exceeded Tom's estimate, with the result that, in the desperate process of extracting the baby from the cradle, the cradle had been overset, and now lay on its beam-ends.

"Hsh — hsh!" Tom entreated, shooing and balancing as best he could.

Then, without warning, Tom's spirit leapt into anger.

"Will you be silent, sir!" he demanded fiercely from the baby, imitating Uncle Henry's tone. "Will you be silent, sir!" He shook the infant, who was astounded into a momentary silence.

The next thing was the sound of footsteps approaching rapidly along the passage. Tom had no leisure to right the cradle; he merely dropped the baby on the floor by the side of it, and sprang to the window.

"You naughty, naughty boy!" Aunt Annie shrieked. "You've taken baby out of his cradle! Oh, my pet! my poor darling! my mumsy! Did they, then?"

"I didn't! I didn't!" Tom asserted passionately. "I've never stirred from here all the time you were out. It fell out itself!"

"Oh!" screamed Aunt Annie. "There's a black place on his poor little forehead!"

In an instant the baby's parents were to the rescue, and Tom was declaring his innocence to the united family.

"It fell out itself!" he repeated; and soon he began to think of interesting details. "I saw it. It put its hand on the edge of the cradle and pulled up, and then it leaned to one side, and then the cradle toppled over."

Of course the preposterous lie was credited by nobody.

"There's one thing!" said Mrs. Knight, weeping for the second time that morning. "I won't have him christened with a black forehead, that I won't!"

At this point, Aunt Annie, who had scurried to the kitchen for some butter, flew back and anointed the bruise.

"It fell out itself!" Tom said again.

"Whatever would the minister think?" Mrs. Knight wondered.

"It fell out itself!" said Tom.

Mr. Knight whipped Tom, and his Aunt Annie put him to bed for the rest of the day. In the settled opinion of Mrs. Knight, Tom was punished for attempting to murder her baby. But Mr. Knight insisted that the punishment was for lying. As for the baptism, it had necessarily to be postponed for four weeks, since the ceremony was performed at the Great Queen Street Chapel only on the first Sunday in the month.

"I never touched it!" Tom asseverated solemnly the next day. "It fell out itself!"

And he clung to the statement, day after day, with such obstinacy that at length the three adults, despite the protests of reason, began to think that conceivably, just conceivably, the impossible was possible—in regard to one particular baby. Mrs. Knight had often commented on the perfectly marvellous muscular power of her baby's hand when it clutched hers, and signs were not wanting to convince the parents and the aunt that the infant was no ordinary infant, but indeed extraordinary and wonderful to the last degree.

On the fourth day, when Tom had asserted for about the hundredth time, "It fell out itself," his Aunt Susan kissed him and gave him a sweetmeat. Tom threw it away, but in the end, after much coaxing, he consented to enjoy it. Aunt Susan detected the finger of Providence in recent events, and one night she whispered to her husband: 'Lovey, I want you to call him what you said."

And so it occurred, at the christening, that when the minister leaned over the Communion-rail to take the wonder-child from its mother's arms, its father whispered into the minister's ear a double name.

"Henry Shakspere——" began the minister with lifted hand.

And the baby smiled confidently upwards.

CHAPTER IV

AGED TWELVE

"QUICK! He's coming!"

It was Aunt Annie who uttered the dramatic whisper, and as she did so she popped a penknife on to an empty plate in front of an empty chair at the breakfast-table. Mr. Knight placed a silver watch and also, separately, a silver chain by the side of the weapon; and, lastly, Mrs. Knight had the happy inspiration of covering these articles with the empty slop-basin.

The plotters sat back in their chairs and tried to keep their guilty eyes off the overturned basin. "Two slices, Annie?" said Mr. Knight in a loud tone, elaborately casual. "Yes, please," said Aunt Annie. Mrs. Knight began to pour out coffee. They all three looked at each other, joyous, naughty, strategic; and the thing of which they were least conscious, in that moment of expectancy, was precisely the thing that the lustrous trifles hidden beneath the basin were meant to signalize: namely, the passage of years and the approach of age. Mr. Knight's hair was grey; Mrs. Knight, once a slim bride of twenty-seven, was now a stout matron of thirty-nine, with a tendency to pant after the most modest feats of stair-climbing; and Aunt Annie, only the other day a pretty girl with a head full of what is wrongly called nonsense, was a spinster—a spinster. Fortunately, they were blind to these obvious facts. Even Mr. Knight, accustomed as he was to survey fundamental truths with the detachment of a philosopher, would have been shocked to learn that his hair was grey. Before the glass, of a morning, he sometimes remarked, in the tone of a man whose passion for candour permits him to conceal nothing: "It's *getting* grey."

Then young Henry burst into the room.

It was exactly twelve years since he had been born, a tiny, shapeless, senseless, helpless, toothless, speechless, useless, feeble, deaf, myopic creature; and now he was a schoolboy, strong, healthy, big, and clever, who could define a dodecahedron and rattle off the rivers of Europe like a house on fire. The change amounted to a miracle, and it was esteemed as such by those who had spent twelve years chiefly in watching it. One evening, in the very earliest stages, while his mother was nursing him, his father had come into the darkened chamber, and, after bending over the infant, had struck a match to ignite a cigar; and the eyes of the infant had blinked in the sudden light. "*See how he takes notice!*" the mother had cried in ecstatic wonderment. And from that moment she, and the other two, had never ceased to marvel, and to fear. It seemed impossible that this extraordinary fragment of humanity, which at first could not be safely ignored for a single instant night or day, should survive the multitudinous perils that surrounded it. But it did survive, and it became an intelligence. At eighteen months the intelligence could walk, sit up, and say "Mum." These performances were astounding. And the fact that fifty thousand other babies of eighteen months in London were similarly walking, sitting up, and saying "Mum," did not render these performances any the less astounding. And when, half a year later, the child could point to a letter and identify it plainly and unmistakably —"O"—the parents' cup was full. The mother admitted frankly that she had not expected this final proof of understanding. Aunt Annie and father pretended not to be surprised, but it was a pretence merely. Why, it seemed scarcely a month since the miraculous child had not even sense enough to take milk out of a spoon! And here he was identifying "O" every time he tried, with the absolute assurance of a philologist! True, he had once or twice shrieked "O" while putting a finger on "Q," but that was the fault of the printers, who had printed the tail too small.

After that the miracles had followed one another so rapidly, each more amazing than the last, that the watchers had unaffectedly abandoned themselves to an attitude of permanent delighted astonishment. They lived in a world of magic. And their entire existence was based on the tacit assumption—tacit because the truth of it was so manifest—that their boy was the most prodigious boy that ever was. He went into knickerbockers. He learnt hymns. He went to school—and came back alive at the end of the first day and said he had enjoyed it! Certainly, other boys went to school. Yes, but there was something special, something indefinable, something incredible, about Henry's going to school that separated his case from all the other cases, and made it precious in its wonder. And he began to study arithmetic, geometry, geography, history, chemistry, drawing, Latin, French, mensuration, composition, physics,

Scripture, and fencing. His singular brain could grapple simultaneously with these multifarious subjects. And all the time he was growing, growing, growing. More than anything else it was his growth that stupefied and confounded and enchanted his mother. His limbs were enormous to her, and the breadth of his shoulders and the altitude of his head. It puzzled her to imagine where the flesh came from. Already he was as tall as she, and up to Aunt Annie's lips, and up to his father's shoulder. She simply adored his colossal bigness. But somehow the fact that a giant was attending the Bloomsbury Middle School never leaked out.

"What's this?" Henry demanded, mystified, as he sat down to breakfast. There was a silence.

"What's what?" said his father gruffly. "Get your breakfast."

"Oh my!" Henry had lifted the basin.

"Had you forgotten it was your birthday?" Mrs. Knight asked, beaming.

"Well, I'm blest!" He had in truth forgotten that it was his birthday.

"You've been so wrapped up in this Speech Day business, haven't you?" said Aunt Annie, as if wishful to excuse him to himself for the extraordinary lapse.

They all luxuriated in his surprise, his exclamations, his blushes of delight, as he fingered the presents. For several days, as Henry had made no reference to his approaching anniversary, they had guessed that he had overlooked it in the exciting preparations for Speech Day, and they had been anticipating this moment with the dreadful joy of conspirators. And now they were content. No hitch, no anticlimax had occurred.

"I know," said Henry. "The watch is from father, and you've given me the chain, mother, and the knife is from Aunt Annie. Is there a thing in it for pulling stones out of horses' hoofs, auntie?" (Happily, there was.)

"You must make a good breakfast, dear; you've got a big day before you," enjoined his mother, when he had thanked them politely, and assumed the watch and chain, and opened all the blades and other pleasant devices of the penknife.

"Yes, mother," he answered obediently.

He always obeyed injunctions to eat well. But it would be unfair to Henry not to add that he was really a most obedient boy—in short, a good boy, a nice boy. The strangest thing of all in Henry's case was that, despite their united and unceasing efforts, his three relatives had quite failed to spoil him. He was too self-possessed for his years, too prone to add the fanciful charm of his ideas to no matter what conversation might be proceeding in his presence; but spoiled he was not.

The Speech Day which had just dawned marked a memorable point in his career. According to his mother's private notion, it would be a demonstration, and a triumphant demonstration, that, though the mills of God grind slowly, they grind exceeding small. For until that term, of which the Speech Day was the glittering conclusion, the surpassing merits and talents of her son had escaped recognition at the Bloomsbury Middle School. He had never reached the top of a form; he had never received a prize; he had never earned pedagogic praise more generous than "Conduct fair—progress fair." But now, out of the whole school, he had won the prize for Good

Conduct. And, as if this was not sufficiently dazzling, he had also taken to himself, for an essay on " Streets," the prize for English Composition. And, thirdly, he had been chosen to recite a Shaksperean piece at the ceremony of prize-giving. It was the success in Composition which tickled his father's pride, for was not this a proof of heredity? Aunt Annie flattered herself on the Good Conduct prize. Mrs. Knight exulted in everything, but principally in the prospective sight of her son at large on the platform delivering Shakspere to a hushed, attentive audience of other boys' parents. It was to be the apotheosis of Henry, was that night!

" Will you hear me, father?" Henry requested meekly, when he had finished the first preparations for his big day, and looked at the time, and cut a piece of skin from the palm of his hand, to the horror of his mother and aunt. " Will you hear me, father?"

(No! I assure you he was not a destestable little prig. He had been brought up like that.)

And Mr. Knight took Staunton's Shakspere from the bookcase and opened it at *Othello*, Act I. scene iii., and Henry arose and began to explain to the signiors of Venice in what manner Desdemona had fallen in love with him and he with Desdemona; how he told Desdemona that even from his boyish days he had experienced moving accidents by flood and field, and had been sold into slavery, and all about the cannibals and the—but he came to utter grief at the word " Anthropophagi."

" An-thro-poph-a-gi," said his father.

" It's a very difficult word, I'm sure," said his mother.

Difficult or not, Henry mastered it, and went on

to the distressful strokes his youth had suffered, and then to Desdemona's coy hint :

> "Upon this hint I spoke—spake, I mean :
> She loved me for the dangers I had passed ;
> And I loved her that she did pity them.
> This only is the witchcraft I have used.
> Here comes the lady ; let her witness it."

"Have a bit of toast, my pet," Mrs. Knight suggested.

The door opened at the same moment.

"Enter Desdemona," said a voice. "Now do go light on the buttered toast, Othello. You know you'll be ill."

It was Cousin Tom. He was always very late for breakfast.

CHAPTER V

MARRONS GLACÉS

AND Tom was always being inconvenient,
always producing intellectual discomfort. On
this occasion there can be no doubt that if
Tom had not come in just then Henry would have
accepted and eaten the buttered toast, and would
have enjoyed it; and his father, mother, and aunt
would have enjoyed the spectacle of his bliss; and
all four of them would have successfully pretended
to their gullible consciences that an indiscretion had
not been committed. Here it must be said that the
Achilles' heel of Henry Shakspere Knight lay in
his stomach. Despite his rosy cheeks and pervading
robustness, despite the fact that his infancy had
been almost immune from the common ailments—
even measles—he certainly suffered from a form of
chronic dyspepsia. Authorities differed upon the
cause of the ailment. Some, such as Tom, diagnosed
the case in a single word. Mr. Knight, less abrupt,
ascribed the evil to Mrs. Knight's natural but too
solicitous endeavours towards keeping up the
strength of her crescent son. Mrs. Knight and
Aunt Annie regarded it as a misfortune simply,
inexplicable, unjust, and cruel. But even Mrs.
Knight and Aunt Annie had perceived that there
was at least an apparent connection between hot

buttered toast and the recurrence of the malady. Hence, though the two women would not admit that this connection was more than a series of unfortunate coincidences, Henry had been advised to deprive himself of hot buttered toast. And here came Tom, with his characteristic inconvenience, to catch them in the very midst of their folly, and to make even Mr. Knight, that mask of stern rectitude, a guilty accessory before the fact.

"It's only this once!" Mrs. Knight protested.

"You're quite right," said Tom. "It's only this once."

Henry took the piece of toast, and then, summoning for one supreme effort all the spiritual courage which he had doubtless inherited from a long line of Puritan ancestors, he nobly relinquished it.

Mr. Knight's eyes indicated to Tom that a young man who was constantly half an hour late for breakfast had no moral right to preach abstinence to a growing boy, especially on his birthday. But the worst thing about Tom was that he was never under any circumstances abashed.

"As nothing is worse than hot toast cold," Tom imperturbably remarked, "I'll eat it at once." And he ate the piece of toast.

No one could possibly blame Tom. Nevertheless, every soul round the table did the impossible and blamed him. The atmosphere lost some of its festive quality.

Tom Knight was nineteen, thin, pale, and decidedly tall; and his fair hair still curled slightly on the top of his head. In twelve years his development, too, had amounted to a miracle, or would have amounted to a miracle had there been anyone present sufficiently interested to observe and believe in it. Miracles, however, do not begin to exist until at least one person believes, and the available credence in the household had been monopolized by Tom's young cousin. The great difference between Tom and Henry was that Tom had faults, whereas Henry had none—yet Tom was the elder by seven years and ought to have known better! Mr. Knight had always seen Tom's faults, but it was only since the advent of Henry that Mrs. Knight, and particularly Aunt Annie, had begun to see them. Before Henry arrived, Tom had been Aunt Annie's darling. The excellent spinster took pains never to show that Henry had supplanted him; nevertheless, she showed it all the time. Tom's faults flourished and multiplied. There can be no question that he was idle, untruthful, and unreliable. In earliest youth he had been a merry prank; he was still a prank, but not often merry. His spirit seemed to be overcast; and the terrible fact came out gradually that he was not "nicely disposed." His relatives failed to understand him, and they gave him up like a puzzle. He was self-contradictory. For instance, though a shocking liar, he was lavish of truth whenever truth happened to be disconcerting and inopportune. He it was who told the forewoman of his uncle's millinery department, in front of a customer, that she had a moustache. His uncle thrashed him. "She *has* a moustache, anyhow!" said this Galileo when his uncle had finished. Mr. Knight wished Tom to go into the drapery, but Tom would not. Tom wanted to be an artist; he was always drawing. Mr. Knight had only heard of artists; he had never seen one. He thought Tom's desire for art was mere wayward naughtiness. However, after Tom had threatened to burn the house down if he was not allowed to go to an art school, and had carried out his threat so far as to

set fire to a bale of cotton goods in the cellar,
Mr. Knight yielded to the whim for the sake of
peace and a low temperature. He expansively
predicted ultimate disaster for Tom. But at the
age of eighteen and a half, Tom, with his habit of
inconvenience, simply fell into a post as designer
to a firm of wholesale stationers. His task was to
design covers for coloured boxes of fancy notepaper,
and his pay was two guineas a week. The richness
of the salary brought Mr. Knight to his senses; it
staggered, sobered, and silenced him. Two guineas
a week at eighteen and a half! It was beyond the
verge of the horizons of the drapery trade. Mr.
Knight had a shopwalker, aged probably thirty-
eight and a half, who was receiving precisely two
guineas a week, and working thirty hours a week
longer than Tom.

On the strength of this amazing two guineas,
Tom, had he chosen, might easily have regained
the long-lost esteem of his relatives. But he did
not choose. He became more than ever a mystery
to them, and a troubling mystery, not a mystery
that one could look squarely in the face and then
pass by. His ideals, if they could be called ideals,
were always in collision with those of the rest of
the house. Neither his aunts nor his uncle could
ever be quite sure that he was not enjoying some
joke which they were not enjoying. Once he had
painted Aunt Annie's portrait. "Never let me see
that thing again!" she exclaimed when she beheld
it complete. She deemed it an insult, and she was
not alone in her opinion. "Do you call this art?"
said Mr. Knight. "If this is art, then all I can say
is I'm glad I wasn't brought up to understand art,
as you call it." Nevertheless, somehow the painting
was exhibited at South Kensington in the national

competition of students' works, and won a medal. "Portrait of my Aunt," Tom had described it in the catalogue, and Aunt Annie was furious a second time. "However," she said, "no one'll recognize me, that's one comfort!" Still, the medal weighed heavily; it was a gold medal. Difficult to ignore its presence in the house!

Tom's crowning sin was that he was such a bad example to Henry. Henry worshipped him, and the more Tom was contemned the more Henry worshipped.

"You'll surely be very late, Tom," Mrs. Knight ventured to remark at half-past nine.

Mr. Knight had descended into the shop, and Aunt Annie also.

"Oh no," said Tom—"not more than is necessary." And then he glanced at Henry. "Look here, my bold buccaneer, you've got nothing to do just now, have you! You can stroll along with me a bit, and we'll see if we can buy you a twopenny toy for a birthday present."

Tom always called Henry his "bold buccaneer." He had picked up the term of endearment from the doctor with the black bag twelve years ago. Henry had his cap on in two seconds, and Mrs. Knight beamed at this unusual proof of kindly thought on Tom's part.

In the street Tom turned westwards instead of to the City, where his daily work lay.

"Aren't you going to work to-day?" Henry asked in surprise.

"No," said Tom. "I told my benevolent employers last night that it was your birthday to-day, and I asked whether I could have a holiday. What do you think they answered?"

"You didn't ask them," said Henry.

"They answered that I could have forty holidays. And they requested me to wish you, on behalf of the firm, many happy returns of the day."

"Don't rot," said Henry.

It was a beautiful morning, sunny, calm, inspiriting, and presently Tom began to hum. After a time Henry perceived that Tom was humming the same phrase again and again: "Some streets are longer than others. Some streets are longer than others."

"*Don't rot*, Tom," Henry pleaded.

The truth was that Tom was intoning a sentence from Henry's prize essay on streets. Tom had read the essay and pronounced it excellent, and till this very moment on the pavement of Oxford Street Henry had imagined Tom's verdict to be serious. He now knew that it was not serious.

Tom continued to chant, with pauses: "Some streets are longer than others. . . . Very few streets are straight. . . . But we read in the Bible of the street which is called Straight. . . . Oxford Street is nearly straight. . . . A street is what you go along. . . . It has a road and two footpaths."

Henry would have given his penknife not to have written that essay. The worst of Tom was that he could make anything look silly without saying that it was silly—a trick that Henry envied.

Tom sang further: "In the times before the French Revolution the streets of Paris had no pavements. . . . *e.g.* they were all road. . . . It was no infrequent occurrence for people to be maimed for life, or even seriously injured, against walls by passing carriages of haughty nobles."

"I didn't put 'haughty,'" Henry cried passionately.

"Didn't you?" Tom said with innocence. "But you put 'or even seriously injured.'"

"Well?" said Henry dubiously.

"And you put 'It was no infrequent occurrence.' Where did you steal that from, my bold buccaneer?"

"I didn't steal it," Henry asserted. "I made it up."

"Then you will be a great writer," Tom said. "If I were you, I should send a telegram to Tennyson, and tell him to look out for himself. Here's a telegraph-office. Come on."

And Tom actually did enter a doorway. But it proved to be the entrance to a large and magnificent confectioner's shop. Henry followed him timidly.

"A pound of marrons glacés," Tom demanded.

"What are they?" Henry whispered up at Tom's ear.

"Taste," said Tom, boldly taking a sample from the scales while the pound was being weighed out.

"It's like chestnuts," Henry mumbled through the delicious brown frosted morsel. "But nicer."

"They are rather like chestnuts, aren't they?" said Tom.

The marrons glacés were arranged neatly in a beautiful box; the box was wrapped in paper of one colour, and then further wrapped in paper of another colour, and finally bound in pink ribbon.

"Golly!" murmured Henry in amaze, for Tom had put down a large silver coin in payment, and received no change.

They came out, Henry carrying the parcel.

"But will they do me any harm?" the boy asked apprehensively,

The two cousins had reached Hyde Park, and were lying on the grass, and Tom had invited Henry to begin the enterprise of eating his birthday present.

"Harm! I should think not. They are the best things out for the constitution. Not like sweets at all. Doctors often give them to patients when they are getting better. And they're very good for sea-sickness too."

So Henry opened the box and feasted. One half of the contents had disappeared within twenty minutes, and Tom had certainly not eaten more than two marrons.

"They're none so dusty!" said Henry, perhaps enigmatically. "I could go on eating these all day."

A pretty girl of eighteen or so wandered past them.

"Nice little bit of stuff, that!" Tom remarked reflectively.

"What say?"

"That little thing there!" Tom explained, pointing with his elbow to the girl.

"Oh!" Henry grunted. "I thought you said a nice little bit of stuff."

And he bent to his chestnuts again. By slow and still slower degrees they were reduced to one.

"Have this," he invited Tom.

"No," said Tom. "Don't want it. You finish up."

"I think I can't eat any more," Henry sighed.

"Oh yes, you can," Tom encouraged him. "You've shifted about fifty. Surely you can manage fifty-one."

Henry put the survivor to his lips, but withdrew it.

"No," he said. "I tell you what I'll do: I'll put it in the box and save it."

"But you can't cart that box about for the sake of one chestnut, my bold buccaneer."

"Well, I'll put it in my pocket."

And he laid it gently by the side of the watch in his waistcoat pocket.

"You can find your way home, can't you?" said Tom. "It's just occurred to me that I've got some business to attend to."

A hundred yards off the pretty girl was reading on a seat. His business led him in that direction.

CHAPTER VI

A CALAMITY FOR THE SCHOOL

IT was a most fortunate thing that there was cold mutton for dinner. The economic principle governing the arrangement of the menu was that the simplicity of the mutton atoned for the extravagance of the birthday pudding, while the extravagance of the birthday pudding excused the simplicity of the mutton. Had the first course been anything richer than cold mutton, Henry could not have pretended even to begin the repast. As it was, he ate a little of the lean, leaving a wasteful margin of lean round the fat, which he was not supposed to eat; he also nibbled at the potatoes, and compressed the large remnant of them into the smallest possible space on the plate; then he unobtrusively laid down his knife and fork.

"Come, Henry," said Aunt Annie, "don't leave a saucy plate."

Henry had already pondered upon a plausible explanation of his condition.

"I'm too excited to eat," he promptly answered.

"You aren't feeling ill, are you?" his mother asked sharply.

"No," he said. "But can I have my birthday pudding for supper, after it's all over, instead of now?"

Mrs. Knight and Aunt Annie looked at one another. "That might be safer," said Aunt Annie, and she added: "You can have some cold rice pudding now, Henry."

"No, thank you, auntie; I don't want any."

"The boy's ill," Mrs. Knight exclaimed. "Annie, where's the Mother Seigel?"

"The boy's no such thing," said Mr. Knight, pouring calmness and presence of mind over the table like oil. "Give him some Seigel by all means, if you think fit; but don't go and alarm yourself about nothing. The boy's as well as I am."

"I think I *should* like some Seigel," said the boy.

Tom was never present at the midday meal; only Mrs. Knight knew that Henry had been out with him; and Mrs. Knight was far too simple a soul to suspect the horrid connection between the morning ramble and this passing malaise of Henry's. As for Henry, he volunteered nothing.

"It will pass off soon," said Aunt Annie two hours later. The time was then half-past three; the great annual ceremony of Speech Day began at half-past seven. Henry reclined on the sofa, under an antimacassar, and Mrs. Knight was bathing his excited temples with eau de Cologne.

"Oh yes," Mr. Knight agreed confidently; he had looked in from the shop for a moment. "Oh yes! It will pass off. Give him a cup of strong tea in a quarter of an hour, and he'll be as right as a trivet."

"Of course you will, won't you, my dear?" Mrs. Knight demanded fondly of her son.

Henry nodded weakly.

The interesting and singular fact about the situation is that these three adults, upright, sincere, strictly moral, were all lying, and consciously lying.

They knew that Henry's symptoms differed in no particular from those of his usual attacks, and that his usual attacks had a minimum duration of twelve hours. They knew that he was decidedly worse at half-past three than he had been at half-past two, and they could have prophesied with assurance that he would be still worse at half-past four than he was then. They knew that time would betray them. Yet they persisted in falsehood, because they were incapable of imagining the Speech Day ceremony without Henry in the midst. If any impartial friend had approached at that moment and told them that Henry would spend the evening in bed, and that they might just as well resign themselves first as last, they would have cried him down, and called him unfriendly and unfeeling, and, perhaps, in the secrecy of their hearts thrown rotten eggs at him.

It proved to be the worst dyspeptic visitation that Henry had ever had. It was not a mere "attack"—it was a revolution, beginning with slight insurrections, but culminating in universal upheaval, the overthrowing of dynasties, the establishment of committees of public safety, and a reign of terror. As a series of phenomena it was immense, variegated, and splendid, and was remembered for months afterwards.

"Surely he'll be better *now*!" said Mrs. Knight, agonized.

But no! And so they carried Henry to bed.

At six the martyr uneasily dozed.

"He may sleep a couple of hours," Aunt Annie whispered.

Not one of the three had honestly and openly withdrawn from the position that Henry would be able to go to the prize-giving. They seemed to

have silently agreed to bury the futile mendacity
of the earlier afternoon in everlasting forgetfulness.

" Poor little thing !" observed Mrs. Knight.

His sufferings had reduced him, in her vision, to
about half his ordinary size.

At seven Mr. Knight put on his hat.

" Are you going out, father ?" his wife asked,
shocked.

" It is only fair," said Mr. Knight, " to warn the
school people that Henry will not be able to be
present to-night. They will have to alter their
programme. Of course I shan't stay."

In pitying the misfortune of the school, thus
suddenly and at so critical a moment deprived of
Henry's presence and help, Mrs. Knight felt less
keenly the pang of her own misfortune and that
of her son. Nevertheless, it was a night sufficiently
tragic in Oxford Street.

Mr. Knight returned with Henry's two prizes
—*Self-Help* and *The Voyage of the " Fox" in the
Arctic Seas.*

The boy had wakened once, but dozed again.

" Put them on the chair where he can see them
in the morning," Aunt Annie suggested.

" Yes," said the father, brightening. " And I'll
wind up his watch for him. . . . Bless us ! what's
he been doing to the watch ? What *is* it,
Annie ?"

" Why did you do it ?" Mr. Knight asked Tom.

" That's what I can't understand. Why did you
do it ?"

They were alone together the next morning in
the sitting-room. (" I will speak to that young
man privately," Mr. Knight had said to the two
women in a formidable tone.) Henry was still in

bed, but awake and reading Smiles with precocious gusto.

"Did the kid tell you all about it, then?"

"The kid," said Mr. Knight, marking by a peculiar emphasis his dissatisfaction with Tom's choice of nouns, "was very loyal. I had to drag the story out of him bit by bit. I repeat: why did you do it? Was this your idea of a joke? If so, I can only say——"

"You should have seen how he enjoyed them! It was tremendous," Tom broke in. "Tremendous! I've no doubt the afternoon was terrible, but the morning was worth it. Ask Henry himself. I wanted to give him a treat, and it seems I gave you all one."

"And then the headmaster!" Mr. Knight complained. "He was very upset. He told me he didn't know what they should do without Henry last night."

"Oh yes. I know old Pingles. Pingles is a great wit. But seriously, uncle," said Tom—he gazed at the carpet; "seriously——" He paused. "If I had thought of the dreadful calamity to the school, I would only have bought half a pound."

"Pah!" Mr. Knight whiffed out.

"It's a mercy we're all still alive," murmured Tom.

"And, may I ask, sir——" Mr. Knight began afresh, in a new vein, sarcastic and bitter. "Of course you're an independent member of society, and your own master; but may I venture to ask what you were doing in Hyde Park yesterday at eleven o'clock?"

"You may," Tom replied. "The truth is, Bollingtons Limited and me, just me, have had a row. I didn't like their style, nor their manners. So the day before yesterday I told them to go to the devil——"

"You told them to go to the——!"

"And I haven't seen anything of Bollingtons since, and I don't want to."

"That is where you are going to yourself, sir," thundered Mr. Knight. "Mark my words. That is where you are going to yourself. Two guineas a week, at your age, and you tell them——! I suppose you think you can get a place like that any day."

"Look here, uncle. Listen. Mark my words. I have two to say to you, and two only. Good-morning."

Tom hastened from the room, and went down into the shop by the shop-stairs. The cashier of the establishment was opening the safe.

"Mr. Perkins," said Tom lightly, "uncle wants change for a ten-pound note, in gold."

"Certainly, Mr. Tom. With pleasure."

"Oh!" Tom explained, as though the notion had just struck him, taking the sovereigns, "the note! I'll bring it down in a jiffy."

"That's all right, Mr. Tom," said the cashier, smiling with suave confidence.

Tom ran up to his room, passing his uncle on the way. He snatched his hat and stick, and descended rapidly into the street by the house-stairs. He chose this effective and picturesque method of departing for ever from the hearth and home of Mr. Knight.

CHAPTER VII

CONTAGIOUS

"THERE'S only the one slipper here," said Aunt Annie, feeling in the embroidered slipper-bag which depended from a glittering brass nail in the recess to the right of the fireplace. And this fireplace was on the ground-floor, and not in Oxford Street.

"I was mending the other this morning," said Mrs. Knight, springing up with all her excessive stoutness from the easy-chair. "I left it in my work-basket, I do believe."

"I'll get it," said Aunt Annie.

"No, I'll get it," said Mrs. Knight.

So it occurred that Aunt Annie laid the left slipper (sole upwards) in front of the brisk red fire, while Mrs. Knight laid the right one.

Then the servant entered the dining-room—a little simple fat thing of sixteen or so, proud of her cap and apron and her black afternoon dress. She was breathing quickly.

"Please'm, Dr. Dancer says he'll come at nine o'clock, or as soon after as makes no matter."

In delivering the message the servant gave a shrewd, comprehending, sympathetic smile, as if to say: "I am just as excited about your plot as you are."

40

"Thank you, Sarah. That will do." Aunt Annie dismissed her frigidly.

"Yes'm."

Sarah's departing face fell to humility, and it said now : "I'm sorry I presumed to be as excited about your plot as you are."

The two sisters looked at each other interrogatively, disturbed, alarmed, shocked.

"Can she have been listening at doors?" Aunt Annie inquired in a whisper.

Wherever the sisters happened to be, they never discussed Sarah save in a whisper. If they had been in Alaska and Sarah in Timbuctoo, they would have mentioned her name in a whisper, lest she might overhear. And, by the way, Sarah's name was not Sarah, but Susan. It had been altered in deference to a general opinion that it was not nice for a servant to bear the same name as her mistress, and, further, that such an anomaly had a tendency to subvert the social order.

"I don't know," said Mrs. Knight. "I put her straight about those lumps of sugar."

"Did you tell her to see to the hot-water bottle?"

"Bless us, no!"

Aunt Annie rang the bell.

"Sarah, put a hot-water bottle in your master's bed. And be sure the stopper is quite tight."

"Yes'm. Master's just coming down the street now, mum."

Sarah spoke true. The master was in fact coming down the wintry gas-lit street. And the street was Dawes Road, Fulham, in the day of its newness. The master stopped at the gate of a house of two storeys with a cellar kitchen. He pushed open the creaking iron device and entered the garden, sixteen feet by four, which was the symbol of the park in which the house would have stood if it had been a mansion. In a stride he walked from one end to the other of the path, which would have been a tree-lined, winding carriage drive had the garden been a park. As he fumbled for his latch-key, he could see the beaming face of the representative of the respectful lower classes in the cellar kitchen. The door yielded before him as before its rightful lord, and he passed into his sacred domestic privacy with an air which plainly asserted: "Here I am king, absolute, beneficent, worshipped."

"Come to the fire, quick, Henry," said Aunt Annie, fussing round him actively.

It would be idle to attempt to conceal, even for a moment, that this was not Henry the elder, but Henry Shakspere, aged twenty-three, with a face made grave, perhaps prematurely, by the double responsibilties of a householder and a man of affairs. Henry had lost some of his boyish plumpness, and he had that night a short, dry cough.

"I'm coming," he replied curtly, taking off his blue Melton. "Don't worry."

And in a fraction of a second, not only Aunt Annie, but his mother in the dining-room and his helot in the cellar kitchen, knew that the master was in a humour that needed humouring.

Henry the younger had been the master for six years, since the death of his father. The sudden decease of its head generally means financial calamity for a family like the Knights. But somehow the Knights were different from the average. In the first place, Henry Knight was insured for a couple of thousand pounds. In the second place, Aunt Annie had a little private income of thirty pounds a year. And in the third place, there was Henry Shakspere. The youth had just left school; he left

it without special distinction (the brilliant successes
of the marred Speech Day were never repeated),
but the state of his education may be inferred from
the established fact that the headmaster had said
that if he had stayed three months longer he would
have gone into logarithms.   Instead of going into
logarithms, Henry went into shorthand.   And shorthand, at that date, was a key to open all doors, a
cure for every ill, and the finest thing in the world.
Henry had a talent for shorthand; he took to it;
he revelled in it; he dreamt it; he lived for it
alone.   He won a speed medal, the gold of which
was as pure as the gold of the medal won by his
wicked cousin Tom for mere painting.   Henry's
mother was at length justified before all men in her
rosy predictions.

Among the most regular attendants at the Great
Queen Street Wesleyan Chapel was Mr. George
Powell, who himself alone constituted and com-
prised the eminent legal firm known throughout
Lincoln's Inn Fields, New Court, the Temple, Broad
Street, and Great George Street, as "Powells."   It
is not easy, whatever may be said to the contrary,
to reconcile the exigencies of the modern solicitor's
profession with the exigencies of active Wesleyan
Methodism; but Mr. George Powell succeeded in
the difficult attempt, and his fame was, perhaps,
due mainly to this success.   All Wesleyan solicitors
in large practice achieve renown, whether they
desire it or not; Wesleyans cannot help talking
about them, as one talks about an apparent defiance
of natural laws.   Most of them are forced into
Parliament, and compelled against their wills to
accept the honour of knighthood.   Mr. George
Powell, however, had so far escaped both Parliament
and the prefix—a fact which served only to increase

his fame. In fine, Mr. George Powell, within the
frontiers of Wesleyan Methodism, was a lion of
immense magnitude, and even beyond the frontiers,
in the vast unregenerate earth, he was no mean
figure. Now, when Mr. Powell heard of the death
of Henry Knight, whom he said he had always
respected as an upright tradesman and a sincere
Christian, and of the shorthand speed medal of
Henry Shakspere Knight, he benevolently offered
the young Henry a situation in his office at twenty-
five shillings a week, rising to thirty.

Young Henry's fortune was made. He was in
Powells, and under the protecting ægis of the
principal. He shared in the lustre of Powells.
When people mentioned him they also mentioned
Powells, as if that settled the matter—whatever
the matter was. Mr. Powell invested Mrs. Knight's
two thousand pounds on mortgage of freehold
security at five per cent., and upon this interest,
with Henry's salary and Aunt Annie's income, the
three lived in comfort at Dawes Road. Nay, they
saved, and Henry travelled second-class between
Walham Green and the Temple. The youth was
serious, industrious, and trustworthy, and in shorthand incomparable. No one acquainted with the
facts was surprised when, after three years, Mr.
Powell raised him to the position of his confidential
clerk, and his salary to fifty-two shillings and
sixpence.

And then Mr. Powell, who had fought for so
long against meaningless honours, capitulated and
accepted a knighthood. The effect upon Dawes
Road was curious and yet very natural. It was
almost as though Henry himself had accepted a
knighthood. Both Mrs. Knight and Aunt Annie
seemed to assume that Henry had at least con-

tributed to the knighthood, and that the knighthood was in some subtle way the reward of Henry's talent, rectitude, and strenuousness. "Sir George" —those two syllables which slipped smoothly off the tongue with no effort to the speaker—entered largely into all conversations in the house at Dawes Road; and the whole street, beginning with the milkman, knew that Henry was Sir George's—no, not Sir George's confidential clerk, no such thing!— private secretary.

His salary was three guineas a week. He had a banking account at Smith, Payne, and Smiths, and a pew at the Munster Park Wesleyan Chapel. He was a power at the Regent Street Polytechnic. He bought books, including encyclopædias and dictionaries. He wrote essays which were read and debated upon at the sessions of the Debating Society. (One of the essays was entitled: "The Tendencies of Modern Fiction"; he was honestly irate against the stream of trashy novels constantly poured forth by the Press.) He took out a life insurance policy for two hundred and fifty pounds, and an accident policy which provided enormous sums for all sorts of queer emergencies. Indeed, Henry was armed at every point. He could surely snap his fingers at Chance.

If any young man in London had the right to be bumptious and didactic, Henry had. And yet he remained simple, unaffected, and fundamentally kind. But he was very serious. His mother and aunt strained every nerve, in their idolatrous treatment of him, to turn him into a conceited and unbearable jackanapes—and their failure to do so was complete. They only made him more serious. His temper was, and always had been, what is called even.

And yet, on this particular evening when Sarah had been instructed to put a hot-water bottle in his bed, Henry's tone, in greeting his aunt, had been curt, fretful, peevish, nearly cantankerous. "Don't worry me!" he had irascibly protested, well knowing that his good aunt was guiltless of the slightest intention to worry him. Here was a problem, an apparent contradiction, in Henry's personality.

His aunt, in the passage, and his mother, who had overheard in the dining-room, instantly and correctly solved the problem by saying to themselves that Henry's tone was a Symptom. They had both been collecting symptoms for four days. His mother had first discovered that he had a cold; Aunt Annie went further and found that it was a feverish cold. Aunt Annie saw that his eyes were running; his mother wormed out of him that his throat tickled and his mouth was sore. When Aunt Annie asked him if his eyes ached as well as ran, he could not deny it. On the third day, at breakfast, he shivered, and the two ladies perceived simultaneously the existence of a peculiar rash behind Henry's ears. On the morning of the fourth day Aunt Annie, up early, scored one over her sister by noticing the same rash at the roots of his still curly hair. It was the second rash, together with Henry's emphatic and positive statement that he was perfectly well, which had finally urged his relatives to a desperate step—a step involving intrigue and prevarication. And to justify this step had come the crowning symptom of peevishness—peevishness in Henry! It wanted only that!

"I've asked Dr. Dancer to call in to-night," said Aunt Annie casually, while Henry was assuming his toasted crimson carpet slippers. Mrs. Knight was brewing tea in the kitchen.

"What for?" Henry demanded quickly, and as if defensively. Then he added: "Is mother wrong again?"

Mrs. Knight had a recurrent "complaint."

"Well," said Aunt Annie darkly, "I thought it would be as well to be on the safe side. . . ."

"Certainly," said Henry.

This was Aunt Annie's neat contribution to the necessary prevarication.

They had tea and ham and eggs, the latter specially chosen because it was a dish that Henry doted upon. However, he ate but little.

"You're overtired, dear," his mother ventured.

"Overtired or not, mater," said Henry with a touch of irony, "I must do some work to-night. Sir George has asked me to——"

"My dear love," Mrs. Knight cried out, moved, "you've no right——"

But Aunt Annie quelled the impulsive creature with a glance full of meaning. "Sir George what?" she asked, politely interested.

"The governor has asked me to look through his Christmas appeal for the Clerks' Society, and to suggest any alterations that occur to me."

It became apparent to the ladies, for the thousand and first time, that Sir George would be helpless without Henry, utterly helpless.

After tea the table was cleared, and Henry opened his bag and rustled papers, and the ladies knitted and sewed with extraordinary precautions to maintain the silence which was the necessary environment of Henry's labours. And in the calm and sane domestic interior, under the mild ray of the evening lamp, the sole sounds were

Henry's dry, hacking cough and the cornet-like blasts of his nose into his cambric handkerchief.

"I think I'll do no more to-night," he said at length, yawning.

"That's right, dear," his mother ejaculated.

Then the doctor entered, and, for all the world as if by preconcerted action, the ladies disappeared. Dr. Dancer was on friendly terms with the household, and, his age being thirty, he was neither too old nor too young to address Henry as Old Man.

"Hallo, old man," he began, after staring hard at Henry. "What's the matter with your forehead?"

"Forehead?" Henry repeated questioningly.

"Yes. Let's have a look."

The examination was thorough, and it ended with the thrusting of a thermometer into Henry's unwilling mouth.

"One hundred and two," said the doctor, and, smiling faintly, he whispered something to Henry.

"You're joking," Henry replied, aghast.

"No, I'm not. Of course it's not serious. But it means bed for a fortnight or so, and you must go immediately."

The ladies, who had obviously and shamelessly been doing that which they so strongly deprecated in Sarah, came back into the room.

In half an hour Henry was in bed, and a kettle containing eucalyptus was steaming over a bright fire in the bedroom; and his mother was bent upon black-currant tea in the kitchen; and Aunt Annie was taking down from dictation, in her angular Italian hand, a letter which began: "Dear Sir George,—I much regret to say"; and little Sarah was standing hooded and girt up, ready to fly upon errands of the highest importance at a second's notice.

"Sarah," said Mrs. Knight solemnly, when Sarah had returned from the post and the doctor's, "I am going to trust you. Your master has got the measles, but, of course, we don't want anyone to know, so you mustn't breathe a word."

"No'm," said Sarah.

"He never had them as a boy," Mrs. Knight added proudly.

"Didn't he, mum?" said Sarah.

The doctor, whose gift for seriousness was not marked, showed a tendency to see humour in the situation of Sir George's private secretary being down with measles. But he was soon compelled to perceive his mistake. By a united and tremendous effort Mrs. Knight and Aunt Annie made measles august. As for Sarah, she let slip the truth to the milkman. It came out by itself, as the spout of a teapot had once come off by itself in her hand.

The accident policy appeared to provide for every emergency except measles.

CHAPTER VIII

CREATIVE

THE sick-room—all due solemnity and importance must be imported into the significance of that word—the sick-room became a shrine, served by two ageing priestesses and a naïve acolyte. Everything was done to make Henry an invalid in the grand manner. His bed of agony became the pivot on which the household life flutteringly and soothingly revolved. No detail of delicate attention which the most ingenious assiduity could devise was omitted from the course of treatment. And if the chamber had been at the front instead of at the back, the Fulham Vestry would certainly have received an application for permission to lay down straw in the street.

The sole flaw in the melancholy beauty of the episode was that Henry was never once within ten miles of being seriously ill. He was incapable of being seriously ill. He happened to be one of those individuals who, when they "take" a disease, seem to touch it only with the tips of their fingers: such was his constitution. He had the measles, admittedly. His temperature rose one night to a hundred and three, and for a few brief moments his mother and Aunt Annie enjoyed visions of fighting the grim spectre of Death. The tiny round pink spots covered his face and then ran together into a general vermilion. He coughed exquisitely. His beard grew. He supported life on black-currant tea and an atmosphere impregnated with eucalyptus. He underwent the examination of the doctor every day at eleven. But he was not personally and genuinely ill. He did not feel ill, and he said so. His most disquieting symptom was boredom. This energetic organism chafed under the bed-clothes and the black-currant tea and the hushed eucalyptic calm of the chamber. He fervently desired to be up and active and stressful. His mother and aunt cogitated in vain to hit on some method of allaying the itch for work. And then one day—it was the day before Christmas—his mother chanced to say:

"You might try to write out that story you told us about—when you are a little stronger. It would be something for you to do."

Henry shook his head sheepishly.

"Oh no!" he said; "I was only joking."

"I'm sure you could write it quite nicely," his mother insisted.

And Henry shook his head again, and coughed. "No," he said. "I hope I shall have something better to do than write stories."

"But just to pass the time!" pleaded Aunt Annie.

The fact was that, several weeks before, while his thoughts had been engaged in analysing the detrimental qualities of the Stream of Trashy Novels Constantly Poured Forth by the Press, Henry had himself been visited by a notion for a story. He had scornfully ejected it as an inopportune intruder; but it had returned, and at length, to get rid for ever of this troublesome guest, he had instinctively related the outline of the tale over the tea-table. And the outline had been pronounced wonderful. "It might be called *Love in Babylon*—Babylon being London, you know," he had said. And Aunt Annie had exclaimed: "What a pretty title!" Whereupon Henry had remarked contemptuously and dismissingly: "Oh, it was just an idea I had, that's all!" And the secret thought of both ladies had been, "That busy brain is never still."

As the shades of Christmas Eve began to fall, Aunt Annie was seated by the sick-bed, engaged in making entries in the household washing-book with a lead pencil. Henry lay with his eyes closed. Mrs. Knight was out shopping. Presently there was a gentle *ting* of the front-door bell; then a protracted silence; then another gentle *ting*.

"Bless the girl! Why doesn't she answer the door?" Aunt Annie whispered to herself, listening hard.

A third time the bell rang, and Aunt Annie, anathematizing the whole race of servants, got up, put the washing-book on the dressing-table, lighted the gas and turned it low, and descended to answer the door in person and to behead Sarah.

More than an hour elapsed before either sister re-entered Henry's room—events on the ground-floor had been rather exciting—and then they appeared together, bearing a bird, and some mince-tarts on a plate, and a card. Henry was wide awake.

"This *is* a surprise, dear," began Mrs. Knight. "Just listen: 'With Sir George Powell's hearty greetings and best wishes for a speedy recovery!' A turkey and six mince-tarts. Isn't it thoughtful of him?"

"It's just like the governor," said Henry, smiling, and feeling the tenderness of the turkey.

"He is a true gentleman," said Aunt Annie.

"And we've sent round to the doctor to ask, and he says there's no harm in your having half a mince-tart; so we've warmed it. And you are to have a slice off the breast of the turkey to-morrow."

"Good!" was Henry's comment. He loved a savoury mouthful, and these dainties were an unexpected bliss, for the ladies had not dreamt of Christmas fare in the sad crisis, even for themselves.

Aunt Annie, as if struck by a sudden blow, glanced aside at the gas.

"I could have been certain I left the gas turned down," she remarked.

"I turned it up," said Henry.

"You got out of bed! Oh, Henry! And your temperature was a hundred and two only the day before yesterday!"

"I thought I'd begin that thing—just for a lark, you know," he explained.

He drew from under the bed-clothes the household washing-book. And there, nearly at the top of a page, were Aunt Annie's last interrupted strokes:

"2 Ch——"

and underneath:

"LOVE IN BABYLON"

and the commencement of the tale. The marvellous man had covered nine pages of the washing-book.

Within twenty-four hours, not only Henry, but his mother and aunt, had become entirely absorbed in Henry's tale. The ladies wondered how he

thought of it all, and Henry himself wondered a
little, too. It seemed to "come," without trouble
and almost without invitation. It cost no effort.
The process was as though Henry acted merely as
the amanuensis of a great creative power concealed
somewhere in the recesses of his vital parts.
Fortified by two halves of a mince-tart and several
slices of Sir George's turkey, he filled the washing-
book full up before dusk on Christmas Day; and on
Boxing Day, despite the faint admiring protests of
his nurses, he made a considerable hole in a quire
of the best ruled essay paper. Instead of showing
signs of fatigue, Henry appeared to grow stronger
every hour, and to revel more and more in the sweet
labour of composition; while the curiosity of the
nurses about the exact nature of what Henry termed
the dénouement increased steadily and constantly.
The desires of those friends who had wished a
Happy Christmas to the household were generously
gratified.

It was a love tale, of course. And it began thus,
the first line consisting of a single word, and the
second of three words:

"*Babylon!*

"*And in winter!*

"*The ladies' waiting-room on the arrival platform of
one of our vast termini was unoccupied save for the
solitary figure of a young and beautiful girl, who, clad
in a thin but still graceful costume, crouched shivering
over the morsel of fire which the greed of a great
company alone permitted to its passengers. Outside resounded the roar and shriek of trains, the ceaseless ebb
and flow of the human tide which beats for ever on the
shores of modern Babylon. Enid Anstruther gazed
sadly into the embers. She had come to the end of her
resources. Suddenly the door opened, and Enid looked*

up, naturally expecting to see one of her own sex. But it was a man's voice, fresh and strong, which exclaimed : ' Oh, I beg pardon !' The two glanced at each other, and then Enid sank backwards."

Such were the opening sentences of *Love in Babylon*.

Enid was an orphan, and had come to London in order to obtain a situation in a draper's shop. Unfortunately she had lost her purse on the way. Her reason for sinking back in the waiting-room was that she had fainted from cold, hunger, and fatigue. Thus she and the man, Adrian Tempest, became acquainted, and Adrian's first gift to her was seven drops of brandy, which he forced between her teeth. His second was his heart. Enid obtained a situation, and Adrian took her to the Crystal Palace one Saturday afternoon. It was a pity that he had not already proposed to her, for they got separated in the tremendous Babylonian crowd, and Enid, unused to the intricacies of locomotion in Babylon, arrived home at the emporium at an ungodly hour on Sunday morning. She was dismissed by a proprietor with a face of brass. Adrian sought her in vain. She sought Adrian in vain—she did not know his address. Thenceforward the tale split itself into two parts : the one describing the life of Adrian, a successful barrister, on the heights of Babylon, and the other the life of Enid, reduced to desperate straits, in the depths thereof. The contrasts were vivid and terrific.

Mrs. Knight and Aunt Annie could not imagine how Henry would bring the two lovers, each burning secretly the light torch of love in Babylon, together again. But Henry did not hesitate over the problem for more than about fifty seconds. Royal Academy. Private view. Adrian present thereat as a celebrity. Picture of the year, "The Enchantress." He recognises her portrait. She had, then, been forced to sell her beauty for eighteenpence an hour as an artist's model. To discover the artist and Enid's address was for Adrian the work of a few minutes.

This might have finished the tale, but Henry opined that the tale was a trifle short. As a fact, it was. He accordingly invented a further and a still more dramatic situation. When Adrian proposed to Enid, she conscientiously told him, told him quietly but firmly, that she could not marry him for the reason that her father, though innocent of a crime imputed to him, had died in worldly disgrace. She could not consent to sully Adrian's reputation. Now, Adrian happened to be the real criminal. But he did not know that Enid's father had suffered for him, and he had honestly lived down that distant past. "If there is a man in this world who has the right to marry you," cried Adrian, "I am that man. And if there is a man in this world whom you have the right to spurn, I am that man also." The extreme subtlety of the thing must be obvious to every reader. Enid forgave and accepted Adrian. They were married in a snowy January at St. Paul's, Knightsbridge, and the story ended thus:

"*Babylon in winter.*

"*Babylon !*"

Henry achieved the entire work in seven days, and, having achieved it, he surveyed it with equal pride and astonishment. It was a matter of surprise to him that the writing of interesting and wholesome fiction was so easy. Some parts of the book he read over and over again, for the sheer joy of reading.

" Of course it isn't good enough to print," he said one day while sitting up in the arm-chair.

" I should think any publisher would be glad to print it," said his mother. " I'm not a bit prejudiced, I'm sure, and I think it's one of the best tales I ever read in all my life."

" Do you really?" Henry smiled, his natural modesty fighting against a sure conviction that his mother was right.

Aunt Annie said little, but she had copied out *Love in Babylon* in her fine, fair Italian hand, keeping pace day by day with Henry's extraordinary speed, and now she accomplished the transcription of the last pages.

The time arrived for Henry to be restored to a waiting world. He was cured, well, hearty, vigorous, radiant. But he was still infected, isolate, one might almost say *taboo*; and everything in his room, and everything that everyone had worn while in the room, was in the same condition. Therefore the solemn process, rite, and ceremony of purification had to be performed. It began upon the last day of the old year at dusk.

Aunt Annie made a quantity of paste in a basin; Mrs. Knight bought a penny brush; and Henry cut up a copy of the *Telegraph* into long strips about two inches wide. The sides and sash of the window were then hermetically sealed; the register of the fireplace was closed, and sealed also. Clothes were spread out in open order, the bed stripped, rugs hung over chairs.

" Henry's book?" Mrs. Knight demanded.

" Of course it must be disinfected with the other things," Aunt Annie continued.

" Yes, of course," Henry agreed.

"And it will be safer to lay the sheets separately on the floor," Aunt Annie continued.

There were fifty-nine sheets of Aunt Annie's fine, finicking caligraphy, and the scribe and her nephew went down on their knees, and laid them in numerical sequence on the floor. The initiatory "*Babylon*" found itself in the corner between the window and the fireplace beneath the dressing-table, and the final "*Babylon*" was hidden in gloomy retreats under the bed.

Then Sarah entered, bearing sulphur in a shallow pan, and a box of matches. The paste and the paste-brush and the remnants of the *Telegraph* were carried out into the passage. Henry carefully ignited the sulphur, and, captain of the ship, was the last to leave. As they closed the door the odour of burning, microbe-destroying sulphur impinged on their nostrils. Henry sealed the door on the outside with "London Day by Day," "Sales by Auction," and a leading article or so.

"There!" said Henry.

All was over.

At intervals throughout the night he thought of the sanative and benign sulphur smouldering, smouldering always with ghostly yellow flamelets in the midst of his work of art, while the old year died and the new was born.

CHAPTER IX

SPRING ONIONS

THE return to the world and to Powells, while partaking of the nature of a triumph, was at the same time something of a cold, fume-dispersing, commonsense-bestowing bath for Henry. He had meant to tell Sir George casually that he had taken advantage of his enforced leisure to write a book. "Taken advantage of his enforced leisure" was the precise phrase which Henry had in mind to use. But, when he found himself in the strenuous, stern, staid, sapient and rational atmosphere of Powells, he felt with a shock of perception that in rattling off *Love in Babylon* he had been guilty of one of those charming weaknesses to which great and serious men are sometimes tempted, but of which great and serious men never boast. And he therefore confined his personal gossip with Sir George to the turkey, the mince-tarts, and the question of contagion. He plunged into his work with a feeling akin to dignified remorse, and Sir George was vehemently and openly delighted by the proofs which he gave of undiminished loyalty and devotion.

Nevertheless Henry continued to believe in the excellence of his book, and he determined that, in duty to himself, his mother and aunt, and the cause of wholesome fiction, he must try to get it published. From that moment he began to be worried, for he had scarcely a notion how sagaciously to set about the business. He felt like a bachelor of pronounced views who has been given a baby to hold. He knew no one in the realms of literature, and no one who knew anyone. Sir George, warily sounded, appeared to be unaware that such a thing as fiction existed. Not a soul at the Polytechnic enjoyed the acquaintance of either an author or a publisher, though various souls had theories about these classes of persons. Then one day a new edition of the works of Carlyle burst on the world, and Henry bought the first volume, *Sartor Resartus,* a book which he much admired, and which he had learnt from his father to call simply and familiarly —*Sartor.* The edition, though inexpensive, had a great air of dignity. It met, in short, with Henry's approval, and he suddenly decided to give the publishers of it the opportunity of publishing *Love in Babylon.* The deed was done in a moment. He wrote a letter explaining the motives which had led him to write *Love in Babylon,* and remarked that, if the publishers cared for the story, mutually satisfactory terms might be arranged later; and Aunt Annie did *Love in Babylon* up in a neat parcel. Henry was in the very act of taking the parcel to the post, on his way to town, when Aunt Annie exclaimed :

" Of course you'll register it ? "

He had not thought of doing so, but the advisability of such a step at once appealed to him.

" Perhaps I'd better," he said.

" But that only means two pounds if it's lost, doesn't it ? " Mrs. Knight inquired.

Henry nodded and pondered.

" Perhaps I'd better insure it," he suggested.

" If I were you, I should insure it for a hundred pounds," said Aunt Annie positively.

" But that will cost one and a penny," said Henry, who had all such details by heart. " I could insure it for twenty pounds for five-pence."

" Well, say twenty pounds then," Aunt Annie agreed, relenting.

So he insured *Love in Babylon* for twenty pounds and dispatched it. In three weeks it returned like the dove to the ark (but soiled), with a note to say that, though the publishers' reader regarded it as promising, the publishers could not give themselves the pleasure of making an offer for it. Thenceforward Henry and the manuscript suffered all the usual experiences, and the post-office reaped all the usual profits. One firm said the story was good, but too short. (" A pitiful excuse," thought Henry. ' As if length could affect merit.") Another said nothing. Another offered to publish it if Henry would pay a hundred pounds down. (At this point Henry ceased to insure the parcel.) Another sent it back minus the last leaf, the matter of which Henry had to reinvent and Aunt Annie to recopy. Another returned it insufficiently stamped, and there was fourpence to pay. Another kept it four months, and disgorged it only under threat of a writ; the threat was launched forth on Powells' formidable notepaper. At length there arrived a day when even Henry's pertinacity was fatigued, and he forgot, merely forgot, to send out the parcel again. It was put in a drawer, after a year of ceaseless adventures, and Mrs. Knight and Aunt Annie discreetly forbore to mention it. During that year Henry's opinion on his work had fluctuated. There had been moments, days perhaps, of dis-

couragement, when he regarded it as drivel, and
himself as a fool—in so far, that is, as he had
trafficked with literature. On the other hand, his
original view of it reasserted itself with frequency.
And in the end he gloomily and proudly decided,
once and for all, that the Stream of Trashy Novels
Constantly Poured Forth by the Press had killed
all demand for wholesome fiction; he came reluctantly to the conclusion that modern English
literature was in a very poor way. He breathed
a sigh, and dismissed the episode utterly from his
mind.

And *Love in Babylon* languished in the drawer
for three months.

Then, upon an April morning, the following
telegram was received at Dawes Road, Fulham:
"*Please bring manuscript me immediately top left
take cab Henry.*"

Mrs. Knight was alone in the house with Sarah
when the imperious summons of the telegraph-boy
and the apparition of the orange envelope threw
the domestic atmosphere into a state of cyclonic
confusion. Before tearing the envelope she had
guessed that Aunt Annie had met with an accident,
that Henry was dead, and that her own Aunt
Eliza in Glossop had died without making a will;
and these imaginings had done nothing to increase
the efficiency of her intellectual powers. She could
not read sense into the message, not even with the
aid of spectacles and Sarah.

Happily Aunt Annie returned, with her masculine
grasp of affairs.

"He means *Love in Babylon*," said Aunt Annie.
"It's in the top left-hand drawer of his desk.
That's what he means. Perhaps I'd better take
it. I'm ready dressed."

"Oh yes, sister," Mrs. Knight replied hastily.
You had better take it."

Aunt Annie rang the bell with quick decision.

"Sarah," she said, "run out and get me a cab,
four-wheeler. You understand, a four-wheeler."

"Yes'm. Shall I put my jacket on, mum?"
arah asked, glancing through the window.

"No. Go instantly!"

"Yes'm."

"I wonder what he wants it for," Aunt Annie
emarked, after she had found the manuscript and
ut it under her arm. "Perhaps he has mentioned
: to Sir George, and Sir George is going to do
omething."

"I thought he had forgotten all about it," said
Irs. Knight. "But he never gives a thing up,
Ienry doesn't."

Sarah drove dashingly up to the door in a hansom.

"Take that back again," commanded Aunt Annie,
autiously putting her nose outside the front-door.
t was a snowy and sleety April morning, and she
ad already had experience of its rigour. "I said a
our-wheeler."

"Please'm, there wasn't one," Sarah defended
erself.

"None on the stand, lady," said the cabman
rightly. "You'll never get a four-wheeler on a
ay like this."

Aunt Annie raised her veil and looked at her
ister. Like many strong-minded and vigorous
omen, she had a dislike of hansoms which
mounted to dread. She feared a hansom as
hough it had been a revolver—something that
ight go off unexpectedly at any moment and
estroy her.

"I daren't go in that," she admitted frankly.

She was torn between her allegiance to the darling Henry and her fear of the terrible machine.

"Suppose I go with you?" Mrs. Knight suggested.

"Very well," said Aunt Annie, clenching her teeth for the sacrifice.

Sarah flew for Mrs. Knight's bonnet, fur mantle, gloves, and muff; and with remarkably little delay the sisters and the manuscript started. First they had the window down because of the snow and the sleet; then they had it up because of the impure air; and lastly Aunt Annie wedged a corner of the manuscript between the door and the window, leaving a slit of an inch or so for ventilation. The main body of the manuscript she supported by means of her muff.

Alas! her morbid fear of hansoms was about to be justified—at any rate, justified in her own eyes. As the machine was passing along Walham Green it began to overtake a huge market-cart laden, fraught, and piled up with an immense cargo of spring onions from Isleworth; and just as the head of the horse of the hansom drew level with the tail of the market-cart, the off hind wheel of the cart succumbed, and a ton or more of spring onions wavered and slanted in the snowy air. The driver of the hansom did his best, but he could not prevent his horse from premature burial amid spring onions. The animal nobly resisted several hundredweight of them, and then tottered and fell and was lost to view under spring onions. The ladies screamed in concert, and discovered themselves miraculously in the roadway, unhurt, but white and breathless. A constable and a knife-grinder picked them up.

The accident was more amusing than tragic, though neither Mrs. Knight nor Aunt Annie was capable of perceiving this fact. The horse emerged gallantly, unharmed, and the window of the hansom was not even cracked. The constable congratulated everyone, and took down the names of the two drivers, the two ladies, and the knife-grinder. The condition of the weather, fortunately, militated against the formation of a large crowd.

Quite two minutes elapsed before Aunt Annie made the horrible discovery that *Love in Babylon* had disappeared. *Love in Babylon* was smothered up in spring onions.

"Keep your nerve, madam," said the constable, seeing signs of an emotional crisis, "and go and stand in that barber's doorway—both of you."

The ladies obeyed.

In due course *Love in Babylon* was excavated, chapter by chapter, and Aunt Annie held it safely once more, rumpled but complete.

By the luckiest chance an empty four-wheeler approached.

The sisters got into it, and Aunt Annie gave the address.

"As quick as you can," she said to the driver, "but do drive slowly."

CHAPTER X

MARK SNYDER

THREE-QUARTERS of an hour later Henry might have been seen—in fact, was seen by a number of disinterested wayfarers—to enter a magnificent new block of offices and flats in Charing Cross Road. *Love in Babylon* was firmly gripped under his right arm. Partly this strange burden and partly the brilliant aspect of the building made him feel self-conscious and humble and rather unlike his usual calm self. For, although Henry was accustomed to offices, he was not accustomed to magnificent offices. There are offices in Lincoln's Inn Fields, offices of extreme wealth, which, were they common lodging-houses, would be instantly condemned by the County Council. Powells' was such a one—and Sir George had a reputed income of twenty thousand a year. At Powells the old Dickensian tradition was kept vigorously alive by every possible means. Dirt and gloom were omnipresent. Cleanliness and ample daylight would have been deemed unbusinesslike, as revolutionary and dangerous as a typewriter. One day, in winter, Sir George had taken cold, and he had attributed his misfortune, in language which he immediately regretted, to the fact that "that d——d woman had cleaned the windows"—probably with a damp

cloth. "That d——d woman" was the caretaker,
a grey-haired person usually dressed in sackcloth,
who washed herself, incidentally, while washing the
stairs. At Powells', nothing but the stairs was ever
put to the indignity of a bath.

That Henry should be somewhat diffident about
invading Kenilworth Mansions was therefore not
surprising. He climbed three granite steps, passed
through a pair of swinging doors, traversed eight
feet of tesselated pavement, climbed three more
granite steps, passed through another pair of swinging doors, and discovered himself in a spacious
marble hall, with a lift-cabinet resembling a con-
fessional, and broad stairs behind curving up to
Paradise. On either side of him, in place of
priceless works by old masters, were great tablets
inscribed with many names in gold characters. He
scanned these tablets timidly, and at length found
what he wanted, "Mark Snyder, Literary Agent,"
under the heading "Third Floor." At the same
moment a flunkey in chocolate and cream approached
him.

"Mr. Snyder?" asked Henry.

"Third-floor, left," pronounced the flunkey, thus
giving the tablets the force of his authority.

As Henry was wafted aloft in the elevator, with
the beautiful and innocuous flunkey as travelling
companion, he could not help contrasting that
official with the terrible Powellian caretaker who
haunted the Powellian stairs.

On the third-floor, which seemed to be quite a
world by itself, an arrow with the legend "Mark
Snyder, Literary Agent," directed his mazed feet
along a corridor to a corner where another arrow
with the legend "Mark Snyder, Literary Agent,"
pointed along another corridor. And as he pro-

gressed, the merry din of typewriters grew louder
and louder. At length he stood in front of a
glassy door, and on the face of the door, in a
graceful curve, was painted the legend, "Mark
Snyder, Literary Agent." Shadows of vague
moving forms could be discerned on the opalescent
glass, and the chatter of typewriters was almost
disconcerting.

Henry paused.

That morning Mr. Mark Snyder had been to
Powells on the business of one of his clients, a
historian of the Middle Ages, and in the absence
of Sir George had had a little talk with Henry.
And Henry had learnt for the first time what a
literary agent was, and, struck by the man's
astuteness and geniality, had mentioned the matter
of *Love in Babylon*. Mr. Snyder had kindly
promised to look into the matter of *Love in
Babylon* himself if Henry could call on him
instantly with the manuscript. The reason for
haste was that on the morrow Mr. Snyder was
leaving England for New ·York on a professional
tour of the leading literary centres of the United
States. Hence Henry's telegram to Dawes Road.

Standing there in front of Mr. Snyder's door,
Henry wondered whether, after all, he was not
making a fool of himself. But he entered.

Two smart women in tight and elegant bodices,
with fluffy bows at the backs of their necks, looked
up from two typewriters, and the one with golden
hair rose smiling and suave.

"Well, you seem a fairly nice sort of boy—I shall
be kind to you," her eyes appeared to say. Her
voice, however, said nothing except, "Will you take
a seat a moment?" and not even that until Henry
had asked if Mr. Snyder was in.

The prospective client examined the room. It had a carpet, and lovely almanacs on the walls, and in one corner, on a Japanese table, was a tea-service in blue and white. Tables more massive bore enormous piles of all shapes and sizes of manuscripts, scores and hundreds of unprinted literary works, and they all carried labels, "Mark Snyder, Literary Agent." *Love in Babylon* shrank so small that Henry could scarcely detect its presence under his arm.

Then Goldenhair, who had vanished, came back, and, with the most enchanting smile that Henry had ever seen on the face of a pretty woman, lured him by delicious gestures into Mr. Mark Snyder's private office.

"Well," exclaimed Mr. Snyder, full of good-humour, "here we are again." He was a fair, handsome man of about forty, and he sat at a broad table playing with a revolver. "What do you think of that, Mr. Knight?" he asked sharply, holding out the revolver for inspection.

"It seems all right," said Henry lamely.

Mr. Snyder laughed heartily. "I'm going to America to-morrow. I told you, didn't I? Never been there before. So I thought I'd get a revolver. Never know, you know. Eh?" He laughed again.

Then he suddenly ceased laughing, and sniffed the air.

"Is this a business office?" Henry asked himself. "Or is it a club?"

His feet were on a Turkey carpet. He was seated in a Chippendale chair. A glorious fire blazed behind a brass fender, and the receptacle for coal was of burnished copper. Photogravures in rich oaken frames adorned the roseate walls. The ceiling was an expanse of ornament, with an electric chandelier for centre.

"Have a cigarette?" said Mr. Snyder, pushing across towards Henry a tin of Egyptians.

"Thanks," said Henry, who did not usually smoke, and he put *Love in Babylon* on the table.

Mr. Snyder sniffed the air again.

"Now, what can I do for you?" said he abruptly.

Henry explained the genesis, exodus, and vicissitudes of *Love in Babylon*, and Mr. Snyder stretched out an arm and idly turned over a few leaves of the manuscript as it lay before its author.

"Who's your amanuensis?" he demanded, smiling.

"My aunt," said Henry.

"Ah yes!" said Mr. Snyder, smiling still. "It's too short, you know," he added, grave. "Too short. What length is it?"

"Nearly three hundred folios."

"None of your legal jargon here," Mr. Snyder laughed again. "What's a folio?"

"Seventy-two words."

"About twenty thousand words then, eh? Too short!"

"Does that matter?" Henry demanded. "I should have thought——"

"Of course it matters," Mr. Snyder snapped. "If you went to a concert, and it began at eight and finished at half-past, would you go out satisfied with the performers' assurance that quality and not quantity was the thing? Ha, ha!"

Mr. Snyder sniffed the air yet again, and looked at the fire inquisitively, still sniffing.

"There's only one price for novels—six shillings," Mr. Snyder proceeded. "The public likes six shillings' worth of quality. But it absolutely insists on six shillings' worth of quantity, and doesn't

object to more. What can I do with this?" he
went on, picking up *Love in Babylon* and weighing
it as in a balance. "What *can* I do with a thing
like this?"

"If Carlyle came to Kenilworth Mansions!"
Henry speculated. At the same time Mr. Snyder's
epigrammatic remarks impressed him. He saw the
art of Richardson and Balzac in an entirely new
aspect. It was as though he had walked round the
house of literature and peeped in at the back door.

Mr. Snyder suddenly put *Love in Babylon* to his
nose.

"Oh, it's *that!*" he murmured, enlightened.

Henry had to narrate the disaster of the onion-
cart, at which Mr. Snyder was immensely amused.

"Good!" he ejaculated. "Good! By the way,
might send it to Onions Winter. Know Onions
Winter? No? He's always called Spring Onions
in the trade. Pushing man. What a joke it would
be!" Mr. Snyder roared with laughter. "But
seriously, Winter might——"

Just then Goldenhair entered the room with a
slip of paper, and Mr. Snyder begged to be excused
a moment. During his absence Henry reflected
upon the singularly unbusinesslike nature of the
conversation, and decided that it would be well to
import a little business into it.

"I'm called away," said Mr. Snyder, re-entering.

"I must go too," said Henry. "May I ask,
Mr. Snyder, what are your terms for arranging
publication?"

"Ten per cent.," said Mr. Snyder, succinctly.
"On gross receipts. Generally, to unknown men,
I charge a preliminary fee, but, of course, with
you——"

"Ten per cent.?" Henry inquired.

"Ten per cent.," repeated Mr. Snyder.

"Does that mean—ten per cent.?" Henry demanded, dazed.

Mr. Snyder nodded.

"But do you mean to say," said the author of *Love in Babylon* impressively, "that if a book of mine makes a profit of ten thousand pounds, you'll take a thousand pounds just for getting it published?"

"It comes to that," Mr. Snyder admitted.

"Oh!" cried Henry, aghast, astounded. "A thousand pounds!"

And he kept saying: "A thousand pounds! A thousand pounds!"

He saw now where the Turkey carpets and the photogravures and the Teofani cigarettes came from.

"A thousand pounds!"

Mr. Snyder stuck the revolver into a drawer, and began to put on an overcoat and a muffler.

"I'll think it over," said Henry discreetly. "How long shall you be in America?"

"Oh, about a couple of months!" And Mr. Snyder smiled brightly. Henry could not find a satisfactory explanation of the man's eternal jollity.

"Well, I'll think it over," he said once more, very courteously. "And I'm much obliged to you for giving me an interview." And he took up *Love in Babylon* and departed.

It appeared to have been a futile and ludicrous encounter.

CHAPTER XI

SATIN

YES, there had been something wrong with the interview. It had entirely failed to tally with his expectations of it. The fact was that he, Henry, had counted for very little in it. He had sat still and listened, and, after answering Mr. Mark Snyder's questions, he had made no original remark except, "A thousand pounds!" And if he was disappointed with Mr. Snyder, and puzzled by him too, he was also disappointed with himself. He felt that he had displayed none of those business qualities which he knew he possessed. He was a man of affairs, with a sure belief in his own capacity to handle any matter requiring tact and discretion; and yet he had lolled like a simpleton in the Chippendale chair of Mr. Snyder, and contributed naught to the interview save "A thousand pounds!"

Nevertheless, he sincerely thought Mr. Snyder's terms exorbitant. He was not of the race of literary aspirants who are eager to be published at any price. Literature had no fatal fascination for him. His wholly sensible idea now was that, having written a book, he might as well get it printed and make an honest penny out of it, if possible. However, the effect of the visit to Kenilworth Mansions was to persuade him to resolve to abandon the enterprise; Mr. Mark Snyder had indeed discouraged him. And in the evening, when he reached Dawes Road, he gave his mother and aunt a truthful account of the episode, and stated, pleasantly but plainly, that he should burn *Love in Babylon*. And his mother and aunt, perceiving that he was in earnest, refrained from comment.

And after they had gone to bed he took *Love in Babylon* out of the brown paper in which he had wrapped it, and folded the brown paper and tied up the string; and he was in the very act of putting *Love in Babylon* bodily on the fire, when he paused.

"Suppose I give it one more chance?" he reflected.

He had suddenly thought of the name of Mr. Onions Winter, and of Mr. Snyder's interrupted observations upon that publisher. He decided to send *Love in Babylon* to Mr. Winter. He untied the string, unfolded the brown paper, indited a brief letter, and made the parcel anew.

A week later, only a week, Mr. Onions Winter wrote asking Henry to call upon him without delay, and Henry called. The establishment of Mr. Onions Winter was in Leicester Square, between the Ottoman Music Hall and a milliner's shop. Architecturally it presented rather a peculiar appearance. The leading feature of the ground-floor was a vast arch, extending across the entire frontage in something more than a semicircle. Projecting from the keystone of the arch was a wrought-iron sign bearing a portrait in copper, and under the portrait the words "Ye Shakspere Head." Away beneath the arch was concealed the shop-window, an affair of small square panes, and in the middle of every small

pane was stuck a small card, "The Satin Library—
Onions Winter." This mystic phrase was repeated
a hundred and sixty-five times. To the right of
the window was a low green door with a copper
handle in the shape of a sow's tail, and the legend
" Ye Office of Onions Winter."

" Is Mr. Winter in?" Henry demanded of a
young man in a very high collar, after he had
mastered the mechanism of the sow's tail.

" Yes, he's *in*," said the young man rudely, as
Henry thought. (How different from Goldenhair was this high collar!)

" Do you want to see him?" asked the young
man, when he had hummed an air and stared out
of the window.

" No," said Henry placidly. " But he wants to
see me. My name is Knight."

Henry had these flashes of brilliance from time
to time. They came of themselves, as *Love in
Babylon* came. He felt that he was beginning
better with Mr. Onions Winter than he had begun
with Mr. Mark Snyder.

In another moment he was seated opposite
Mr. Winter in a charming but littered apartment
on the first-floor. He came to the conclusion that
all literary offices must be drawing-rooms.

" And so you are the author of *Love in Babylon*?"
began Mr. Winter. He was a tall man, with burning eyes, grey hair, a grey beard which stuck
out like the sun's rays, but no moustache. The
naked grey upper lip was very deep, and somehow
gave him a formidable appearance. He wore a
silk hat at the back of his head, and a Melton
overcoat rather like Henry's own, but much
longer.

" You like it?" said Henry boldly.

"I think—— The fact is, I will be frank with you, Mr. Knight." Here Mr. Onions Winter picked up *Love in Babylon,* which lay before him, and sniffed at it exactly as Mr. Snyder had done. "The fact is, I shouldn't have thought twice about it if it hadn't been for this peculiar odour——"

Here Henry explained the odour.

"Ah yes. Very interesting!" observed Mr. Winter without a smile. "Very curious! We might make a par out of that. Onions—onions. The public like these coincidences. Well, as I tell you, I shouldn't have thought twice about it if it hadn't been for this——" (Sniff, sniff.) "Then I happened to glance at the title, and the title attracted me. I must admit that the title attracted me. You have hit on a very pretty title, Mr. Knight, a very pretty title indeed. I took your book home and read it myself, Mr. Knight. I didn't send it to any of my readers. Not a soul in this office has read it except me. I'm a bit superstitious, you know. We all are— everyone is, when it comes to the point. And that —Onions—onions! And then the pretty title! I like your book, Mr. Knight. I tell you candidly, I like it. It's graceful and touching, and original. It's got atmosphere. It's got that indefinable something—*je ne sais quoi*—that we publishers are always searching for. Of course it's crude— very crude in places. It might be improved. What do you want for it, Mr. Knight? What are you asking?"

Mr. Onions Winter rose and walked to the window in order, apparently, to drink his fill of the statue of Shakspere in the middle of the square.

"I don't know," said Henry, overjoyed but none the less perplexed. "I have not considered the question of price."

"Will you take twenty-five pounds cash down for it—lock, stock, and barrel? You know it's very short. In fact, I'm just about the only publisher in London who would be likely to deal with it."

Henry kept silence.

"Eh?" demanded Mr. Onions Winter, still perusing the Shaksperean forehead. "Cash down. Will you take it?"

"No, I won't, thank you," said Henry.

"Then what will you take?"

"I'll take a hundred."

My dear young man!" Mr. Onions Winter turned suddenly to reason blandly with Henry. "Are you aware that that means five pounds a thousand words? Many authors of established reputation would be glad to receive as much. No, I should like to publish your book, but I am neither a philanthropist nor a millionaire."

"What I should really prefer," said Henry, "would be so much on every copy sold."

"Ah! A royalty?"

"Yes. A royalty. I think that is fairer to both parties," said Henry judicially.

"So you'd prefer a royalty," Mr. Onions Winter addressed Shakspere again. "Well. Let me begin by telling you that first books by new authors never pay expenses. Never! Never! I always lose money on them. But you believe in your book? You believe in it, don't you?" He faced Henry once more.

"Yes," said Henry.

"Then, you must have the courage of your

convictions. I will give you a royalty of three halfpence in the shilling on every copy after the first five thousand. Thus, if it succeeds, you will share in the profit. If it fails, my loss will be the less. That's fair, isn't it?"

It seemed fair to Henry. But he was not Sir George's private secretary for nothing.

"You must make it twopence in the shilling," he said in an urbane but ultimatory tone.

"Very well," Mr. Onions Winter surrendered at once. "We'll say twopence, and end it."

"And what will the price of the book be?" Henry inquired.

"Two shillings, naturally. I intend it for the Satin Library. You know about the Satin Library? You don't know about the Satin Library? My dear sir, I hope it's going to be *the* hit of the day. Here's a dummy copy." Mr. Winter picked up an orange-tinted object from a side-table. "Feel that cover! Look at it! Doesn't it feel like satin? Doesn't it look like satin? But it isn't satin. It's paper — a new invention, the latest thing. You notice the book-marker *is* of satin — real satin. Now observe the shape — isn't that original? And yet quite simple — it's exactly square! And that faint design of sunflowers! These books will be perfect bibelots; that's what they'll be—bibelots. Of course, between you and me, there isn't going to be very much for the money—a hundred and fifty quite small pages. But that's between you and me. And the satin will carry it off. You'll see these charming bijou volumes in every West End drawing-room, Mr. Knight, in a few weeks. Take my word for it. By the way, will you sign our form of agreement now?"

So Henry perpended legally on the form of
agreement, and, finding nothing in it seriously
to offend the legal sense, signed it with due
ceremony.

"Can you correct the proofs instantly, if I send
them?" Mr. Winter asked at parting.

"Yes," said Henry, who had never corrected
a proof in his life. "Are you in a hurry?"

"Well," Mr. Winter replied, "I had meant to
inaugurate the Satin Library with another book.
In fact, I have already bought five books for it.
But I have a fancy to begin it with yours. I have
a fancy, and when I have a fancy, I—I generally
act on it. I like the title. It's a very pretty
title. I'm taking the book on the title. And,
really, in these days a pretty, attractive title is half
the battle."

Within two months, *Love in Babylon*, by Henry
S. Knight, was published as the first volume of
Mr. Onions Winter's Satin Library, and Henry
saw his name in the papers under the heading
"Books Received." The sight gave him a passing
thrill, but it was impossible for him not to observe
that in all essential respects he remained the same
person as before. The presence of six author's
copies of *Love in Babylon* at Dawes Road alone
indicated the great step in his development. One
of these copies he inscribed to his mother, another
to his aunt, and another to Sir George. Sir George
accepted the book with a preoccupied air, and
made no remark on it for a week or more. Then
one morning he said: "By the way, Knight, I ran
through that little thing of yours last night
Capital! Capital! I congratulate you. Take
down this letter."

Henry deemed that Sir George's perspective was somewhat awry, but he said nothing. Worse was in store for him. On the evening of that same day he bought the *Whitehall Gazette* as usual to read in the train, and he encountered the following sentences:

Twaddle in Satin.

"Mr. Onions Winter's new venture, the Satin Library, is a pretty enough thing in its satinesque way The *format* is pleasant, the book-marker voluptuous, the binding Arty-and-Crafty. We cannot, however, congratulate Mr. Winter on the literary quality of the first volume. Mr. Henry S. Knight, the author of *Love in Babylon* (2s.), is evidently a beginner, but he is a beginner from whom nothing is to be expected. That he has a certain gross facility in the management of sentimental narrative we will not deny. It is possible that he is designed to be the delight of "the great public." It is possible—but improbable. He has no knowledge of life, no feeling for style, no real sense of the dramatic. Throughout, from the first line to the last, his story moves on the plane of tawdriness, theatricality, and ballad pathos. There are some authors of whom it may be said that they will never better themselves. They are born with a certain rhapsodic gift of commonness, a gift which neither improves or deteriorates. Richly dowered with crass mediocrity, they proceed from the cradle to the grave at one low dead level. We suspect that Mr. Knight is of these. In saying that it is a pity that he ever took up a pen, we have no desire to seem severe. He is doubtless a quite excellent and harmless person. But he has mistaken his vocation, and that is always a pity. We do not care to see the admirable grocery trade robbed by the literary trade of a talent which was clearly intended by Providence to adorn it. As for the *Satin Library*, we hope superior things from the second volume."

Henry had the fortitude to read this pronouncement aloud to his mother and Aunt Annie at the tea-table.

"The cowards!" exclaimed Mrs. Knight.

Aunt Annie flushed. "Let me look," she

whispered; she could scarcely control her voice. Having looked, she cast the paper with a magnificent gesture to the ground. It lay on the hearthrug, open at a page to which Henry had not previously turned. From his arm-chair he could read in the large displayed type of one of Mr. Onions Winter's advertisments: "Onions Winter. The Satin Library. The success of the year. *Love in Babylon.* By Henry S. Knight. Two shillings. Eighteenth thousand.—Onions Winter. The Satin Library. The success of the year. *Love in Babylon.* By Henry S. Knight. Two shillings. Eighteenth thousand."

And so it went on, repeated and repeated, down the whole length of the twenty inches which constitute a column of the *Whitehall Gazette.*

CHAPTER XII

HIS FAME

HENRY'S sleep was feverish, and shot with the iridescence of strange dreams. And during the whole of the next day one thought burned in his brain, the thought of the immense success of *Love in Babylon*. It burned so fiercely and so brightly, it so completely preoccupied Henry, that he would not have been surprised to overhear men whisper to each other in the street as he passed: "See that extraordinary thought blazing away there in that fellow's brain?" It was, in fact, curious to him that people did not stop and gaze at his cranium, so much the thing felt like a hollowed turnip illuminated by this candle of an idea. But nobody with whom he came into contact appeared to be aware of the immense success of *Love in Babylon*. In the office of Powells were seven full-fledged solicitors and seventeen other clerks, without counting Henry, and not a man or youth of the educated lot of them made the slightest reference to *Love in Babylon* during all that day. (It was an ordinary, plain, common, unromantic, dismal Tuesday in Lincoln's Inn Fields.) Eighteen thousand persons had already bought *Love in Babylon*; possibly several hundreds of copies had been sold since nine o'clock that morning; doubtless someone was every minute inquiring for it and demanding it in bookshop or library, just as someone is born every minute. And yet here was the author, the author himself, the veritable and only genuine author, going about his daily business unhonoured, unsung, uncongratulated, even unnoticed! It was incredible, and, besides being incredible, it was exasperating. Henry was modest, but there are limits to modesty, and more than once in the course of that amazing and endless Tuesday, Henry had a narrow escape of dragging *Love in Babylon* bodily into the miscellaneous conversation of the office. However, with the aid of his natural diffidence he refrained from doing so.

At five-fifty Sir George departed, as usual, to catch the six-five for Wimbledon, where he had a large residence, which outwardly resembled at once a Bloomsbury boarding-house, a golf-club, and a Riviera hotel. Henry, after Sir George's exit, lapsed into his principal's chair and into meditation. The busy life of the establishment died down until only the office-boys and Henry were left. And still Henry sat, in the leathern chair at the big table in Sir George's big room, thinking, thinking, thinking, in a vague but golden and roseate manner, about the future.

Then the door opened, and Foxall, the emperor of the Powellian office-boys, entered.

"Here's someone to see you," Foxall whispered archly; he economized time by licking envelopes the while. Every night Foxall had to superintend and participate in the licking of about two hundred envelopes and as many stamps.

"Who is it?" Henry asked, instantly perturbed and made self-conscious by the doggishness, the waggishness, the rakishness, of Foxall's tone. It must be explained that, since Henry did not happen to be an "admitted" clerk, Foxall and himself, despite the difference in their ages and salaries, were theoretically equals in the social scale of the office. Foxall would say "sir" to the meanest articled clerk that ever failed five times in his intermediate, but he would have expired on the rack before saying "sir" to Henry. The favour accorded to Henry in high quarters, the specialty of his position, gave rise to a certain jealousy of him—a jealousy, however, which his natural simplicity and good-temper prevented from ever becoming formidable. Foxall, indeed, rather liked Henry, and would do favours for him in matters connected with press-copying, letter-indexing, dispatching, and other mysteries of the office-boy's peculiar craft.

"It's a girl," said Foxall, smiling with the omniscience of a man of the world.

"A girl!" Somehow Henry had guessed it was a girl. "What's she like?"

"She's a bit of all right," Foxall explained. "Miss Foster she says her name is. Better show her in here, hadn't I? The old woman's in your room now. It's nearly half-past six."

"Yes," said Henry; "show her in here. Foster? Foster? I don't know——"

His heart began to beat like an engine under his waistcoat.

And then Miss Foster tripped in. And she was Goldenhair!

"Good-afternoon, Mr. Knight," she said, with a charming affectation of a little lisp. "I'm so glad I've caught you. I thought I should. What a lovely room you've got!"

He wanted to explain that this was Sir George's room, not his own, and that anyway he did not consider it lovely ; but she gave him no chance.

"I'm awfully nervous, you know, and I always talk fast and loud when I'm nervous," she continued rapidly. "I shall get over it in a few minutes. Meanwhile you must bear with me. Do you think you can? I want you to do me a favour, Mr. Knight. Only you can do it. May I sit down? Oh, thanks! What a huge chair! If I get lost in it, please advertise. Is this where your clients sit? Yes, I want you to do me a favour. It's quite easy for you to do. You won't say No, will you? You won't think I'm presuming on our slight acquaintanceship?"

The words babbled and purled out of Miss Foster's mouth like a bright spring out of moss. It was simply wonderful. Henry did not understand quite precisely how the phenomenon affected him, but he was left in no doubt that his feelings were pleasurable. She had a manner of looking— of looking up at him and to him, of relying on him as a great big wise man who could get poor little silly her out of a difficulty. And when she wasn't talking she kept her mouth open, and showed her teeth and the tip of her red, red tongue. And there was her golden fluffy hair! But, after all, perhaps the principal thing was her dark-blue, tight-fitting bodice—not a wrinkle in all those curves!

It is singular how a man may go through life absolutely blind to a patent, obvious, glaring fact, and then suddenly perceive it. Henry perceived that his mother and his aunt were badly dressed —in truth, dowdy. It struck him as a discovery.

"Anything I can do, I'm sure——" he began.

"Oh, thank you, Mr. Knight, I felt I could count on your good-nature. You know——"

She cleared her throat, and then smiled intimately, dazzlingly, and pushed a thin gold bangle over the wrist of her glove. And as she did so Henry thought what bliss it would be to slip a priceless diamond bracelet on to that arm. It was just an arm, the usual feminine arm; every normal woman in this world has two of them; and yet——! But at the same time, such is the contradictoriness of human nature, Henry would have given a considerable sum to have had Miss Foster magically removed from the room, and to be alone. The whole of his being was deeply disturbed, as if by an earthquake. And, moreover, he could scarce speak coherently.

"You know," said Miss Foster, "I want to interview you."

He did not take the full meaning of the phrase at first.

"What about?" he innocently asked.

"Oh, about yourself, and your work, and your plans, and all that sort of thing. The usual sort of thing, you know."

"For a newspaper?"

She nodded.

He took the meaning. He was famous, then! People—that vague, vast entity known as "people" —wished to know about him. He had done something. He had arrested attention—he, Henry, son of the draper's manager; aged twenty-three; eater of bacon for breakfast every morning like ordinary men; to be observed daily in the Underground, and daily in the A B C shop in Chancery Lane.

"You are thinking of *Love in Babylon*?" he inquired.

She nodded again. (The nod itself was an enchantment. "She's just about my age," said Henry to himself. And he thought, without realizing that he thought: "She's lots older than me *practically*. She could twist me round her little finger.")

"Oh, Mr. Knight," she recommenced at a tremendous rate, sitting up in the great client's chair, "you must let me tell you what I thought of *Love in Babylon*! It's the sweetest thing! I read it right off, at one go, without looking up! And the title! How *did* you think of it? Oh! if I could write, I would write a book like that. Old Spring Onions has produced it awfully well, too, hasn't he? It's a boom, a positive, unmistakable boom! Everyone's talking about you, Mr. Knight. Personally, I tell everyone I meet to read your book."

Henry mildly protested against this excess of enthusiasm.

"I must," Miss Foster explained. "I can't help it."

Her admiration was the most precious thing on earth to him at that moment. He had not imagined that he could enjoy anything so much as he enjoyed her admiration.

"I'm going now, Mr. Knight," Foxall sang out from the passage.

"Very well, Foxall," Henry replied, as who should say: "Foxall, I benevolently permit you to go."

They were alone together in the great suite of rooms.

"You know *Home and Beauty*, don't you?" Miss Foster demanded.

"*Home and Beauty?*"

"Oh, you don't! I thought perhaps you did. But then, of course, you're a man. It's one of the new ladies' penny papers. I believe it's doing rather well now. I write interviews for it. You see, Mr. Knight, I have a great ambition to be a regular journalist, and in my spare time at Mr. Snyder's, and in the evenings, I write—things. I'm getting quite a little connection. What I want to obtain is a regular column in some really good paper. It's rather awkward, me being engaged all day, especially for interviews. However, I just thought if I ran away at six I might catch you before you left. And so here I am. I don't know what you think of me, Mr. Knight, worrying you and boring you like this with my foolish chatter. . . . Ah! I see you don't want to be interviewed."

"Yes, I do," said Henry. "That is, I shall be most happy to oblige you in any way, I assure you. If you really think I'm sufficiently——"

"Why, of course you are, Mr. Knight," she urged forcefully. "But, like most clever men, you're modest; you've no idea of it—of your success, I mean. By the way, you'll excuse me, but I do trust you made a proper bargain with Mr. Onions Winter."

"I think so," said Henry. "You see, I'm in the law, and we understand these things."

"Exactly," she agreed, but without conviction. "Then you'll make a lot of money. You must be very careful about your next contracts. I hope you didn't agree to let Mr. Winter have a second book on the same terms as this one."

Henry recalled a certain clause of the contract which he had signed.

"I am afraid I did," he admitted sheepishly. "But the terms are quite fair. I saw to that."

"Mr. Knight! Mr. Knight!" she burst out. "Why are all you young and clever men the same? Why do you perspire in order that publishers may grow fat? *I* know what Spring Onions' terms would be. Seriously, you ought to employ an agent. He'd double your income. I don't say Mr. Snyder particularly——"

"But Mr. Snyder is a very good agent, isn't he?"

"Yes," affirmed Miss Foster gravely. "He acts for all the best men."

"Then I shall come to him," said Henry. "I had thought of doing so. You remember when I called that day—it was mentioned then."

He made this momentous decision in an instant, and even as he announced it he wondered why. However, Mr. Snyder's ten per cent. no longer appeared to him outrageous.

"And now can you give me some paper and a pencil, Mr. Knight? I forgot mine in my hurry not to miss you. And I'll sit at the table. May I? Thanks awfully."

She sat near to him, while he hastily and fumblingly searched for paper. The idea of being alone with her in the offices seemed delightful to him. And just then he heard a step in the passage, and a well-known dry cough, and the trailing of a long brush on the linoleum. Of course the caretaker, the inevitable and omnipresent Mrs. Mawner, had invested the place, according to her nightly custom.

Mrs. Mawner opened the door of Sir George's room, and stood on the mat, calmly gazing within, the brush in one hand and a duster in the other.

"I beg pardon, sir," said she inimically. "I thought Sir George was gone."

"Sir George has gone," Henry replied.

Mrs. Mawner enveloped the pair in her sinister glance.

"Shall you be long, sir?"

"I can't say." Henry was firm.

Giving a hitch to her sackcloth, she departed and banged the door.

Henry and Miss Foster were solitary again. And as he glanced at her he thought deliciously: "I am a gay spark." Never before had such a notion visited him.

"What first gave you the idea of writing *Love in Babylon*, Mr. Knight?" began Miss Foster, smiling upon him with a marvellous allurement.

Henry was nearly an hour later than usual in arriving home, but he offered no explanation to his mother and aunt beyond saying that he had been detained by a caller, after Sir George's departure. He read in the faces of his mother and aunt their natural pride that he should be capable of conducting Sir George's business for him after Sir George's departure of a night. Yet he found himself incapable of correcting the false impression which he had wittingly given. In plain terms, he could not tell the ladies, he could not bring himself to tell them, that a well-dressed young woman had called upon him at a peculiar hour and interviewed him in the strict privacy of Sir George's own room on behalf of a lady's paper called *Home and Beauty*. He wanted very much to impart to them these quite harmless and, indeed, rather agreeable and honourable facts, but his lips would not frame the communicating words. Not even when the talk turned, as of course it did, to *Love in Babylon*, did he contrive to mention the interview. It was ridiculous; but so it was.

"By the way——" he began once, but his mother happened to speak at the same instant.

"What were you going to say, Henry?" Aunt Annie asked when Mrs. Knight had finished.

"Oh, nothing. I forget," said the miserable poltroon.

"The next advertisement will say twentieth thousand, that's what it will say—you'll see!" remarked Mrs. Knight.

"What an ass you are!" murmured Henry to Henry. "You'll have to tell them some time, so why not now? Besides, what in thunder's the matter?"

Vaguely, dimly, he saw that Miss Foster's tight-fitting bodice was the matter. Yes, there was something about that bodice, those teeth, that tongue, that hair, something about *her*, which seemed to challenge the whole system of his ideas, all his philosophy, self-satisfaction, seriousness, smugness, and general invincibility. And he thought of her continually—no particular thought, but a comprehensive, enveloping, brooding, static thought. And he was strangely jolly and uplifted, full of affectionate, absent-minded good-humour towards his mother and Aunt Annie.

There was a *ting-ting* of the front-door bell.

"Perhaps Dr. Dancer has called for a chat," said Aunt Annie with pleasant anticipation.

Sarah was heard to ascend and to run along the hall. Then Sarah entered the dining-room.

"Please, sir, there's a young lady to see you."

Henry flushed.

The sisters looked at one another.

"What name, Sarah?" Aunt Annie whispered.

"I didn't ask, mum."

"How often have I told you always to ask strangers' names when they come to the door!" Aunt Annie's whisper became angry. "Go and see."

Henry hoped and feared, feared and hoped. But he knew not where to look.

Sarah returned and said: "The young lady's name is Foster, sir."

"Oh!" said Henry, bursting into speech as some plants burst suddenly and brilliantly into blossom. "Miss Foster, eh? It's the lady who called at the office to-night. Show her into the front-room, Sarah, and light the gas. I'll come in a minute. I wonder what she wants."

"You didn't say it was a lady," said his mother.

"No," he admitted; his tongue was unloosed now on the subject. "And I didn't say it was a lady-journalist, either. The truth is," this liar proceeded with an effrontery which might have been born of incessant practice, but was not, "I meant it as a surprise for you. I've been interviewed this afternoon, for a lady's paper. And I wouldn't mind betting—I wouldn't mind betting," he repeated, "that she's come for my photograph."

All this was whispered.

Henry had guessed correctly. It was the question of a portrait which Miss Foster plunged into immediately he entered the drawing-room. She had forgotten it utterly—she had been so nervous. "So I ran down here to-night," she said, "because if I send in my stuff and the portrait to-morrow morning, it may be in time for next week's issue. Now, don't say you haven't got a photograph of yourself, Mr. Knight. Don't say that! What a pretty, old-fashioned drawing-room! Oh, there's the very thing!"

She pointed to a framed photograph on the plush-covered mantelpiece.

"The very thing, is it?" said Henry. He was feeling his feet now, the dog. "Well, you shall have it, then." And he took the photograph out of the frame and gave it to her.

No! she wouldn't stay, not a minute, not a
second. One moment her delicious presence filled
the drawing-room (he was relieved to hear her call it a
pretty, old-fashioned drawing-room, because, as the
drawing-room of a person important enough to be
interviewed, it had seemed to him somewhat less
than mediocre), and the next moment she had
gone. By a singular coincidence, Aunt Annie was
descending the stairs just as Henry showed Miss
Foster out of the house; the stairs commanded the
lobby and the front-door.

On his return to the dining-room and the com-
panionship of his relatives, Henry was conscious of
a self-preserving instinct which drove him to make
conversation as rapidly and in as large quantities as
possible. In a brief space of time he got round to
Home and Beauty.

" Do you know it ? " he demanded.

" No," said Aunt Annie. " I never heard of it.
But I dare say it's a very good paper."

Mrs. Knight rang the bell.

" What do you want, sister? " Aunt Annie
inquired.

" I'm going to send Sarah out for a copy of
Home and Beauty," said Mrs. Knight, with the air
of one who has determined to indulge a wild whim
for once in a way. " Let's see what it's like."

" Don't forget the name, Sarah — *Home and
Beauty* ! " Aunt Annie enjoined the girl when
Mrs. Knight had given the order.

" Not me, mum," said Sarah. " I know it. It's a
beautiful paper. I often buys it myself. But it's like
as if what must be—I lighted the kitchen fire with
this week's this very morning, paper pattern and all."

" That will do, thank you, Sarah," said Aunt
Annie crushingly.

CHAPTER XIII

A LION IN HIS LAIR

THE respectable portion of the male sex in England may be divided into two classes, according to its method and manner of complete immersion in water. One class, the more dashing, dashes into a cold tub every morning. Another, the more cleanly, sedately takes a warm bath every Saturday night. There can be no doubt that the former class lends tone and distinction to the country, but the latter is the nation's backbone. Henry belonged to the Saturday-nighters, to the section which calls a bath a bath, not a tub, and which contrives to approach godliness without having to boast of it on frosty mornings.

Henry performed the weekly rite in a zinc receptacle exactly circular, in his bedroom, because the house in Dawes Road had been built just before the craze for washing had spread to such an extent among the lower middle-classes that no builder dared build a tenement without providing for it specially; in brutal terms, the house in Dawes Road had no bathroom. The preparations for Henry's immersion were always complex and thorough. Early in the evening Sarah began by putting two kettles and the largest saucepan to boil on the range. Then she took an old blanket and spread

t out upon the master's bedroom floor, and drew
he bathing-machine from beneath the bed and
oaxed it, with considerable clangor, to the mathematical centre of the blanket. Then she filled
ewers with cold water and arranged them round
he machine, Then Aunt Annie went upstairs to
ee that the old blanket was well and truly laid,
not too near the bed and not too near the mirror of
he wardrobe, and that the machine did indeed rest
n the mathematical centre of the blanket. (As a
act, Aunt Annie's mathematics never agreed with
Sarah's.) Then Mrs. Knight went upstairs to bear
witness that the window was shut, and to decide
he question of towels. Then Sarah went upstairs,
panting, with the kettles and the large saucepan, two
ourneys being necessary; and Aunt Annie followed
her in order to indicate to Sarah every step upon
which Sarah had spilled boiling-water. Then Mrs.
Knight moved the key of Henry's door from the
inside to the outside; she was always afraid lest he
might lock himself in and be seized with a sudden
and fatal illness. Then the women dispersed, and
Aunt Annie came down to the dining-room, and in
accents studiously calm (as though the preparation
of Henry's bath was the merest nothing) announced:
"Henry dear, your bath is waiting."
And Henry would disappear at once and begin
by mixing his bath, out of the ewers, the kettles,
and the saucepan, according to a recipe of which
he alone had the secret. The hour would be about
nine o'clock, or a little after. It was not his custom
to appear again. He would put one kettle out on
an old newspaper, specially placed to that end on
the doormat in the passage, for the purposes of
Sunday's breakfast; the rest of the various para-
phernalia remained in his room till the following

morning. He then slept the sleep of one who is
aware of being the nation's backbone.

Now, he was just putting a toe or so into the
zinc receptacle, in order to test the accuracy of his
dispensing of the recipe, when he heard a sharp tap
at the bedroom door.

"What is it?" he cried, withdrawing the toe.

"Henry!"

"Well?"

"Can I open the door an inch?" It was Aunt
Annie's voice.

"Yes. What's the matter?"

"There's come a copy of *Home and Beauty* by
the last post, and on the wrapper it says, 'See
page 16.'"

"I suppose it contains that—thing?"

"That interview, you mean?"

"Yes, I suppose so."

"Shall I open it?"

"If you like," said Henry. "Certainly, with
pleasure."

He stepped quietly and unconcernedly into the
bath. He could hear the sharp ripping of paper.

"Oh yes!" came Aunt Annie's voice through the
chink. "And there's the portrait! Oh! and what
a smudge across the nose! Henry, it doesn't make
you look at all nice. You're too black. Oh
Henry! what *do* you think it's called? 'Lions in
their Lairs. No. 19. Interview with the brilliant
author of *Love in Babylon*.' And you told us her
name was Foster."

"Whose name?" Henry demanded, reddening in
the hot water.

"You know—that lady's name, the one that
called."

"So it is."

"No, it isn't, dear.   It's Flossie Brighteye.   Oh,
I beg pardon, Henry!   I'm sure I beg pardon!"

Aunt Annie, in the excitement of discovering
Miss Foster's real name, and ground withal for
her original suspicion that the self-styled Miss
Foster was no better than she ought to be, had
leaned too heavily against the door, and thrust it
wide open.   She averted her eyes and drew it to
in silence.

"Shall I show the paper to your mother at
once?" she asked, after a fit pause.

"Yes, do," said Henry.

"And then bring it up to you again for you to
read in bed?"

"Oh," replied Henry in the grand manner, "I
can read it to-morrow morning."

He said to himself that he was not going to get
excited about a mere interview, though it was his
first interview.   During the past few days the
world had apparently wakened up to his existence.
Even the men at the office had got wind of his
achievement, and Sir George had been obliged to
notice it.   At Powells everyone pretended that
this was the same old Henry Knight who arrived
so punctually each day, and yet everyone knew
secretly that it was not the same old Henry
Knight.   Everyone, including Henry, felt — and
could not dismiss the feeling — that Henry was
conferring a favour on the office by working as
usual.   There seemed to be something provisional,
something unreal, something uncanny, in the continuance of his position there.   And Sir George,
when he demanded his services to take down
letters in shorthand, had the air of saying apolo-
getically: "Of course, I know you're only here for
fun; but, since you are here, we may as well carry

4

out the joke in a practical manner." Similar phenomena occurred at Dawes Road. Sarah's awe of Henry, always great, was enormously increased. His mother went about in a state of not being quite sure whether she had the right to be his mother, whether she was not taking a mean advantage of him in remaining his mother. Aunt Annie did not give herself away, but on her face might be read a continuous, proud, gentle surprise that Henry should eat as usual, drink as usual, talk simply as usual, and generally behave as though he was not one of the finest geniuses in England.

Further, Mr. Onions Winter had written to ask whether Henry was proceeding with a new book, and how pleased he was at the prospective privilege of publishing it. Nine other publishers had written to inform him that they would esteem it a favour if he would give them the refusal of his next work. Messrs Antonio, the eminent photographers of Regent Street, had written offering to take his portrait gratis, and asking him to deign to fix an appointment for a séance. The editor of *Which is Which*, a biographical annual of inconceivable utility, had written for intimate details of his age, weight, pastimes, works, ideals, and diet. The proprietary committee of the Park Club in St. James's Square had written to suggest that he might join the club without the formality of paying an entrance fee. The editor of a popular magazine had asked him to contribute his views to a "symposium" about the proper method of spending quarter-day. Twenty-five charitable institutions had invited subscriptions from him. Three press-cutting agencies had sent him cuttings of reviews of *Love in Babylon*, and the reviews grew kinder and more laudatory every day. Lastly, Mr. Onions Winter was advertising the thirty-first thousand of that work.

It was not to be expected that the recipient of all these overtures, the courted and sought-for author of *Love in Babylon*, should disarrange the tenor of his existence in order to read an interview with himself in a ladies' penny paper. And Henry repeated, as he sat in the midst of the zinc circle, that he would peruse Flossie Brighteye's article on Sunday morning at breakfast. Then he began thinking about Flossie's tight-fitting bodice, and wondered what she had written. Then he murmured: "Oh, nonsense! I'll read it to-morrow. Plenty soon enough." Then he stopped suddenly and causelessly while applying the towel to the small of his back, and stood for several moments in a state of fixity, staring at a particular spot on the wall-paper. And soon he clearly perceived that he had been too hasty in refusing Aunt Annie's suggestion. However, he had made his bed, and so he must lie on it, both figuratively and factually. . . .

The next thing was that he found himself, instead of putting on his pyjamas, putting on his day-clothes. He seemed to be doing this while wishing not to do it. He did not possess a dressing-gown — Saturday-nighters and backbones seldom do. Hence he was compelled to dress himself completely, save that he assumed a silk muffler instead of a collar and necktie, and omitted the usual stockings between his slippers and his feet. In another minute he unostentatiously entered the dining-room.

"Nay," his mother was saying, "I can't read it." Tears of joyous pride had rendered her spectacles worse than useless. "Here, Annie, read it aloud."

Henry smiled, and he tried to make his smile carry so much meaning, of pleasant indifference, careless amusement, and benevolent joy in the joy of others, that it ended by being merely foolish.

And Aunt Annie began:

"'It is not too much to say that Mr. Henry Knight, the author of *Love in Babylon*, the initial volume of the already world-famous Satin Library, is the most-talked-of writer in London at the present moment. I shall therefore make no apology for offering to my readers an account of an interview which the young and gifted novelist was kind enough to give to me the other evening. Mr. Knight is a legal luminary well known in Lincoln's Inn Fields, the right-hand man of Sir George Powell, the celebrated lawyer. I found him in his formidable room seated at a——'"

"What does she mean by 'formidable,' Henry? I don't think that's quite nice," said Mrs. Knight.

"No, it isn't," said Aunt Annie. "But perhaps she means it frightened her."

"That's it," said Henry. "It was Sir George's room, you know."

"She doesn't *look* as if she would be easily frightened," said Aunt Annie. "However—'seated at a large table littered with legal documents. He was evidently immersed in business, but he was so good as to place himself at my disposal for a few minutes. Mr. Knight is twenty-three years of age. His father was a silk-mercer in Oxford Street, and laid the foundation of the fortunes of the house now known as Duck and Peabody Limited.'"

"That's very well put," said Mrs. Knight.

" Yes, isn't it?" said Aunt Annie, and continued in her precise, even tones:

"'"What first gave you the idea of writing, Mr. Knight?" I inquired, plunging at once *in medias res.* Mr. Knight hesitated a few seconds, and then answered: " I scarcely know. I owe a great deal to my late father. My father, although first and foremost a business man, was devoted to literature. He held that Shakspere, besides being our greatest poet, was the greatest moral teacher that England has ever produced. I was brought up on Shakspere," said Mr. Knight, smiling. " My father often sent communications to the leading London papers on subjects of topical interest, and one of my most precious possessions is a collection of these which he himself put into an album.'"'"

Mrs. Knight removed her spectacles and wiped her eyes.

"'"With regard to *Love in Babylon,* the idea came to me — I cannot explain how. And I wrote it while I was recovering from a severe illness——"'"

" I didn't say 'severe,'" Henry interjected. " She's got that wrong."

" But it *was* severe, dear," said Aunt Annie, and once more continued: "'"I should never have written it had it not been for the sympathy and encouragement of my dear mother——"'"

At this point Mrs. Knight sobbed aloud, and waved her hand deprecatingly.

"Nay, nay!" she managed to stammer at length. " Read no more. I can't stand it. I'll try to read it myself to-morrow morning while you're at chapel and all's quiet."

And she cried freely into her handkerchief.

Henry and Aunt Annie exchanged glances, and

Henry retired to bed with *Home and Beauty* under his arm. And he read through the entire interview twice, and knew by heart what he had said about his plans for the future, and the state of modern fiction, and the tendency of authors towards dyspepsia, and the question of realism in literature, and the Stream of Trashy Novels Constantly Poured Forth by the Press. The whole thing seemed to him at first rather dignified and effective. He understood that Miss Foster was no common Fleet Street hack.

But what most impressed him, and coloured his dreams, was the final sentence: "As I left Mr. Knight, I could not dismiss the sensation that I had been in the presence of a man who is morally certain, at no distant date, to loom large in the history of English fiction.—Flossie Brighteye."

A passing remark about his "pretty suburban home" was the sauce to this dish.

CHAPTER XIV

HER NAME WAS GERALDINE

A FEW mornings later, in his post, whose proportions grew daily nobler and more imposing, Henry found a letter from Mark Snyder. "I have been detained in America by illness," wrote Mark in his rapid, sprawling, inexcusable hand, "and am only just back. I wonder whether you have come to any decision about the matter which we discussed when you called here. I see you took my advice and went to Onions Winter. If you could drop in to-morrow at noon or a little after, I have something to show you which ought to interest you." And then there was a postscript: "My congratulations on your extraordinary success go without saying."

After Henry had deciphered this invitation, he gave a glance at the page as a whole, which had the air of having been penned by Planchette in a state of violent hysteria, and he said to himself: "It's exactly like Snyder, that is. He's a clever chap. He knows what he's up to. As to my choosing Onions Winter, yes, of course it was due to him."

Henry was simple, but he was not a fool. He was modest and diffident, but, as is generally the case with modest and diffident persons, there

existed, somewhere within the recesses of his consciousness, a very good conceit of himself. He
had already learnt, the trout, to look up through
the water from his hole and compare the skill of
the various anglers on the bank who were fishing
for the rise. And he decided that morning, finally :
"Snyder shall catch me." His previous decision
to the same effect, made under the influence of
the personal magnetism of Miss Foster, had been
annulled only the day before. And the strange
thing was that it had been annulled because of
Miss Foster's share in it, and in consequence of
the interview in *Home and Beauty*. For the more
Henry meditated upon that interview the less he
liked it. He could not have defined its offence in
his eyes, but the offence was nevertheless there.
And, further, the interview seemed now scarcely
a real interview. Had it dealt with any other
celebrity it would have been real enough, but in
Henry's view Henry was different. He was only
an imitation celebrity, and Miss Foster's production
was an imitation interview. The entire enterprise,
from the moment when he gave her Sir George's
lead pencil to write with, to the moment when he
gave her his own photograph out of the frame on
the drawing-room mantelpiece, had been a pretence,
and an imposition on the public. Surely if the
public knew . . . ! And then, "pretty suburban
home"! It wasn't ugly, the house in Dawes Road ;
indeed, he esteemed it rather a nice sort of place,
but "pretty suburban home" meant—well, it meant
the exact opposite of Dawes Road : he was sure of
that. As for Miss Foster, he suspected, he allowed
himself to suspect, he audaciously whispered when
he was alone in a compartment on the Underground, that Miss Foster was a pushing little

thing.   A reaction had set in against Flossie Brighteye.

And yet, when he called upon Mark Snyder for the purpose of being caught, he was decidedly piqued, he was even annoyed, not to find her in her chair in the outer room.   "She must have known I was coming," he reflected swiftly.   "No, perhaps she didn't.   The letter was not dictated. . . . But then it was press-copied; I am sure of that by the smudges on it.   She must certainly have known I was coming."   And, despite the verdict that she was a pushing young thing, Henry felt it to be in the nature of a personal grievance that she was not always waiting for him there, in that chair, with her golden locks and her smile and her tight bodice, whenever he cared to look in.   His right to expect her presence seemed part of his heritage as a man, and it could not be challenged without disturbing the very foundations of human society.   He did not think these thoughts clearly as he crossed the outer room into the inner under the direction of Miss Foster's unexciting colleague, but they existed vaguely and furtively in his mind.   Had anyone suggested that he cared twopence whether Miss Foster was there or not, he would have replied with warm sincerity that he did not care three halfpence, nor two straws, nor a bilberry, nor even a jot.

"Well," cried Mark Snyder, with his bluff and jolly habit of beginning interviews in the middle, and before the caller had found opportunity to sit down.   "All you want now is a little bit of judicious engineering!"   And Mark's rosy face said : "I'll engineer you."

Upon demand Henry produced the agreement with Onions Winter, and he produced it with a shamed countenance. He knew that Mark Snyder would criticize it.

"Worse than I expected," Mr. Snyder observed. "Worse than I expected. A royalty of twopence in the shilling is all right. But why did you let him off the royalty on the first five thousand copies? You call yourself a lawyer! Listen, young man. I have seen the world, but I have never seen a lawyer who didn't make a d——d fool of himself when it came to his own affairs. Supposing *Love in Babylon* sells fifty thousand—which it won't; it won't go past forty—you would have saved my ten per cent. commission by coming to me in the first place, because I should have got you a royalty on the first five thousand. See?"

"But you weren't here," Henry put in.

"I wasn't here! God bless my soul! Little Geraldine Foster would have had the sense to get that!"

(So her name was Geraldine.)

"It isn't the money," Mark Snyder proceeded. "It's the idea of Onions Winter playing his old game with new men. And then I see you've let yourself in for a second book on the same terms, if he chooses to take it. That's another trick of his. Look here," Mr. Snyder smiled persuasively, "I'll thank you to go right home and get that second book done. Make it as short as you can. When that's out of the way—— Ah!" He clasped his hands in a sort of ecstasy.

"I will," said Henry obediently. But a dreadful apprehension which had menaced him for several weeks past now definitely seized him.

"And I perceive further," said Mr. Snyder, growing sarcastic, "that in case Mr. Onions Winter chooses to copyright the book in America, you are to have half-royalties on all copies sold over there. Now about America," Mark continued after an impressive pause, at the same time opening a drawer and dramatically producing several paper-covered volumes therefrom. "See this—and this—and this —and this! What are they? They're pirated editions of *Love in Babylon,* that's what they are. You didn't know? No, of course not. I'm told that something like a couple of hundred thousand copies have been sold in America up to date. I brought these over with me as specimens."

"Then Onions Winter didn't copyright——"

"No, sir, he didn't. That incredible ass did not. He's just issued what he calls an authorised edition there at half a dollar, but what will that do in the face of this at twenty cents, and this wretched pamphlet at ten cents?" Snyder fingered the piracies. "Twopence in the shilling on two hundred thousand copies at half a dollar means over three thousand pounds. That's what you might well have made if Providence, doubtless in a moment of abstraction, had not created Onions Winter an incredible ass, and if you had not vainly imagined that because you were a lawyer you had nothing to learn about contracts."

"Still," faltered Henry, after he had somewhat recovered from these shrewd blows, "I shall do pretty well out of the English edition."

"Three thousand pounds is three thousand pounds," said Mark Snyder with terrible emphasis. And suddenly he laughed. "You really wish me to act for you?"

"I do," said Henry.

"Very well. Go home and finish book number two. And don't let it be a page longer than the first one. I'll see Onions Winter. With care we may clear a couple of thousand out of book number two, even on that precious screed you call an agreement. Perhaps more. Perhaps I may have a pleasant little surprise for you. Then you shall do a long book, and we'll begin to make money, real money. Oh, you can do it! I've no fear at all of you fizzling out. You simply go home and sit down and *write*. I'll attend to the rest. And if you think Powells can struggle along without you, I should be inclined to leave."

"Surely not yet?" Henry protested.

"Well," said Snyder in a different tone, looking up quickly from his desk, "perhaps you're right. Perhaps it will be as well to wait a bit, and just make quite sure about the quality of the next book. Want any money?"

"No," said Henry.

"Because if you do, I can let you have whatever you need. And you can carry off these piracies if you like."

As he thoughtfully descended the stairways of Kenilworth Mansions, Henry's mind was an arena of emotions. Undoubtedly, then, a considerable number of hundreds of pounds were to come from *Love in Babylon,* to say nothing of three thousand lost! Two thousand from the next book! And after that "money, real money"! Mark Snyder had awakened the young man's imagination. He had entered the parlour of Mark Snyder with no knowledge of the Transatlantic glory of *Love in Babylon* beyond the fact, gathered from a newspaper cutting, that the book had attracted attention in America; and in five minutes Mark had opened wide to him the doors of Paradise. Or, rather, Mark had pointed out to him that the doors of Paradise were open wide. Mr. Snyder, as Henry perceived, was apt unwittingly to give the impression that he, and not his clients, earned the wealth upon which he received ten per cent. commission. But Henry was not for a single instant blind to the certitude that, if his next book realized two thousand pounds, the credit would be due to himself, and to no other person whatever. Henry might be tongue-tied in front of Mark Snyder, but he was capable of estimating with some precision their relative fundamental importance in the scheme of things.

In the clerks' office Henry had observed numerous tin boxes inscribed in white paint with the names of numerous eminent living authors. He wondered if Mr. Snyder played to all these great men the same rôle—half the frank and bluff uncle, half the fairy-godmother. He was surprised that he could remember no word said about literature, ideas, genius or even talent. No doubt Mr. Snyder took such trifles for granted. No doubt he began where they left off.

He sighed. He was dazzled by golden visions, but beneath the dizzy and delicious fabric of the dream, eating away at the foundations, lurked always that dreadful apprehension.

As he reached the marble hall on the ground-floor a lady was getting into the lift. She turned sharply, gave a joyous and yet timid commencement of a scream, and left the lift to the lift-man.

"I'm so glad I've not missed you," she said, holding out her small gloved hand, and putting her golden head on one side, and smiling. "I was afraid I should. I had to go out. Don't tell me that interview was too awful. Don't crush me. I know it was pretty bad."

So her name was Geraldine.

"I thought it was much too good for its subject," said Henry. He saw in the tenth of a second that he had been wholly wrong, very unjust, and somewhat cruel, to set her down as a pushing little thing. She was nothing of the kind. She was a charming and extremely stylish woman, exquisitely feminine; and she admired him with a genuine admiration. "I was just going to write and thank you," he added. And he really believed that he was.

What followed was due to the liftman. The impatient liftman, noticing that the pair were enjoying each other's company, made a disgraceful gesture behind their backs, slammed the gate, and ascended majestically alone in the lift towards some high altitude whence emanated an odour of boiled Spanish onions. Geraldine Foster glanced round carelessly at the rising and beautiful flunkey, and it was the sudden curve of her neck that did it. It was the sudden curve of her neck, possibly assisted by Henry's appreciation of the fact that they were now unobserved and solitary in the hall.

Henry was made aware that women are the only really interesting phenomena in the world. And just as he stumbled on this profound truth, Geraldine, for her part, caught sight of the pirated editions in his hand, and murmured: "So Mr. Snyder has told you! *What a shame*, isn't it?"

The sympathy in her voice, the gaze of her eyes under the lashes, finished him.

"Do you live far from here?" he stammered, he knew not why.

"In Chenies Street," she replied. "I share a little flat with my friend upstairs. You must come and have tea with me some afternoon — some Saturday or Sunday. Will you? Dare I ask?"

He said he should like to, awfully.

"I was dining out last night, and we were talking about you," she began a few seconds later.

Women! Wine! Wealth! Joy! Life itself! He was swept off his feet by a sudden and tremendous impulse.

"I wish," he blurted out, interrupting her—"I wish you'd come and dine with *me* some night, at a restaurant."

"Oh!" she exclaimed, "I should love it."

"And we might go somewhere afterwards." He was certainly capable of sublime conceptions."

And she exclaimed again: "I should love it!" The naïve and innocent candour of her bliss appealed to him with extraordinary force.

In a moment or so he had regained his self-control, and he managed to tell her in a fairly usual tone that he would write and suggest an evening.

He parted from her in a whirl of variegated ecstasies. "Let us eat and drink, for to-morrow we die," he remarked to the street. What he meant was that, after more than a month's excogitation, he had absolutely failed to get any single shred of a theme for the successor to *Love in Babylon* — that successor out of which a mere couple of thousand pounds was to be made; and that he didn't care.

CHAPTER XV

HIS TERRIBLE QUANDARY

THERE was to be an important tea-meeting at the Munster Park Chapel on the next Saturday afternoon but one, and tea was to be on the tables at six o'clock. The gathering had some connection with an attempt on the part of the Wesleyan Connexion to destroy the vogue of Confucius in China. Mrs. Knight and Aunt Annie had charge of the department of sandwiches, and they asked Henry whether he should be present at the entertainment. They were not surprised, however, when he answered that the exigencies of literary composition would make his attendance impossible. They lauded his self-denial, for Henry's literary work was quite naturally now the most important and the most exacting work in the world, the crusade against Confucius not excepted. Henry wrote to Geraldine and invited her to dine with him at the Louvre Restaurant on that Saturday night, and Geraldine replied that she should be charmed. Then Henry changed his tailor, and could not help blushing when he gave his order to the new man, who had a place in Conduit Street and a way of looking at the clothes Henry wore that reduced those neat garments to shapeless and shameful rags.

The first fatal steps in a double life having been irrevocably taken, Henry drew a long breath, and once more seriously addressed himself to book number two. But ideas obstinately refused to show themselves above the horizon. And yet nothing had been left undone which ought to have been done in order to persuade ideas to arrive. The whole domestic existence of the house in Dawes Road revolved on Henry's precious brain as on a pivot. The drawing-room had not only been transformed into a study; it had been re-christened "the study." And in speaking of the apartment to each other or to Sarah, Mrs. Knight and Aunt Annie employed a vocal inflection of peculiar impressiveness. Sarah entered the study with awe, the ladies with pride. Henry sat in it nearly every night and laboured hard, with no result whatever. If the ladies ventured to question him about his progress, he replied with false gaiety that they must ask him again in a month or so; and they smiled in sure anticipation of the beautiful thing that was in store for them and the public.

He had no one to consult in his dilemma. Every morning he received several cuttings, chiefly of an amiable character, about himself from the daily and weekly press; he was a figure in literary circles; he had actually declined two invitations to be interviewed; and yet he knew no more of literary circles than Sarah did. His position struck him as curious, bizarre, and cruel. He sometimes felt that the history of the last few months was a dream from which he would probably wake up by falling heavily out of bed, so unreal did the events seem. One day, when he was at his wits' end, he saw in a newspaper an advertisement of a book entitled *How to become a Successful Novelist*, price half a crown. Just above it was an advertisement of the thirty-eighth thousand of *Love in Babylon*. He went into a large bookseller's shop in the Strand and demanded *How to become a Successful Novelist*. The volume had to be searched for, and while he was waiting Henry's eyes dwelt on a high pile of *Love in Babylon*, conspicuously placed near the door. Two further instalments of the Satin Library had been given to the world since *Love in Babylon*, but Henry noted with satisfaction that no excessive prominence was accorded to them in that emporium of literature. He paid the half-crown and pocketed *How to become a Successful Novelist* with a blush, just as if the bookseller had been his new tailor. He had determined, should the bookseller recognize him—a not remote contingency—to explain that he was buying *How to become a Successful Novelist* on behalf of a young friend. However, the suspicions of the bookseller happened not to be aroused, and hence there was no occasion to lull them.

That same evening, in the privacy of his study, he eagerly read *How to become a Successful Novelist*. It disappointed him; nay, it desolated him. He was shocked to discover that he had done nothing that a man must do who wishes to be a successful novelist. He had not practised style; he had not paraphrased choice pages from the classics; he had not kept note-books; he had not begun with short stories; he had not even performed the elementary, obvious task of studying human nature. He had never thought of "atmosphere" as "atmosphere"; nor had he considered the important question of the "functions of dialogue." As for the "significance of scenery," it had never occurred to him. In brief, he was a lost man. And he could detect in the book no practical hint towards salvation. "Having decided

pon your theme——" said the writer in a chapter
ntitled "The Composition of a Novel." But what
Henry desired was a chapter entitled "The Finding
f a Theme." He suffered the aggravated dis-
ress of a starving man who has picked up a
ookery-book.

There was a knock at the study door, and Henry
astily pushed *How to become a Successful Novelist*
nder the blotting-paper, and assumed a meditative
ir. Not for worlds would he have been caught
eading it.

"A letter, dear, by the last post," said Aunt
Annie, entering ; and then discreetly departed.

The letter was from Mark Snyder, and it
nclosed a cheque for a hundred pounds, saying
hat Mr. Onions Winter, though under no obli-
gation to furnish a statement until the end of the
ear, had sent this cheque on account out of
ourtesy to Mr. Knight, and in the hope that
Mr. Knight would find it agreeable ; also in the
hope that Mr. Knight was proceeding satisfactorily
with book number two. The letter was type-
written, and signed "Mark Snyder, per G. F.,"
and the "G. F." was very large and distinct.

Henry instantly settled in his own mind that he
would attempt no more with book number two
until the famous dinner with "G. F." had come to
pass. He cherished a sort of hopeful feeling that
after he had seen her, and spent that about-to-be-
wonderful evening with her, he might be able to
invent a theme. The next day he cashed the
cheque. The day after that was Saturday, and
he came home at two o'clock with a large flat box,
which he surreptitiously conveyed to his bedroom.
Small parcels had been arriving for him during
the week. At half-past four Mrs. Knight and

Aunt Annie, invading the study, found him reading *Chambers's Encyclopædia.*

" We're going now, dear," said Aunt Annie.

" Sarah will have your tea ready at half-past five," said his mother. " And I've told her to be sure and boil the eggs three and three-quarter minutes."

" And we shall be back about half-past nine," said Aunt Annie.

" Don't stick at it too closely," said his mother.

" You ought to take a little exercise. It's a beautiful afternoon."

" I shall see," Henry answered gravely. I shall be all right."

He watched the ladies down the road in the direction of the tea-meeting, and no sooner were they out of sight than he nipped upstairs and locked himself in his bedroom. At half-past five Sarah tapped at his door and announced that tea was ready. He descended to tea in his overcoat, and the collar of his overcoat was turned up and buttoned across his neck. He poured out some tea, and drank it, and poured some more into the slop-basin. He crumpled a piece or two of bread-and-butter and spread crumbs on the cloth. He shelled the eggs very carefully, and, climbing on to a chair, dropped the eggs themselves into a large blue jar which stood on the top of the bookcase. After these singular feats he rang the bell for Sarah.

" Sarah," he said in a firm voice, " I've had my tea, and I'm going out for a long walk. Tell my mother and aunt that they are on no account to wait up for me, if I am not back."

" Yes, sir," said Sarah timidly. " Was the eggs hard enough, sir?"

"Yes, thank you."   His generous, kindly approval of the eggs cheered this devotee.

Henry brushed his silk hat, put it on, and stole out of the house, feeling, as all livers of double lives must feel, a guilty thing.   It was six o'clock. The last domestic sound he heard was Sarah singing in the kitchen.   "Innocent, simple creature!" he thought, and pitied her, and turned down the collar of his overcoat.

CHAPTER XVI

DURING THE TEA-MEETING

IN spite of the sincerest intention not to arrive too soon, Henry reached the Louvre Restaurant a quarter of an hour before the appointed time. He had meant to come in an omnibus, and descend from it at Piccadilly Circus, but his attire made him feel self-conscious, and he had walked on, allowing omnibus after omnibus to pass him, in the hope of being able to get into an empty one; until at last, afraid that he was risking his fine reputation for exact promptitude, he had suddenly yielded to the alluring gesture of a cabman.

The commissionaire of the Louvre, who stood six feet six and a half inches high, who wore a coat like the side of a blue house divided by means of pairs of buttons into eighty-five storeys, who had the face of a poet addicted to blank verse, and who was one of the glories of the Louvre, stepped across the pavement in one stride and assisted Henry to alight. Henry had meant to give the cabman eighteenpence, but the occult influence of the glorious commissionaire mysteriously compelled him, much against his will, to make it half a crown. He hesitated whether to await Geraldine within the Louvre or without; he was rather bashful about entering (hitherto he

...ad never flown higher than Sweeting's).   The
...ommissionaire, however, attributing this indecision
...o Henry's unwillingness to open doors for himself,
...tepped back across the pavement in another stride,
...nd held the portal ajar.   Henry had no alternative
...ut to pass beneath the commissionaire's bended
...nd respectful head.   Once within the gorgeous
...wilit hall of the Louvre, Henry was set upon by
...wo very diminutive and infantile replicas of the
...ommissionaire, one of whom staggered away with
his overcoat, while the other secured the remainder
of the booty in the shape of his hat, muffler, and
stick, and left Henry naked.   I say "naked"
purposely.   Anyone who has dreamed the familiar
dream of being discovered in a state of nudity amid
a roomful of clothed and haughty strangers may,
by recalling his sensations, realize Henry's feelings
as he stood alone and unfriended there, exposed for
the first time in his life in evening dress to the
vulgar gaze.   Several minutes passed before Henry
could conquer the delusion that everybody was
staring at him in amused curiosity.   Having conquered it, he sank sternly into a chair, and
surreptitiously felt the sovereigns in his pocket.

Soon an official bore down on him, wearing a
massive silver necklet which fell gracefully over his
chest.   Henry saw and trembled.

"Are you expecting someone, sir?" the man
whispered in a velvety and confidential voice, as
who should say: "Have no secrets from me.   I am
discretion itself."

"Yes," answered Henry boldly, and he was
inclined to add: "But it's all right, you know.
I've nothing to be ashamed of."

"Have you booked a table, sir?" the official
proceeded with relentless suavity.   As he stooped

towards Henry's ear his chain swung in the air
and gently clanked.

"No," said Henry, and then hastened to assure
the official: "But I want one." The idea of
booking tables at a restaurant struck him as a
surprising novelty.

"Upstairs or down, sir? Perhaps you'd prefer
the balcony? For two, sir? I'll *see*, sir. We're
always rather full. What name, sir?"

"Knight," said Henry majestically.

He was a bad starter, but once started he could
travel fast. Already he was beginning to feel at
home in the princely foyer of the Louvre, and to
stare at new arrivals with a cold and supercilious
stare. His complacency, however, was roughly
disturbed by a sudden alarm lest Geraldine might
not come in evening-dress, might not have quite
appreciated what the Louvre was.

"Table No. 16, sir," said the chain-wearer in his
ear, as if depositing with him a state-secret.

"Right," said Henry, and at the same instant
she irradiated the hall like a vision.

"Am I not prompt?" she demanded sweetly, as
she took a light wrap from her shoulders.

Henry began to talk very rapidly and rather
loudly. "I thought you'd prefer the balcony," he
said with a tremendous air of the man about town;
"so I got a table upstairs. No. 16, I fancy it is."

She was in evening-dress. There could be no
doubt about that; it was a point upon which
opinions could not possibly conflict. She was in
evening-dress.

"Now tell me all about *your*self," Henry
suggested. They were in the middle of the
dinner.

"Oh, you can't be interested in the affairs of poor little me!"

"Can't I?"

He had never been so ecstatically happy in his life before. In fact, he had not hitherto suspected even the possibility of that rapture. In the first place, he perceived that in choosing the Louvre he had builded better than he knew. He saw that the Louvre was perfect. Such napery, such argent, such crystal, such porcelain, such flowers, such electric and glowing splendour, such food and so many kinds of it, such men, such women, such chattering gaiety, such a conspiracy on the part of menials to persuade him that he was the Shah of Persia, and Geraldine the peerless Circassian odalisque! The reality left his fancy far behind. In the second place, owing to his prudence in looking up the subject in *Chambers's Encyclopædia* earlier in the day, he, who was almost a teetotaler, had cut a more than tolerable figure in handling the wine-list. He had gathered that champagne was in truth scarcely worthy of its reputation among the uninitiated, that the greatest of all wines was burgundy, and that the greatest of all burgundies was Romanée-Conti. "Got a good Romanée-Conti?" he said casually to the waiter. It was immense, the look of genuine respect that came into the face of the waiter. The Louvre had a good Romanée-Conti. Its price, two pounds five a bottle, staggered Henry, and he thought of his poor mother and aunt at the tea-meeting, but his impassive features showed no sign of the internal agitation. And when he had drunk half a glass of the incomparable fluid, he felt that a hundred and two pounds five a bottle would not have been too much to pay for it. The physical,

moral and spiritual effects upon him of that wine
were remarkable in the highest degree. That wine
banished instantly all awkwardness, diffidence,
timidity, taciturnity, and meanness. It filled him
with generous emotions and the pride of life. It
ennobled him.

And, in the third place, Geraldine at once furnished him with a new ideal of the feminine and
satisfied it. He saw that the women of Munster
Park were not real women; they were afraid to
be real women, afraid to be joyous, afraid to be
pretty, afraid to attract; they held themselves in
instead of letting themselves go; they assumed
that every pleasure was guilty until it was |proved
innocent, thus transgressing the fundamental
principle of English justice; their watchful eyes
seemed to be continually saying: "Touch me—
and I shall scream for help!" In costume, any
elegance, any elaboration, any coquetry, was
eschewed by them as akin to wantonness. Now
Geraldine reversed all that. Her frock was
candidly ornate. She told him she had made it
herself, but it appeared to him that there were
more stitches in it than ten women could have
accomplished in ten years. She openly revelled
in her charms; she openly made the most of them.
She did not attempt to disguise her wish to please,
to flatter, to intoxicate. Her eyes said nothing
about screaming for help. Her eyes said: "I'm
a woman; you're a man. How jolly!" Her
eyes said: "I was born to do what I'm doing now."
Her eyes said: "Touch me—and we shall see."
But what chiefly enchanted Henry was her intellectual courage and her freedom from cant. In
conversing with her you hadn't got to tread lightly
and warily, lest at any moment you might put your

ot through the thin crust of a false modesty, and
mble into eternal disgrace. You could talk to
r about anything; and she did not pretend to
blind to the obvious facts of existence, to the
vious facts of the Louvre Restaurant, for example.
oreover, she had a way of being suddenly and
liciously serious, and of indicating by an earnest
ance that of course she was very ignorant really,
d only too glad to learn from a man like him.

"Can't I!" he replied, after she had gazed at
m in silence over the yellow roses and the fowl.

So she told him that she was an orphan, and
d a brother who was a solicitor in Leicester.
hy Henry should have immediately thought
at her brother was a somewhat dull and tedious
rson cannot easily be explained; but he did
ink so.

She went on to tell him that she had been in
ondon five years, and had begun in a milliner's
op, had then learnt typewriting and shorthand,
dvertised for a post, and obtained her present
tuation with Mark Snyder.

"I was determined to earn my own living," she
id, with a charming smile. "My brother would
ave looked after me, but I preferred to look after
yself." A bangle slipped down her arm.

"She's perfectly wonderful!" Henry thought.

And then she informed him that she was doing
airly well in journalism, and had attempted sensa-
ional fiction, but that none saw more clearly than
he how worthless and contemptible her sort of
ork was, and none longed more sincerely than she
o produce good work, serious work. . . . However,
he knew she couldn't.

"Will you do me a favour?" she coaxed.

"What is it?" he said.

"Oh! No! You must promise."

"Of course, if I can."

"Well, you can. I want to know what yo
next book's about. I won't breathe a word to
soul. But I would like you to tell me. I wou
like to feel that it was you that had told me. Y
can't imagine how keen I am."

"Ask me a little later," he said. "Will you?"

"To-night?"

She put her head on one side.

And he replied audaciously: "Yes."

"Very well," she agreed. "And I shan't forge
I shall hold you to your promise."

Just then two men passed the table, and or
of them caught Geraldine's eye, and Geraldin
bowed.

"Well, Mr. Doxey," she exclaimed. "What ag
since I saw you!"

"Yes, isn't it?" said Mr. Doxey.

They shook hands and talked a moment.

"Let me introduce you to Mr. Henry Knight,
said Geraldine. "Mr. Knight—Mr. Doxey,
the P.A."

"*Love in Babylon*?" murmured Mr. Doxe
inquiringly. "Very pleased to meet you, sir."

Henry was not favourably impressed by M
Doxey's personal appearance, which was attenuate
and riggish. He wondered what "P.A." mean
Not till later in the evening did he learn that i
stood for Press Association, and had no connectio
with Pleasant Sunday Afternoons. Mr. Doxe
stated that he was going on to the Alhambra t
"do" the celebrated Toscato, the inventor of th
new vanishing trick, who made his first publi
appearance in England at nine forty-five tha
night.

"You didn't mind my introducing him to you? He's a decent little man in some ways," said Geraldine humbly, when they were alone again.

"Oh, of course not!" Henry assured her. "By the way, what would you like to do to-night?"

"I don't know," she said. "It's awfully late, isn't it? Time flies so when you're interested."

"It's a quarter to nine. What about the Alhambra?" he suggested.

(He who had never been inside a theatre, not to mention a music-hall!)

"Oh!" she burst out. "I adore the Alhambra. What an instinct you have! I was just hoping you'd say the Alhambra!"

They had Turkish coffee. He succeeded very well in pretending that he had been thoroughly accustomed all his life to the spectacle of women smoking—that, indeed, he was rather discomposed than otherwise when they did not smoke. He paid the bill, and the waiter brought him half a crown concealed on a plate in the folds of the receipt; it was the change out of a five-pound note.

Being in a hansom with her, though only for two minutes, surpassed even the rapture of the restaurant. It was the quintessence of Life.

CHAPTER XVII

A NOVELIST IN A BOX

PERHAPS it was just as well that the curtain was falling on the ballet when Henry and Geraldine took possession of their stalls in the superb Iberian auditorium of the Alhambra Theatre. The glimpse which Henry had of the *prima ballerina assoluta* in her final pose and her costume, and of the hundred minor chorographic artists, caused him to turn involuntarily to Geraldine to see whether she was not shocked. She, however, seemed to be keeping her nerve fairly well; so he smothered up his consternation in a series of short, dry coughs, and bought a programme. He said to himself bravely: "I'm in for it, and I may as well go through with it." The next item, while it puzzled, reassured him. The stage showed a restaurant, with a large screen on one side. A lady entered, chattered at an incredible rate in Italian, and disappeared behind the screen, where she knocked a chair over and rang for the waiter. Then the waiter entered and disappeared behind the screen, chattering at an incredible rate in Italian. The waiter reappeared and made his exit, and then a gentleman appeared, and disappeared behind the screen, chattering at an incredible rate in Italian. Kissing was heard behind the screen. Instantly

e waiter served a dinner, chattering always behind
e screen with his customers at an incredible rate
Italian.   Then another gentleman appeared, and
 sooner had he disappeared behind the screen,
attering at an incredible rate in Italian, than a
liceman appeared, and he too, chattering at an
credible rate in Italian, disappeared behind the
reen.   A fearsome altercation was now developing
hind the screen in the tongue of Dante, and from
ne to time one or other of the characters—the
dy, the policeman, the first or second gentleman,
e waiter—came from cover into view of the
dience, and harangued the rest at an incredible
te in Italian.   Then a disaster happened behind
e screen: a table was upset, to an accompaniment
 yells; and the curtain fell rapidly, amid loud
plause, to rise again with equal rapidity on the
ectacle of a bowing and smiling little man in
dinary evening dress.

This singular and enigmatic drama disconcerted
enry.

"What is it?" he whispered.

"Pauletti," said Geraldine, rather surprised at
e question.

He gathered from her tone that Pauletti was a
rsonage of some importance, and, consulting the
ogramme, read: "Pauletti, the world-renowned
ick-change artiste."   Then he figuratively kicked
mself, like a man kicks himself figuratively in bed
hen he wakes up in the middle of the night and
es the point of what has hitherto appeared to be
ther less than a joke.

"He's very good," said Henry, as the excellence
 Pauletti became more and more clear to him.

"He gets a hundred a week," said Geraldine.

When Pauletti had performed two other violent

dramas, and dressed and undressed himself thirt
nine times in twenty minutes, he gave way to l
fellow-countryman Toscato. Toscato began gent
with a little prestidigitation, picking five-poun
notes out of the air, and simplicities of that kin
He then borrowed a handkerchief, produced a
orange out of the handkerchief, a vegetable-marro
out of the orange, a gibus hat out of the vegetabl
marrow, a live sucking-pig out of the gibus ha
five hundred yards of coloured paper out of th
sucking-pig, a Union-jack twelve feet by ten o
of the bunch of paper, and a wardrobe with re
doors and full of ladies' dresses out of the Unio
jack. Lastly, a beautiful young girl stepped for
from the wardrobe.

"*I never saw anything like it!*" Henry gaspe
very truthfully. He had a momentary fancy th
the devil was in this extraordinary defiance
natural laws.

"Yes," Geraldine admitted. "It's not bad, is it?

As Toscato could speak no English, an Englis
man now joined him and announced that Toscat
would proceed to perform his latest and greate:
illusion—namely, the unique vanishing trick—fc
the first time in England; also that Toscato ex
tended a cordial invitation to members of th
audience to come up on to the stage and do the
acutest to pierce the mystery.

"Come along," said a voice in Henry's ea
"I'm going." It was Mr. Doxey's.

"Oh no, thanks!" Henry replied hastily.

"Nothing to be afraid of," said Mr. Doxe
shrugging his shoulders with an air which Henr
judged slightly patronizing.

"Oh yes, do go," Geraldine urged. "It will b
such fun."

He hated to go, but there was no alternative,
and so he went, stumbling after Mr. Doxey up the
step-ladder which had been placed against the
footlights for the ascending of people who prided
themselves on being acute. There were seven such
persons on the stage, not counting himself, but
Henry honestly thought that the eyes of the entire
audience were directed upon him alone. The stage
seemed very large, and he was cut off from the
audience by a wall of blinding rays, and at first he
could only distinguish vast vague semicircles and
a floor of pale, featureless faces. However, he
depended upon Mr. Doxey.

But when the trick-box had been brought on to
the stage—it was a sort of a sentry-box raised on
four legs—Henry soon began to recover his self-
possession. He examined that box inside and out
until he became thoroughly convinced that it was
without guile. The jury of seven stood round the
erection, and the English assistant stated that a
sheet (produced) would be thrown over Toscato,
who would then step into the box and shut the
door. The door would then be closed for ten
seconds, whereupon it would be opened and the
beautiful young girl would step out of the box,
while Toscato would magically appear in another
part of the house.

At this point Henry stooped to give a last glance
under the box. Immediately Toscato held him
with a fiery eye, as though enraged, and, going up
to him, took eight court cards from Henry's sleeve,
a lady's garter from his waistcoat pocket, and a
Bath-bun out of his mouth. The audience received
this professional joke in excellent part, and, indeed,
roared its amusement. Henry blushed, would have
given all the money he had on him—some ninety

pounds—to be back in the stalls, and felt a ho
desire to explain to everyone that the cards, the
Bath-bun, and especially the garter, had not really
been in his possession at all.   That part of the
episode over, the trick ought to have gone forward
but Toscato's Italian temper was effervescing, and
he insisted by signs that one of the jury should
actually get into the box bodily, and so satisfy the
community that the box was a box *et præterea nihil.*
The English assistant pointed to Henry, and Henry,
to save argument, reluctantly entered the box.
Toscato shut the door.   Henry was in the dark,
and quite mechanically he extended his hands and
felt the sides of the box.   His fingers touched a
projection in a corner, and he heard a clicking
sound.   Then he was aware of Toscato shaking the
door of the box, frantically and more frantically,
and of the noise of distant, multitudinous laughter.

"Don't hold the door," whispered a voice.

"I'm not doing so," Henry whispered in reply.

The box trembled.

"I say, old chap, don't hold the door.   They
want to get on with the trick."   This time it was
Mr. Doxey who addressed him in persuasive tones.

"Don't I tell you I'm not holding the door, you
silly fool!" retorted Henry, nettled.

The box trembled anew and more dangerously.
The distant laughter grew immense and formidable.

"Carry it off," said a third voice, "and get him
out in the wings."

The box underwent an earthquake; it rocked;
Henry was thrown with excessive violence from
side to side; the sound of the laughter receded.

Happily, the box had no roof; it was laid with
all tenderness on its flank, and the tenant crawled
out of it into the midst of an interested crowd

consisting of Toscato, some stage-managers, several scene-shifters, and many ballerinas. His natural good-temper reasserted itself at once, and he received apologies in the spirit in which they were offered, while Toscato set the box to rights. Henry was returning to the stage in order to escape from the ballerinas, whose proximity disturbed and frightened him, but he had scarcely shown his face to the house before he was, as it were, beaten back by a terrific wave of jubilant cheers. The great vanishing trick was brilliantly accomplished without his presence on the boards, and an official guided him through various passages back to the floor of the house. Nobody seemed to observe him as he sat down beside Geraldine.

"Of course it was all part of the show, that business," he heard a man remark loudly some distance behind him.

He much enjoyed explaining the whole thing to Geraldine. Now that it was over, he felt rather proud, rather triumphant. He did not know that he was very excited, but he observed that Geraldine was excited.

"You needn't think you are going to escape from telling me all about your new book, because you aren't," said Geraldine prettily.

They were supping at a restaurant of the discreet sort, divided into many compartments, and situated, with a charming symbolism, at the back of St. George's, Hanover Square. Geraldine had chosen it. They did not need food, but they needed their own unadulterated society.

"I'm only too pleased to tell you," Henry replied. "You're about the only person that I would tell.

It's like this. You must imagine a youth growing
up to manhood, and wanting to be a great artist.
I don't mean a painter. I mean a—an actor. Yes,
a very great actor. Shakspere's tragedies, you
know, and all that."

She nodded earnestly.

"What's his name?" she inquired.

Henry gazed at her. "His name's Gerald," he
said, and she flushed. "Well, at sixteen this youth
is considerably over six feet in height, and still
growing. At eighteen his figure has begun to
excite remark in the streets. At nineteen he has
a severe attack of scarlet fever, and while ill he grows
still more, in bed, like people do, you know. And
at twenty he is six feet eight inches high."

"A giant, in fact."

"Just so. But he doesn't want to be a giant.
He wants to be an actor, a great actor. Nobody
will look at him, except to stare. The idea of his
going on the stage is laughed at. He scarcely dare
walk out in the streets because children follow him.
But he *is* a great actor, all the same, in spirit. He's
got the artistic temperament, and he can't be a
clerk. He can only be one thing, and that one
thing is made impossible by his height. He falls
in love with a girl. She rather likes him, but
naturally the idea of marrying a giant doesn't
appeal to her. So that's off, too. And he's got
no resources, and he's gradually starving in a garret.
See the tragedy?"

She nodded, reflective, sympathetically silent.

Henry continued: "Well, he's starving. He
doesn't know what to do. He isn't quite tall
enough to be a show-giant—they have to be over
seven feet—otherwise he might at any rate try the
music-hall stage. Then the manager of a West

End restaurant catches sight of him one day, and offers him a place as doorkeeper at a pound a week and tips. He refuses it indignantly. But after a week or two more of hunger he changes his mind and accepts. And this man who has the soul and the brains of a great artist is reduced to taking sixpences for opening cab-doors.

" Does it end there? "

" No. It's a sad story, I'm afraid. He dies one night in the snow outside the restaurant, while the rich noodles are gorging themselves inside to the music of a band. Consumption."

" It's the most original story I ever heard in all my life," said Geraldine enthusiastically.

" Do you think so? "

" I do, honestly. What are you going to call it —if I may ask? "

" Call it? " He hesitated a second. " *A Question of Cubits*," he said.

" You are simply wonderful at titles," she observed. " Thank you. Thank you so much."

" No one else knows," he finished.

When he had seen her safely to Chenies Street, and was travelling to Dawes Road in a cab, he felt perfectly happy. The story had come to him almost by itself. It had been coming all the evening, even while he was in the box, even while he was lost in admiration of Geraldine. It had cost him nothing. He knew he could write it with perfect ease. And Geraldine admired it! It was the most original story she had ever heard in all her life! He himself thought it extremely original, too. He saw now how foolish and premature had been his fears for the future. Of course he had studied human nature. Of course he had been through the mill, and practised style. Had he not won the prize for composition at the age of twelve? And was there not the tangible evidence of his essays for the Polytechnic, not to mention his continual work for Sir George?

He crept upstairs to his bedroom joyous, jaunty, exultant.

"Is that you, Henry?" It was Aunt Annie's inquiry.

"Yes," he answered, safely within his room.

"How late you are! It's half-past twelve and more."

"I got lost," he explained to her.

But he could not explain to himself what instinct had forced him to conceal from his adoring relatives the fact that he had bought a suit of dress-clothes, put them on, and sallied forth in them to spend an evening with a young lady.

Just as he was dropping off to sleep and beauteous visions, he sprang up with a start, and, lighting a candle, descended to the dining-room. There he stood on a chair, reached for the blue jar on the bookcase, extracted the two eggs, and carried them upstairs. He opened his window and threw the eggs into the middle of Dawes Road, but several houses lower down; they fell with a soft *plup*, and scattered.

Thus ended the miraculous evening.

The next day he was prostrate with one of his very worst dyspeptic visitations. The Knight pew at Munster Park Chapel was empty at both services, and Henry learnt from loving lips that he must expect to be ill if he persisted in working so hard. He meekly acknowledged the justice of the rebuke.

On Monday morning at half-past eight, before he had appeared at breakfast, there came a telegram, which Aunt Annie opened. It had been dispatched from Paris on the previous evening, and it ran: "*Congratulations on the box trick. Worth half a dozen books with the dear simple public. A sincere admirer.*" This telegram puzzled everybody, including Henry; though perhaps it puzzled Henry a little less than the ladies. When Aunt Annie suggested that it had been wrongly addressed, he agreed that no other explanation was possible, and Sarah took it back to the post-office.

He departed to business. At all the newspaper-shops, at all the bookstalls, he saw the placards of morning newspapers with lines conceived thus:

AMUSING INCIDENT AT THE ALHAMBRA.

A NOVELIST'S ADVENTURE.

VANISHING AUTHOR AT A MUSIC-HALL.

A NOVELIST IN A BOX.

CHAPTER XVIII

HIS JACK-HORNERISM

THAT autumn the Chancelleries of Europe happened to be rather less egotistic than usual, and the English and American publics, seeing no war-cloud on the horizon, were enabled to give the whole of their attention to the balloon sent up into the sky by Mr. Onions Winter. They stared to some purpose. There are some books which succeed before they are published, and the commercial travellers of Mr. Onions Winter reported unhesitatingly that *A Question of Cubits* was such a book. The libraries and the booksellers were alike graciously interested in the rumour of its advent. It was universally considered a "safe" novel; it was the sort of novel that the honest provincial bookseller reads himself for his own pleasure and recommends to his customers with a peculiar and special smile of sincerity as being not only "good," but "*really* good." People mentioned it with casual anticipatory remarks who had never previously been known to mention any novel later than *John Halifax, Gentleman.*

This and other similar pleasing phenomena were, of course, due in part to the mercantile sagacity of Mr. Onions Winter. For during a considerable period the Anglo-Saxon race was

not permitted to forget for a single day that at
a given moment the balloon would burst and rain
down copies of *A Question of Cubits* upon a thirsty
earth. *A Question of Cubits* became the universal
question, the question of questions, transcending
in its insistence the liver question, the soap
question, the Encyclopædia question, the whisky
question, the cigarette question, the patent-food
question, the bicycle-tyre question, and even the
formidable uric-acid question. Another powerful
factor in the case was undoubtedly the lengthy
paragraph concerning Henry's adventure at the
Alhambra. That paragraph, having crystallized
itself into a fixed form under the title " A Novelist
in a Box," had started on a journey round the
press of the entire world, and was making a pace
which would have left Jules Verne's hero out of
sight in twenty-four hours. No editor could deny
his hospitality to it. From the New York dailies
it travelled via the *Chicago Inter-Ocean* to the
Montreal Star, and thence back again with the
rapidity of light by way of the *Boston Transcript,*
the *Philadelphia Ledger,* and the *Washington Post,*
down to the *New Orleans Picayune.* Another day,
and it was in the *San Francisco Call,* and soon
afterwards it had reached *La Prensa* at Buenos
Ayres. It then disappeared for a period amid the
Pacific Isles, and was next heard of in the *Sydney
Bulletin,* the *Brisbane Courier,* and the *Melbourne
Argus.* A moment, and it blazed in the *North
China Herald,* and was shooting across India
through the columns of the Calcutta *Englishman*
and the *Allahabad Pioneer.* It arrived in Paris as
fresh as a new pin, and gained acceptance by the
Paris edition of the *New York Herald,* which had
printed it two months before and forgotten it, as

a brand-new item of the most luscious personal gossip. Thence, later, it had a smooth passage to London, and was seen everywhere with a new frontispiece consisting of the words: " Our readers may remember." Mr. Onions Winter reckoned that it had been worth at least five hundred pounds to him.

But there was something that counted more than the paragraph, and more than Mr. Onions Winter's mercantile sagacity, in the immense preliminary noise and rattle of *A Question of Cubits*: to wit, the genuine and ever-increasing vogue of *Love in Babylon,* and the beautiful hopes of future joy which it aroused in the myriad breasts of Henry's public. *Love in Babylon* had falsified the expert prediction of Mark Snyder, and had reached seventy-five thousand in Great Britain alone. What figure it reached in America no man could tell. The average citizen and his wife and daughter were truly enchanted by *Love in Babylon,* and since the state of being enchanted is one of almost ecstatic felicity, they were extremely anxious that Henry in a second work should repeat the operation upon them at the earliest possible instant.

The effect of the whole business upon Henry was what might have been expected. He was a modest young man, but there are two kinds of modesty, which may be called the internal and the external, and Henry excelled more in the former than in the latter. While never free from a secret and profound amazement that people could really care for his stuff (an infallible symptom of authentic modesty), Henry gradually lost the pristine virginity of his early diffidence. His demeanour grew confident and bold. His glance said: " I know exactly who I am, and let no one think otherwise." His self-esteem as a celebrity, stimulated and fattened by a tremendous daily diet of press-cuttings, and letters from feminine admirers all over the vastest of empires, was certainly in no immediate danger of inanition. Nor did the fact that he was still outside the rings known as literary circles injure that self-esteem in the slightest degree; by a curious trick of nature it performed the same function as the press-cuttings and the correspondence. Mark Snyder said: "Keep yourself to yourself. Don't be interviewed. Don't do anything except write. If publishers or editors approach you, refer them to me." This suited Henry. He liked to think that he was in the hands of Mark Snyder, as an athlete in the hands of his trainer. He liked to think that he was alone with his leviathan public; and he could find a sort of mild, proud pleasure in meeting every advance with a frigid, courteous refusal. It tickled his fancy that he, who had shaken a couple of continents or so with one little book, and had written another and a better one with the ease and assurance of a novelist born, should be willing to remain a shorthand clerk, earning three guineas a week. (He preferred now to regard himself as a common shorthand clerk, not as a private secretary to a knight: the piquancy of the situation was thereby intensified.) And as the day of publication of *A Question of Cubits* came nearer and nearer, he more and more resembled a little Jack Horner sitting in his private corner, and pulling out the plums of fame, and soliloquizing, "What a curious, interesting, strange, uncanny, original boy am I!"

Then one morning he received a telegram from Mark Snyder requesting his immediate presence at Kenilworth Mansions.

CHAPTER XIX

HE JUSTIFIES HIS FATHER

HE went at once to Kenilworth Mansions, but
he went against his will. And the reason of
his disinclination was that he scarcely desired
to encounter Geraldine. It was an ordeal for him to
encounter Geraldine. The events which had led to
this surprising condition of affairs were as follows:

Henry was one of those men—and there exist,
perhaps, more of them than may be imagined—
who are capable of plunging off the roof of a
house, and then reconsidering the enterprise and
turning back. With Henry it was never too late
for discretion. He would stop and think at the
most extraordinary moments. Thirty-six hours
after the roseate evening at the Louvre and the
Alhambra, just when he ought to have been laying
a scheme for meeting Geraldine at once by sheer
accident, Henry was coldly remarking to himself:
"Let me see exactly where I am. Let me survey
the position." He liked Geraldine, but now it
was with a sober liking, a liking which is not too
excited to listen to Reason. And Reason said,
after the position had been duly surveyed: "I
have nothing against this charming lady, and
much in her favour. Nevertheless, there need
be no hurry." Geraldine wrote to thank Henry

for the most enjoyable evening she had ever spent in her life, and Henry found the letter too effusive. When they next saw each other, Henry meant to keep strictly private the advice which he had accepted from Reason; but Geraldine knew all about it within the first ten seconds, and Henry knew that she knew. Politeness reigned, and the situation was felt to be difficult. Geraldine intended to be sisterly, but succeeded only in being resentful, and thus precipitated too soon the second stage of the entanglement, the stage in which a man, after seeing everything in a woman, sees nothing in her; this second stage is usually of the briefest, but circumstances may render it permanent. Then Geraldine wrote again, and asked Henry to tea at the flat in Chenies Street on a Saturday afternoon. Henry went, and found the flat closed. He expected to receive a note of bewitching, cajoling, feminine apology, but he did not receive it. They met again, always at Kenilworth Mansions, and in an interview full of pain at the start and full of insincerity at the finish, Henry learnt that Geraldine's invitation had been for Sunday, and not Saturday, that various people of much importance in her eyes had been asked to meet him, and that the company was deeply disappointed and the hostess humiliated. Henry was certain that she had written Saturday. Geraldine was certain that he had misread the day. He said nothing about confronting her with the letter itself, but he determined, in his masculine way, to do so. She gracefully pretended that the incident was closed, and amicably closed, but the silly little thing had got into her head the wild, inexcusable idea that Henry had stayed away from her "at home" on purpose, and Henry felt this.

He rushed to Dawes Road to find the letter, but the letter was undiscoverable; with the spiteful waywardness which often characterizes such letters, it had disappeared. So Henry thought it would be as well to leave the incident alone. Their cheery politeness to each other when they chanced to meet was affecting to witness. As for Henry, he had always suspected in Geraldine the existence of some element, some quality, some factor, which was beyond his comprehension, and now his suspicions were confirmed.

He fell into a habit of saying in his inmost heart: "Women!"

This meant that he had learnt all that was knowable about them, and that they were all alike, and that—the third division of the meaning was somewhat vague.

Just as he was ascending with the beautiful flunkey in the Kenilworth lift, a middle-aged and magnificently-dressed woman hastened into the marble hall from the street, and, seeing the lift in the act of vanishing with its precious burden, gave a slight scream and then a laugh. The beautiful flunkey permitted himself a derisive gesture, such as one male may make to another, and sped the lift more quickly upwards.

"Who's she?" Henry demanded.

"*I* don't know, sir," said the flunkey. "But you'll hear her ting-tinging at the bell in half a second. There!" he added in triumphant disgust, as the lift-bell rang impatiently. "There's some people," he remarked, "as thinks a lift can go up and down at once."

Geraldine with a few bright and pleasant remarks ushered Henry directly into the presence of Mark Snyder. Her companion was not in the office.

"Well," Mr. Snyder expansively and gaily welcomed him, "come and sit down, my young friend."

"Anything wrong?" Henry asked.

"No," said Mark. "But I've postponed publication of the Q. C. for a month."

In his letters Mr. Snyder always referred to *A Question of Cubits* as the Q. C.

"What on earth for?" exclaimed Henry.

He was not pleased. In strict truth, no one of his innumerable admirers was more keenly anxious for the appearance of that book than Henry himself. His appetite for notoriety and boom grew by what it fed on. He expected something colossal, and he expected it soon.

"Both in England and America," said Snyder.

"But why?"

"Serial rights," said Snyder impressively. "I told you some time since I might have a surprise for you, and I've got one. I fancied I might sell the serial rights in England to Macalisters, at my own price, but they thought the end was too sad. However, I've done business in New York with *Gordon's Weekly*. They'll issue the Q. C. in four instalments. It was really settled last week, but I had to arrange with Spring Onions. They've paid cash. I made 'em. How much d'you think?"

"I don't know," Henry said expectantly.

"Guess," Mark Snyder commanded him.

But Henry would not guess, and Snyder rang the bell for Geraldine.

"Miss Foster," he addressed the puzzling creature in a casual tone, "did you draw that cheque for Mr. Knight?"

"Yes, Mr. Snyder."

"Bring it me, please."

And she respectfully brought in a cheque, which Mr. Snyder signed.

"There!" said he, handing it to Henry. "What do you think of that?"

It was a cheque for one thousand and eighty pounds. Gordon and Brothers, the greatest publishing firm of the United States, had paid six thousand dollars for the right to publish serially *A Question of Cubits*, and Mark Snyder's well-earned commission on the transaction amounted to six hundred dollars.

"Things are looking up," Henry stammered, feebly facetious.

"It's nearly a record price," said Snyder complacently. "But you're a sort of a record man. And when they believe in a thing over there, they aren't afraid of making money talk and say so."

"Nay, nay!" thought Henry. "This is too much! This beats everything! Either I shall wake up soon or I shall find myself in a lunatic asylum." He was curiously reminded of the conjuring performance at the Alhambra.

He said:

"Thanks awfully, I'm sure!"

A large grandiose notion swept over him that he had a great mission in the world.

"That's all I have to say to you," said Mark Snyder pawkily.

Henry wanted to breathe instantly the ampler ether of the street, but on his way out he found Geraldine in rapid converse with the middle-aged and magnificently-dressed woman who thought that a lift could go up and down at once. They became silent.

"*Good*-morning, Miss Foster," said Henry hurriedly.

Then a pause occurred, very brief but uncomfortable, and the stranger glanced in the direction of the window.

"Let me introduce you to Mrs. Ashton Portway," said Geraldine. "Mrs. Portway, Mr. Knight."

Mrs. Portway bent forward her head, showed her teeth, smiled, laughed, and finally sniggered.

"So glad to make your acquaintance, Mr. Knight!" she burst out loudly and uncontrollably, as though Geraldine's magic formula had loosened a valve capable of withstanding enormous strains. Then she smiled, laughed, and sniggered : not because she imagined that she had achieved humour, but because that was her way of making herself agreeable. If anybody had told her that she could not open her mouth without sniggering, she would have indignantly disbelieved the statement. Nevertheless it was true. When she said the weather was changeable, she sniggered ; when she hoped you were quite well, she sniggered ; and if circumstances had required her to say that she was sorry to hear of the death of your mother, she would have sniggered.

Henry, however, unaccustomed to the phenomena accompanying her speech, mistook her at first for a woman determined to be witty at any cost.

"I'm glad to meet you," he said, and laughed as if to insinuate that that speech also was funny.

"I was desolated, simply desolated, not to see you at Miss Foster's 'at home,'" Mrs. Ashton Portway was presently sniggering. "Now, will you come to one of my Wednesdays? They begin in November. First and third. I always try to get interesting people, people who have done something."

"Of course I shall be delighted," Henry agreed. He was in a mood to scatter largesse among the crowd.

"That's so good of you," said Mrs. Ashton Portway, apparently overcome by the merry jest. "Now remember, I shall hold you to your promise. I shall write and remind you. I know you great men."

When Henry reached the staircase he discovered her card in his hand. He could not have explained how it came there. Without the portals of Kenilworth Mansions a pair of fine horses were protesting against the bearing-rein, and throwing spume across the street.

He walked straight up to the Louvre, and there lunched to the sound of wild Hungarian music. It was nearly three o'clock when he returned to his seat at Powells.

"The governor's pretty nearly breaking up the happy home," Foxall alarmingly greeted him in the inquiry office.

"Oh!" said Henry with a very passable imitation of guilelessness. "What's amiss?"

"He rang for you just after you went out at a quarter-past twelve." Here Foxall glanced mischievously at the clock. "He had his lunch sent in, and he's been raving ever since."

"What did you tell him?"

"I told him you'd gone to lunch."

"Did he say anything?"

"He asked whether you'd gone to Brighton for lunch. Krikey! He nearly sacked *me*! You know it's his golfing afternoon."

"So it is. I'd forgotten." Henry observed calmly.

Then he removed his hat and gloves, found his

note-book and pencil, and strode forward to joust with the knight.

"Did you want to dictate letters, Sir George?" he asked, opening Sir George's door.

The knight was taken aback.

"Where have you been," the famous solicitor demanded, "since the middle of the morning?"

"I had some urgent private business to attend to," said Henry. "And I've been to lunch. I went out at a quarter-past twelve."

"And it's now three o'clock. Why didn't you tell me you were going out?"

"Because you were engaged, Sir George."

"Listen to me," said Sir George. "You've been getting above yourself lately, my friend. And I won't have it. Understand, I will not have it. The rules of this office apply just as much to you as to anyone."

"I'm sorry," Henry put in coldly, "if I've put you to any inconvenience."

"Sorry be d——d, sir!" exclaimed Sir George. "Where on earth do you go for your lunch?"

"That concerns no one but me, Sir George," was the reply.

He would have given a five-pound note to know that Foxall and the entire staff were listening behind the door.

"You are an insolent puppy," Sir George stated.

"If you think so, Sir George," said Henry, "I resign my position here."

"And a fool!" the knight added.

"And did you say anything about the thousand pounds?" Aunt Annie asked, when, in the evening domesticity of Dawes Road, Henry recounted the doings of that day so full of emotions.

"Not I!" Henry replied. "Not a word!"

"You did quite right, my dear!" said Aunt Annie.
"A pretty thing, that you can't go out for a few
minutes!"

"Yes, isn't it?" said Henry.

"Whatever will Sir George do without you,
though?" his mother wondered.

And later, after he had displayed for her inspection the cheque for a thousand and eighty pounds,
the old lady cried, with moist eyes:

"My darling, your poor father might well insist
on having you called Shakspere! And to think that
I didn't want it! To think that I didn't want it!"

"Mark my words!" said Aunt Annie. "Sir
George will ask you to stay on."

And Aunt Annie was not deceived.

"I hope you've come to your senses," the lawyer
began early the next morning, not unkindly, but
rather with an intention obviously pacific. "Literature, or whatever you call it, may be all very well,
but you won't get another place like this in a hurry.
There's many an admitted solicitor earns less than
you, young man."

"Thanks very much, Sir George," Henry answered. "But I think, on the whole, I had better
leave."

"As you wish," said Sir George, hurt.

"Still," Henry proceeded, "I hope our relations
will remain pleasant. I hope I may continue to
employ you."

"Continue to employ me?" Sir George gasped.

"Yes," said Henry. "I got you to invest some
moneys for me some time ago. I have another
thousand now that I want a sound security for."

It was one of those rare flashes of his—rare, but
blindingly brilliant.

CHAPTER XX

PRESS AND PUBLIC

AT length arrived the eve of the consummation of Mr. Onions Winter's mercantile labours. Forty thousand copies of *A Question of Cubits* No. 8 of the Satin Library) had been printed, and already, twenty-four hours before they were to shine in booksellers' shops and on the counters of libraries, every copy had been sold to the trade and a second edition was in the press. Thus, it was certain that one immortal soul per thousand of the entire British race would read Henry's story. In literature, when nine hundred and ninety-nine souls ignore you, but the thousandth buys your work, or at least borrows it—that is called enormous popularity. Henry retired to bed in Dawes Road that night sure of his enormous popularity. But he did not dream of the devoted army of forty thousand admirers. He dreamt of the reviews, some of which he knew were to appear on the day of publication itself. A hundred copies of *A Question of Cubits* had been sent out for review, and in his dreams he saw a hundred highly-educated men, who had given their lives to the study of fiction, bending anxiously over the tome and seeking with conscientious care the precise phrases in which most accurately to express their expert appreciation of it. He dreamt much

of the reviewer of the *Daily Tribune,* his favouri
morning paper, whom he pictured as a man of fort
five or so, with gold-rimmed spectacles and an a
of generous enthusiasm.   He hoped great thing
from the article in the *Daily Tribune* (which, by
strange accident, had completely ignored *Love*
Babylon), and when he arose in the morning (h
had been lying awake a long time waiting to hea
the scamper of the newsboy on the steps) he di
covered that his hopes were happily realized.   Th
Daily Tribune had given nearly a column of prais
to *A Question of Cubits,* had quoted some choice ex
tracts, had drawn special attention to the wonderfu
originality of the plot, and asserted that the stor
was an advance, "if an advance were possible," o
the author's previous book.   His mother and Aun
Annie consumed the review at breakfast with an ex
cellent appetite, and lauded the insight of the critic

What had happened at the offices of the *Dail*
Tribune was this.   At the very moment whe
Henry was dreaming of its reviewer—namely, half
past eleven p.m.—its editor was gesticulating an
shouting at the end of a speaking-tube :

"Haven't had proof of that review of a boo
called *A Question of Cubits,* or some such idioti
title!   Send it down at once, instantly.   Do you
hear?   What?   Nonsense!"

The editor sprang away from the tube, and dashe
into the middle of a vast mass of papers on his desk,
turning them all over, first in heaps, then singly.
He then sprang in succession to various side-tables
and served their contents in the same manner.

"I tell you I sent it up myself before dinner,"
he roared into the tube.   "It's Mr. Clackmannan's
"copy"—you know that peculiar paper he writes
on.   Just look about.   Oh, conf——!"

Then the editor rang a bell.

"Send Mr. Heeley to me, quick!" he commanded the messenger-boy.

"I'm just finishing that leaderette," began Mr. Heeley, when he obeyed the summons. Mr. Heeley was a young man who had published a book of verse.

"Never mind the leaderette," said the editor. "Run across to the other shop yourself, and see if they've got a copy of *A Question of Cubits*—yes, that's it, *A Question of Cubits*—and do me fifteen inches on it at once. 'I've lost Clackmannan's copy.'" (The "other shop" was a wing occupied by a separate journal belonging to the proprietors of the *Tribune*.)

"What, that thing!" exclaimed Mr. Heeley. "Won't it do to-morrow? You know I hate messing my hands with that sort of piffle."

"No, it won't do to-morrow. I met Onions Winter at dinner on Saturday night, and I told him I'd review it on the day of publication. And when I promise a thing I promise it. Cut, my son! And I say"—the editor recalled Mr. Heeley, who was gloomily departing—"We're under no obligations to anyone. Write what you think, but, all the same, no antics, no spleen. You've got to learn yet that that isn't our speciality. You're not on the *Whitehall* now."

"Oh, all right, chief—all right!" Mr. Heeley concurred.

Five minutes later Mr. Heeley entered what he called his private boudoir, bearing a satinesque volume.

"Here, boys," he cried to two other young men who were already there, smoking clay pipes— "here's a lark! The chief wants fifteen inches on

this charming and pathetic art-work as quick a
you can. And no antics, he says. Here, Jack
here's fifty pages for you"—Mr. Heeley ripped th
beautiful inoffensive volume ruthlessly in pieces—
"and here's fifty for you, Clementina. Tell m
your parts of the plot. I'll deal with the first fift
my noble self."

Presently, after laughter, snipping out of page
with scissors, and some unseemly language, M
Heeley began to write.

"Oh, he's shot up to six foot eight!" exclaime
Jack, interrupting the scribe.

"Snow!" observed the bearded man styled
Clementina. "He dies in the snow. Listen.'
He read a passage from Henry's final scene
ending with, "His spirit had passed." "Chuck
me the scissors, Jack."

Mr. Heeley paused, looked up, and then drew
his pen through what he had written.

"I say, boys," he almost whispered, "I'll praise
it, eh? I'll take it seriously. It'll be simply
delicious."

"What about the chief?"

"Oh, the chief won't notice it! It'll be just for
us three, and a few at the club."

Then there was hard scribbling, and pasting of
extracts into blank spaces, and more laughter.

"'If an advance were possible,'" Clementina
read, over Mr. Heeley's shoulder. "You'll give
the show away, you fool!"

"No, I shan't, Clemmy, my boy," said Mr. Heeley
judicially. "They'll stand simply anything. I bet
you what you like Onions Winter quotes that all
over the place."

And he handed the last sheet of the review to a
messenger, and ran off to the editorial room to

report that instructions had been executed. Jack
and Clementina relighted their pipes with select
bits of *A Question of Cubits,* and threw the remaining
débris of the volume into the waste-paper basket.
The hour was twenty minutes past midnight. . . .

The great majority of the reviews were exceed-
ingly favourable, and even where praise was diluted
with blame, the blame was administered with
respect, as a dentist might respectfully pain a
prince in pulling his tooth out. The public had
voted for Henry, and the press, organ of public
opinion, displayed a wise discretion. The daring
freshness of Henry's plot, his inventive power, his
skill in "creating atmosphere," his gift for pathos,
his unfailing wholesomeness, and his knack in the
management of narrative, were noted and eulogized
in dozens of articles. Nearly every reviewer
prophesied brilliant success for him; several admitted frankly that his equipment revealed genius
of the first rank. A mere handful of papers scorned
him. Prominent among this handful was the
Whitehall Gazette. The distinguished mouthpiece
of the superior classes dealt with *A Question of
Cubits* at the foot of a column, in a brief paragraph
headed "Our Worst Fears realized." The paragraph, which was nothing but a summary of the
plot, concluded in these terms: "So he expired,
every inch of him, in the snow, a victim to the
British Public's rapacious appetite for the sentimental."

The rudeness of the *Whitehall Gazette,* however,
did nothing whatever to impair the wondrous vogue
which Henry now began to enjoy. His first boom
had been great, but it was a trifle compared to his
second. The title of the new book became a
catchword. When a little man was seen walking

with a tall woman, people exclaimed: "It's a question of cubits." When the recruiting regulations of the British army were relaxed, people also exclaimed: "It's a question of cubits." During a famous royal procession, sightseers trying to see the sight over the heads of a crowd five deep shouted to each other all along the route: "It's a question of cubits." Exceptionally tall men were nicknamed "Gerald" by their friends. Henry's Gerald, by the way, had died as doorkeeper at a restaurant called the Trianon. The Trianon was at once recognized as the Louvre, and the tall commissionaire at the Louvre thereby trebled his former renown. "Not dead in the snow yet?" the wits of the West End would greet him on descending from their hansoms, and he would reply, infinitely gratified: "No, sir. No snow, sir." A music-hall star of no mean eminence sang a song with the refrain:

> "You may think what you like,
>   You may say what you like,
>   It was simply a question of cubits."

The lyric related the history of a new suit of clothes that was worn by everyone except the person who had ordered it.

Those benefactors of humanity, the leading advertisers, used "A Question of Cubits" for their own exalted ends. A firm of manufacturers of high-heeled shoes played with it for a month in various forms. The proprietors of an unrivalled cheap cigarette disbursed thousands of pounds in order to familiarize the public with certain facts. As thus: "A Question of Cubits. Every hour of every day we sell as many cigarettes as, if placed on end one on the top of the other, would make a column as lofty as the Eiffel Tower. Owing to the

ct that cigarettes are not once mentioned in
Question of Cubits, we regret to say that the
thor has not authorized us to assert that he was
inking of our cigarettes when he wrote Chapter
II. of that popular novel."

Editors and publishers cried in vain for Henry.
ney could get from him neither interviews, short
ories, nor novels. They could only get polite
ferences to Mark Snyder. And Mark Snyder
d made his unalterable plans for the exploitation
this most wonderful racehorse that he had ever
ained for the Fame Stakes. The supply of
atty paragraphs concerning the hero and the
ook of the day would have utterly failed had
t Mr. Onions Winter courageously come to the
scue and allowed himself to be interviewed. And
en then respectable journals were reduced to this
rt of paragraph: "Apropos of Mr. Knight's
nenomenal book, it may not be generally known
nat the exact measure of a cubit is. There have
en three different cubits — the Scriptural, the
oman, and the English. Of these, the first-
med," etc.

So the thing ran on.

And at the back of it all, supporting it all, was
e steady and prodigious sale of the book, the
nuine enthusiasm for it of the average sensible,
althy-minded woman and man.

Finally, the information leaked out that Mac-
stairs had made august and successful overtures
r the reception of Henry into their fold. Sir
ugh Macalistair, the head of the firm, was (at
at time) the only publisher who had ever been
ighted. And the history of Macalistairs was
e history of all that was greatest and purest in
nglish literature during the nineteenth century.

Without Macalistairs, English literature since Sco
would have been nowhere. Henry was to write
long novel in due course, and Macalistairs were
have the world's rights of the book, and were
use it as a serial in their venerable and lus
Magazine, and to pay Henry, on delivery of tl
manuscript, eight thousand pounds, of which s
thousand was to count as in advance of royalties
the book.

Mr. Onions Winter was very angry at what I
termed an ungrateful desertion. The unfortuna
man died a year or two later of appendicitis, an
his last words were that he, and he alone, ha
"discovered" Henry.

CHAPTER XXI

PLAYING THE NEW GAME

WHEN Henry had seceded from Powells, and had begun to devote several dignified hours a day to the excogitation of a theme for his new novel, and the triumph of *A Question of Cubits* was at its height, he thought that there ought to be some change in his secret self to correspond with the change in his circumstances. But he could perceive none, except, perhaps, that now and then he was visited by the feeling that he had a great mission in the world. That feeling, however, came rarely, and, for the most part, he existed in a state of not being quite able to comprehend exactly how and why his stories roused the enthusiasm of an immense public.

In essentials he remained the same Henry, and the sameness of his simple self was never more apparent to him than when he got out of a cab one foggy Wednesday night in November, and rang at the Grecian portico of Mrs. Ashton Portway's house in Lowndes Square. A crimson cloth covered the footpath. This was his first entry into the truly great world, and though he was perfectly aware that as a lion he could not easily be surpassed in no matter what menagerie, his nervousness and timidity were so acute as to be painful; they

annoyed him, in fact. When, in the wide hall, a
servant respectfully but firmly closed the door after
him, thus cutting off a possible retreat to the
homely society of the cabman, he became resigned,
careless, reckless, desperate, as who should say,
"Now I *have* done it!" And as at the Louvre, so
at Mrs. Ashton Portway's, his outer garments were
taken forcibly from him, and a ticket given to him
in exchange. The ticket startled him, especially as
he saw no notice on the walls that the management
would not be responsible for articles not deposited
in the cloakroom. Nobody inquired about his
identity, and without further ritual he was asked
to ascend towards regions whence came the faint
sound of music. At the top of the stairs a young
and handsome man, faultless alike in costume and in
manners, suavely accosted him.

"What name, sir?"

"Knight," said Henry gruffly. The young man
thought that Henry was on the point of losing
his temper from some cause or causes unknown,
whereas Henry was merely timid.

Then the music ceased, and was succeeded by
violent chatter; the young man threw open a
door, and announced in loud clear tones, which
Henry deemed ridiculously loud and ridiculously
clear:

"Mr. Knight!"

Henry saw a vast apartment full of women's
shoulders and black patches of masculinity; the
violent chatter died into a profound silence; every
face was turned towards him. He nearly fell down
dead on the doormat, and then, remembering that
life was after all sweet, he plunged into the room
as into the sea.

When he came up breathless and spluttering,

Mrs. Ashton Portway (in black and silver) was introducing him to her husband, Mr. Ashton Portway, known to a small circle of readers as Raymond Quick, the author of several mild novels issued at his own expense. Mr. Portway was rich in money and in his wife; he had inherited the money, and his literary instincts had discovered the wife in a publisher's daughter. The union had not been blessed with children, which was fortunate, since Mrs. Portway was left free to devote the whole of her time to the encouragement of literary talent in the most unliterary of cities.

Henry rather liked Mr. Ashton Portway, whose small black eyes seemed to say: "That's all right, my friend. I share your ideas fully. When you want a quiet whisky, come to me."

"And what have you been doing this dark day?" Mrs. Ashton Portway began, with her snigger.

"Well," said Henry, "I dropped into the National Gallery this afternoon, but really it was so——"

"The National Gallery?" exclaimed Mrs. Ashton Portway swiftly. "I must introduce you to Miss Marchrose, the author of that charming hand-book *Pictures in London*. Miss Marchrose," she called out, urging Henry towards a corner of the room, "This is Mr. Knight." She sniggered on the name. "He's just dropped into the National Gallery."

Then Mrs. Ashton Portway sailed off to receive her guests, and Henry was alone with Miss Marchrose in a nook between a cabinet and a monograph. Many eyes were upon them. Miss Marchrose, a woman of thirty, with a thin face and amorphous body draped in two shades of olive, was obviously flattered.

"Be frank, and admit you've never heard of me," she said.

"Oh yes, I have," he lied.

Pause.

"Do you often go to the National Gallery, M Knight?"

"Not as often as I ought."

Pause.

Several observant women began to think th Miss Marchrose was not making the best of Hen —that, indeed, she had proved unworthy of a unmerited honour.

"I sometimes think——" Miss Marchrose essaye

But a young lady got up in the middle of th room, and with extraordinary self-command an presence of mind began to recite Wordsworth "The Brothers." She continued to recite an recite until she had finished it, and then sat dow amid universal joy.

"Matthew Arnold said that was the greate poem of the century," remarked a man near th phonograph.

"You'll pardon me," said Miss Marchrose, turn ing to him. "If you are thinking of Matthe Arnold's introduction to the selected poems, you and——"

"My dear," said Mrs. Ashton Portway, suddenl looming up opposite the reciter, "what a memor you have!"

"Was it so long, then?" murmured a tall ma with spectacles and a light wavy beard.

"I shall send you back to Paris, Mr. Dolbiac said Mrs. Ashton Portway, "if you are too witty The hostess smiled and sniggered, but it w generally felt that Mr. Dolbiac's remark had n been in the best taste.

For a few moments Henry was alone and uncar for, and he examined his surroundings. His fir conclusion was that there was not a pretty woman in the room, and his second, that this fact had not escaped the notice of several other men who were hanging about in corners.   Then Mrs. Ashton Portway, having accomplished the task of receiving, beckoned him, and intimated to him that, being a lion and the king of beasts, he must roar.   "I think everyone here has done something," she said as she took him round and forced him to roar.   His roaring was a miserable fiasco, but most people mistook it for the latest fashion in roaring, and were impressed.

"Now you must take someone down to get something to eat," she apprised him, when he had growled out soft nothings to poetesses, paragraphists, publicists, positivists, penny-a-liners, and other pale persons.   "Whom shall it be?—Ashton! What have you done?"

The phonograph had been advertised to give a reproduction of Ternina in the Liebestod from *Tristan und Isolde,* but instead it broke into the "Washington Post," and the room, braced to a great occasion, was horrified.   Mrs. Portway, abandoning Henry, ran to silence the disastrous consequence of her husband's clumsiness.   Henry, perhaps impelled by an instinctive longing, gazed absently through the open door into the passage, and there, with two other girls on a settee, he perceived Geraldine!   She smiled, rose, and came towards him.   She looked disconcertingly pretty; she was always at her best in the evening; and she had such eyes to gaze on him.

"You here!" she murmured.

Ordinary words, but they were enveloped in layers of feeling, as a child's simple gift may be wrapped in lovely tinted tissue-papers!

6

"She's the finest woman in the place," he thought decisively. And he said to her: "Will you come down and have something to eat?"

"I can talk to *her*," he reflected with satisfaction, as the faultless young man handed them desired sandwiches in the supper-room. What he meant was that she could talk to him; but men often make this mistake.

Before he had eaten half a sandwich, the period of time between that night and the night at the Louvre had been absolutely blotted out. He did not know why. He could think of no explanation. It merely was so.

She told him she had sold a sensational serial for a pound a thousand words.

"Not a bad price—for me," she added.

"Not half enough!" he exclaimed ardently.

Her eyes moistened. He thought what a shame it was that a creature like her should be compelled to earn even a portion of her livelihood by typewriting for Mark Snyder. The faultless young man unostentatiously poured more wine into their glasses. No other guests happened to be in the room. . . .

"Ah, you're here!" It was the hostess, sniggering.

"You told me to bring someone down," said Henry, who had no intention of being outfaced now.

"We're just coming up," Geraldine added.

"That's right!" said Mrs. Ashton Portway. "A lot of people have gone, and now that we shall be a little bit more intimate, I want to try that new game. I don't think it's ever been played in London anywhere yet. I saw it in the *New York Herald*. Of course, nobody who isn't just a little clever could play at it."

" Oh yes !" Geraldine smiled. " You mean
' Characters.' I remember you told me about it."

And Mrs. Ashton Portway said that she did mean
" Characters."

In the drawing-room she explained that in playing the game of " Characters" you chose a subject
for discussion, and then each player secretly thought
of a character in fiction, and spoke in the discussion
as he imagined that character would have spoken.
At the end of the game you tried to guess the
characters chosen.

" I think it ought to be classical fiction only,"
she said.

Sundry guests declined to play, on the ground
that they lacked the needful brilliance. Henry
declined utterly, but he had the wit not to give
his reasons. It was he who suggested that the
non-players should form a jury. At last seven
players were recruited, including Mr. Ashton Portway, Miss Marchrose, Geraldine, Mr. Dolbiac, and
three others. Mrs. Ashton Portway sat down by
Henry as a jurywoman.

" And now what are you going to discuss ? "
said she.

No one could find a topic.

" Let us discuss love," Miss Marchrose ventured.

" Yes," said Mr. Dolbiac, " let's. There's nothing
like leather."

So the seven in the centre of the room assumed
attitudes suitable for the discussion of love.

" Have you all chosen your characters ? " asked
the hostess.

" We have," replied the seven.

" Then begin."

" Don't all speak at once," said Mr. Dolbiac, after
a pause.

"Who is that chap?" Henry whispered.

"Mr. Dolbiac? He's a sculptor from Paris. Quite English, I believe, except for his grand-mother. Intensely clever." Mrs. Ashton Portway distilled these facts into Henry's ear, and then turned to the silent seven. "It *is* rather difficult, isn't it?" she breathed encouragingly.

"Love is not for such as me," said Mr. Dolbiac solemnly. Then he looked at his hostess, and called out in an undertone: "I've begun."

"The question," said Miss Marchrose, clearing her throat, "is, not what love is not, but what it is."

"You must kindly stand up," said Mr. Dolbiac. "I can't hear."

Miss Marchrose glanced at Mrs. Ashton Portway, and Mrs. Ashton Portway told Mr. Dolbiac that he was on no account to be silly.

Then Mr. Ashton Portway and Geraldine both began to speak at once, and then insisted on being silent at once, and in the end Mr. Ashton Portway was induced to say something about Dulcinea.

"He's chosen Don Quixote," his wife informed Henry behind her hand. "It's his favourite novel."

The discussion proceeded under difficulties, for no one was loquacious except Mr. Dolbiac, and all Mr. Dolbiac's utterances were staccato and sense-less. The game had had several narrow escapes of extinction, when Miss Marchrose galvanized it by means of a long and serious monologue treating of the sorts of man with whom a self-respecting woman will never fall in love. There appeared to be about a hundred and thirty-three sorts of that man.

"There is one sort of man with whom no woman, self-respecting or otherwise, will fall in love," said Mr. Dolbiac, "and that is the sort of man she can't kiss without having to stand on the mantelpiece.   Alas!"—he hid his face in his handkerchief—"I am that sort."

"Without having to stand on the mantelpiece?" Mrs. Ashton Portway repeated.   "What can he mean?   Mr. Dolbiac, you aren't playing the game."

"Yes, I am, gracious lady," he contradicted her.

"Well, what character are you, then?" demanded Miss Marchrose, irritated by his grotesque pendant to her oration.

"I'm Gerald in *A Question of Cubits*."

The company felt extremely awkward.   Henry blushed.

"I said classical fiction," Mrs. Ashton Portway corrected Mr. Dolbiac stiffly.   "Of course I don't mean to insinuate that it isn't——" She turned to Henry.

"Oh! did you?" observed Dolbiac calmly. "So sorry.   I knew it was a silly and nincompoopish book, but I thought you wouldn't mind so long as——"

"*Mr.* Dolbiac!"

That particular Wednesday of Mrs. Ashton Portway's came to an end in hurried confusion. Mr. Dolbiac professed to be entirely ignorant of Henry's identity, and went out into the night. Henry assured his hostess that really it was nothing, except a good joke.   But everyone felt that the less said, the better.   Of such creases in the web of social life Time is the best smoother.

CHAPTER XXII

HE LEARNS MORE ABOUT WOMEN

WHEN Henry had rendered up his ticket and recovered his garments, he found Geraldine in the hall, and a servant asking her if she wanted a four-wheeler or a hansom. He was not quite sure whether she had descended before him or after him : things were rather misty.

"I am going your way," he said. "Can't I see you home ?"

He was going her way : the idea of going her way had occurred to him suddenly as a beautiful idea.

Instead of replying, she looked at him. She looked at him sadly out of the white shawl which enveloped her head and her golden hair, and nodded.

There was a four-wheeler at the kerb, and they entered it and sat down side by side in that restricted compartment, and the fat old driver, with his red face popping up out of a barrel consisting of scores of overcoats and aprons, drove off. It was very foggy, but one could see the lamp-posts.

Geraldine coughed.

"These fogs are simply awful, aren't they ?" he remarked.

She made no answer.

"It isn't often they begin as early as this," he proceeded ; "I suppose it means a bad winter."

But she made no answer.

And then a sort of throb communicated itself to him, and then another, and then he heard a smothered sound. This magnificent creature, this independent, experienced, strong-minded, superior, dazzling creature was crying—was, indeed, sobbing. And cabs are so small, and she was so close. Pleasure may be so keen as to be agonizing : Henry discovered this profound truth in that moment. In that moment he learnt more about women than he had learnt during the whole of his previous life. He knew that her sobbing had some connection with *A Question of Cubits,* but he could not exactly determine the connection.

"What's the matter?" the blundering fool inquired nervously. "You aren't well."

"I'm so—so ashamed," she stammered out, when she had patted her eyes with a fragment of lace.

"Why? What of?"

"I introduced her to you. It's my fault."

"But what's your fault?"

"This horrible thing that happened."

She sobbed again frequently.

"Oh, that was nothing!" said Henry kindly. "You mustn't think about it."

"You don't know how I feel," she managed to tell him.

"I wish you'd forget it," he urged her. "He didn't mean to be rude."

"It isn't so much his rudeness," she wept. "It's—anyone saying a thing—like that—about your book. You don't know how I feel."

"Oh, come!" Henry enjoined her. "What's my book, anyhow?"

"It's yours," she said, and began to cry gently, resignedly, femininely.

It had grown dark. The cab had plunged into an opaque sea of blackest fog. No sound could be heard save the footfalls of the horse, which was now walking very slowly. They were cut off absolutely from the rest of the universe. There was no such thing as society, the state, traditions, etiquette; nothing existed, ever had existed, or ever would exist, except themselves, twain, in that lost four-wheeler.

Henry had a box of matches in his overcoat pocket. He struck one, illuminating their tiny chamber, and he saw her face once more, as though after long years. And there were little black marks round her eyes, due to her tears and the fog and the fragment of lace. And those little black marks appeared to him to be the most delicious, enchanting, and wonderful little black marks that the mind of man could possibly conceive. And there was an exquisite, timid, confiding, surrendering look in her eyes, which said "I'm only a weak, foolish, fanciful woman, and you are a big, strong, wise, great man; my one merit is that I know *how* great, *how* chivalrous you are!" And mixed up with the timidity in that look there was something else — something that made him almost shudder. All this by the light of one match. . . .

Good-bye world! Good-bye mother! Good-bye Aunt Annie! Good-bye the natural course of events! Good-bye correctness, prudence, precedents! Good-bye all! Good-bye everything! He dropped the match and kissed her.

And his knowledge of women was still further increased.

Oh, the unique ecstasy of such propinquity!

Eternity set in.   And in eternity one does not light matches. . . .

The next exterior phenomenon was a blinding flash through the window of what, after all, was a cab.   The door opened.

"You'd better get out o' this," said the cabman, surveying them by the ray of one of his own lamps.

"Why?" asked Henry.

"Why?" replied the cabman sourly.   "Look here, governor, do you know where we are?"

"No," said Henry.

"No.   And I'm jiggered if I do, either.   You'd better take the other blessed lamp and ask.   No, not me.   I don't leave my horse.   I ain't agoin' to lose my horse."

So Henry got out of the cab, and took a lamp and moved forward into nothingness, and found a railing and some steps, and after climbing the steps saw a star, which proved ultimately to be a light over a swing-door.   He pushed open the swing-door, and was confronted by a footman.

"Will you kindly tell me where I am?" he asked the footman.

"This is Marlborough House," said the footman.

"Oh, is it?   Thanks," said Henry.

"Well," ejaculated the cabman when Henry had luckily regained the vehicle.   "I suppose that ain't good enough for you!   Buckingham Palace is your doss, I suppose."

They could now hear distant sounds, which indicated other vessels in distress.

The cabman said he would make an effort to reach Charing Cross, by leading his horse and

sticking to the kerb; but not an inch farther than
Charing Cross would he undertake to go.

The passage over Trafalgar Square was so
exciting that, when at length the aged cabman
touched pavement—that is to say, when his horse
had planted two forefeet firmly on the steps of the
Golden Cross Hotel—he announced that that
precise point would be the end of the voyage.

"You go in there and sleep it off," he advised
his passengers. "Chenies Street won't see much
of you to-night. And make it five bob, governor.
I've done my best."

"You must stop the night here," said Henry in
a low voice to Geraldine, before opening the doors
of the hotel. "And I," he added quickly, "will go
to Morley's. It's round the corner, and so I can't
lose my way."

"Yes, dear," she acquiesced. "I dare say that
will be best."

"Your eyes are a little black with the fog," he
told her.

"Are they?" she said, wiping them. "Thanks
for telling me."

And they entered.

"Nasty night, sir," the hall-porter greeted them.

"Very," said Henry. "This lady wants a room.
Have you one?"

"Certainly, sir."

At the foot of the staircase they shook hands,
and kissed in imagination.

"Good-night," he said, and she said the
same.

But when she had climbed three or four stairs,
she gave a little start and returned to him, smiling,
appealing.

"I've only got a shilling or two," she whispered.

"Can you lend me some money to pay the bill with?"

He produced a sovereign. Since the last kiss in the cab, nothing had afforded him one hundredth part of the joy which he experienced in parting with that sovereign. The transfer of the coin, so natural, so right, so proper, seemed to set a seal on what had occurred, to make it real and effective. He wished to shower gold upon her.

As, bathed in joy and bliss, he watched her up the stairs, a little, obscure compartment of his brain was thinking: "If anyone had told me two hours ago that before midnight I should be engaged to be married to the finest woman I ever saw, I should have said they were off their chumps. Curious, I've never mentioned her at home since she called! Rather awkward!"

He turned sharply and resolutely to go to Morley's, and collided with Mr. Dolbiac, who, strangely enough, was standing immediately behind him, and gazing up the stairs, too.

"Ah, my bold buccaneer!" said Mr. Dolbiac familiarly. "Digested those *marrons glacés*? I've fairly caught you out this time, haven't I?"

Henry stared at him, startled, and blushed a deep crimson.

"You don't remember me. You've forgotten me," said Mr. Dolbiac.

"It isn't Cousin Tom?" Henry guessed.

"Oh, isn't it?" said Mr. Dolbiac. "That's just what it is."

Henry shook his hand generously. "I'm awfully glad to see you," he began, and then, feeling that he must be a man of the world: "Come and have a drink. Are you stopping here?"

The episode of Mrs. Ashton Portway's was, then, simply one of Cousin Tom's jokes, and he accepted it as such without the least demure or ill-will.

"It was you who sent that funny telegram, wasn't it?" he asked Cousin Tom.

In the smoking-room Tom explained how he had grown a beard in obedience to the dictates of nature, and changed his name in obedience to the dictates of art. And Henry, for his part, explained sundry things about himself, and about Geraldine.

The next morning, when Henry arrived at Dawes Road, decidedly late, Tom was already there. And more, he had already told the ladies, evidently in a highly-decorated narrative, of Henry's engagement! The situation for Henry was delicate in the extreme, but, anyhow, his mother and aunt had received the first shock. They knew the naked fact, and that was something. And of course Cousin Tom always made delicate situations: it was his privilege to do so. Cousin Tom's two aunts were delighted to see him again, and in a state so flourishing. He was asked no inconvenient questions, and he furnished no information. Bygones were bygones. Henry had never been told about the trifling incident of the ten pounds.

"She's coming down to-night," Henry said, addressing his mother, after the midday meal.

"I'm very glad," replied his mother.

"We shall be most pleased to welcome her," Aunt Annie said. "Well, Tom——"

CHAPTER XXIII

SEPARATION

HENRY'S astonishment at finding himself so suddenly betrothed to the finest woman in the world began to fade and perish in three days or so. As he looked into the past with that searching eye of his, he thought he could see that his relations with Geraldine had never ceased to develop since their commencement, even when they had not been precisely cordial and sincere. He remembered strange things that he had read about love in books, things which had previously struck him as being absurd, but which now became explanatory commentaries on the puzzling text of the episode in the cab. It was not long before he decided that the episode in the cab was almost a normal episode.

He was very proud and happy, and full of sad superior pity for all young men who, through incorrect views concerning women, had neglected to plight themselves.

He imagined that he was going to settle down and live for ever in a state of bliss with the finest woman in the world, rich, famous, honoured; and that life held for him no other experience, and especially no disconcerting, dismaying experience. But in this supposition he was mistaken.

One afternoon he had escorted Tom to Chenies Street, in order that Tom might formally meet Geraldine. It was rather nervous work, having regard to Tom's share in the disaster at Lowndes Square; and the more so because Geraldine's visit to Dawes Road had not been a dazzling success. Geraldine in Dawes Road had somehow the air, the brazen air, of an orchid in a clump of violets; the violets, by their mere quality of being violets, rebuked the orchid, and the orchid could not have flourished for any extended period in that temperature. Still, Mrs. Knight and Aunt Annie said to Henry afterwards that Geraldine was very clever and nice; and Geraldine said to Henry afterwards that his mother and aunt were delightful old ladies. The ordeal for Geraldine was now quite a different one. Henry hoped for the best. It did not follow, because Geraldine had not roused the enthusiasm of Dawes Road, that she would leave Tom cold. In fact, Henry could not see how Tom could fail to be enchanted.

A minor question which troubled Henry, as they ascended the stone stairs at Chenies Street, was this: Should he kiss Geraldine in front of Tom? He decided that it was not only his right, but his duty, to kiss her in the privacy of her own flat, with none but a relative present. "Kiss her I will!" his thought ran. And kiss her he did. Nothing untoward occurred. "Why, of course!" he reflected. "What on earth was I worrying about?" He was conscious of glory. And he soon saw that Tom really was impressed by Geraldine. Tom's eyes said to him: "You're not such a fool as you might have been."

Geraldine scolded Tom for his behaviour at Mrs. Ashton Portway's, and Tom replied in Tom's manner; and then, when they were all at ease, she turned to Henry.

"My poor friend," she said, "I've got bad news."

She handed him a letter from her brother in Leicester, from which it appeared that the brother's two elder children were down with scarlatina, while the youngest, three days old, and the mother, were in a condition to cause a certain anxiety . . . and could Geraldine come to the rescue?

"Shall you go?" Henry asked.

"Oh yes," she said. "I've arranged with Mr. Snyder, and wired Teddy that I'll arrive early to-morrow."

She spoke in an extremely matter-of-fact tone, as though there were no such things as love and ecstasy in the world, as though to indicate that in her opinion life was no joke, after all.

"And what about me?" said Henry. He thought: "My shrewd, capable girl has to sacrifice herself—and me—in order to look after incompetent persons who can't look after themselves!"

"You'll be all right," said she, still in the same tone.

"Can't I run down and see you?" he suggested.

She laughed briefly, as at a pleasantry, and so Henry laughed too.

"With four sick people on my hands!" she exclaimed.

"How long shall you be away?" he inquired.

"My dear—can I tell?"

"You'd better come back to Paris with me for a week or so, my son," said Tom. "I shall leave the day after to-morrow."

And now Henry laughed, as at a pleasantry. But, to his surprise, Geraldine said:

"Yes, do. What a good idea! I should like

you to enjoy yourself, and Paris is so jolly. You've been, haven't you, dearest?"

"No," Henry replied. "I've never been abroad at all."

"*Never?* Oh, that settles it. You must go."

Henry had neither the slightest desire nor the slightest intention to go to Paris. The idea of him being in Paris, of all places, while Geraldine was nursing the sick night and day, was not a pleasant one.

"You really ought to go, you know," Tom resumed. "You, a novelist . . . can't see too much! The monuments of Paris, the genius of the French nation! And there's notepaper and envelopes and stamps, just the same as in London. Letters posted in Paris before six o'clock will arrive in Leicester on the following afternoon. Am I not right, Miss Foster?"

Geraldine smiled.

"No," said Henry. "I'm not going to Paris—not me!"

"But I wish it," Geraldine remarked calmly.

And he saw, amazed, that she did wish it. Pursuing his researches into the nature of women, he perceived vaguely that she would find pleasure in martyrizing herself in Leicester while he was gadding about Paris; and pleasure also in the thought of his uncomfortable thought of her martyrizing herself in Leicester while he was gadding about Paris.

But he said to himself that he did not mean to yield to womanish whims—he, a man.

"And my work?" he questioned lightly.

"Your work will be all the better," said Geraldine with a firm accent.

And then it seemed to be borne in upon him

hat womanish whims needed delicate handling.
And why not yield this once? It would please
her. And he could have been firm had he chosen.

Hence it was arranged.

" I'm only going to please you," he said to her
when he was mournfully seeing her off at St.
Pancras the next morning.

" Yes, I know," she answered, " and it's sweet of
you. But you want someone to make you move,
dearest."

" Oh, do I ? " he thought; " do I ? "

His mother and Aunt Annie were politely surprised at the excursion. But they succeeded in
conveying to him that they had decided to be
prepared for anything now.

CHAPTER XXIV

COSETTE

TOM and Henry put up at the Grand Hotel, Paris. The idea was Tom's. He decried the hotel, its clients and its reputation, but he said that it had one advantage: when you were at the Grand Hotel you knew where you were. Tom, it appeared, had a studio and bedroom up in Montmartre. He postponed visiting this abode, however, until the morrow, partly because it would not be prepared for him, and partly in order to give Henry the full advantage of his society. They sat on the terrace of the Café de la Paix, after a very late dinner, and drank bock, and watched the nocturnal life of the boulevard, and talked. Henry gathered —not from any direct statement, but by inference— that Tom must have acquired a position in the art world of Paris. Tom mentioned the Salon as if the Salon were his pocket, and stated casually that there was work of his in the Luxembourg. Strange that the cosmopolitan quality of Tom's reputation— if, in comparison with Henry's, it might be called a reputation at all—roused the author's envy! He, too, wished to be famous in France, and to be at home in two capitals. Tom retired at what he considered an early hour—namely, midnight—the oceanic part of the journey having saddened him.

efore they separated he borrowed a sovereign from
Henry, and this simple monetary transaction had
he singular effect of reducing Henry's envy.

The next morning Henry wished to begin a
systematic course of the monuments of Paris and
he artistic genius of the French nation. But Tom
could not get up. At eleven o'clock Henry, armed
with a map and the English talent for exploration,
et forth alone to grasp the general outlines of the
city, and came back successful at half-past one.
At half-past two Tom was inclined to consider the
question of getting up, and Henry strolled out
again and lost himself between the Moulin Rouge
and the church of Sacré Cœur. It was turned four
o'clock when he sighted the façade of the hotel,
and by that time Tom had not only arisen, but
departed, leaving a message that he should be back
at six o'clock. So Henry wandered up and down
the boulevard, from the Madeleine to Marguéry's
Restaurant, had an automatic tea at the Express-
Bar, and continued to wander up and down the
boulevard.

He felt that he could have wandered up and
down the boulevard for ever.

And then night fell; and all along the boulevard,
high on seventh storeys and low as the street names,
there flashed and flickered and winked, in red and
yellow and a most voluptuous purple, electric invitations to drink inspiriting liqueurs and to go and
amuse yourself in places where the last word of
amusement was spoken. There was one name,
a name almost revered by the average healthy
Englishman, which wrote itself magically on the
dark blue sky in yellow, then extinguished itself
and wrote itself anew in red, and so on tirelessly:
that name was "Folies-Bergère." It gave birth to

the most extraordinary sensations in Henry's breast And other names, such as "Casino de Paris, "Eldorado," "Scala," glittered, with their guiding arrows of light, from bronze columns full in the middle of the street. And what with these devices, and the splendid glowing windows of the shops, and the enlarged photographs of surpassingly beautiful women which hung in heavy frames from almost every lamp-post, and the jollity of the slowly moving crowds, and the incredible illustrations displayed on the newspaper kiosks, and the moon creeping up the velvet sky, and the thousands of little tables at which the jolly crowds halted to drink liquids coloured like the rainbow—what with all that, and what with the curious gay feeling in the air, Henry felt that possibly Berlin, or Boston or even Timbuctoo, might be a suitable and proper place for an engaged young man, but that decidedly Paris was not.

At six o'clock there was no sign of Tom. He arrived at half-past seven, admitted that he was a little late, and said that a friend had given him tickets for the first performance of the new "revue" at the Folies-Bergère, that night.

"And now, since we are alone, we can talk," said Cosette, adding, "Mon petit."

"Yes," Henry agreed.

"Dolbiac has told me you are very rich—une vogue épatante. . . . One would not say it. . . . But how your ears are pretty!" Cosette glanced admiringly at the lobe of his left ear.

("Anyhow," Henry reflected, "she would insist on me coming to Paris. I didn't want to come.")

They were alone, and yet not alone. They occupied a "loge" in the crammed, gorgeous, noisy

Folies-Bergère. But it resembled a box in an English theatre less than an old-fashioned family pew at the Great Queen Street Wesleyan Chapel. It was divided from other boxes and from the stalls and from the jostling promenade by white partitions scarcely as high as a walking-stick. There were four enamelled chairs in it, and Henry and Cosette were seated on two of them ; the other two were empty. Tom had led Henry like a sheep to the box, where they were evidently expected by two excessively stylish young women, whom Tom had introduced to the overcome Henry as Loulou and Cosette, two artists of the Théâtre des Capucines. Loulou was short and fair and of a full habit, and spoke no English. Cosette was tall and slim and dark, and talked slowly, and with smiles, a language which was frequently a recognizable imitation of English. She had learnt it, she said, in Ireland, where she had been educated in a French convent. She had just finished a long engagement at the Capucines, and in a fortnight she was to commence at the Scala : this was an off-night for her. She protested a deep admiration for Tom.

Cosette and Loulou and Tom had held several colloquies, in incomprehensible French that raced like a mill-stream over a weir, with acquaintances who accosted them on the promenade or in the stalls, and at length Tom and Loulou had left the "loge" for a few minutes in order to accept the hospitality of friends in the great hall at the back of the auditorium. The new "revue" seemed to be the very last thing that they were interested in.

"Don't be afraid," Tom, departing, had said to Henry. "She won't eat you."

"You leave me to take care of myself," Henry had replied, lifting his chin.

Cosette transgressed the English code governing the externals of women in various particulars. And the principal result was to make the English code seem insular and antique. She had an extremely large white hat, with a very feathery feather in it, and some large white roses between the brim and her black hair. Her black hair was positively sable, and one single immense lock of it was drawn level across her forehead. With the large white hat she wore a low evening-dress, lace-covered, with loose sleeves to the elbow, and white gloves running up into the mystery of the sleeves. Round her neck was a tight string of pearls. The combination of the hat and the evening-dress startled Henry, but he saw in the theatre many other women similarly contemptuous of the English code, and came to the conclusion that, though queer and un-English, the French custom had its points. Cosette's complexion was even more audacious in its contempt of Henry's deepest English convictions. Her lips were most obviously painted, and her eyebrows had received some assistance, and once, in a manner absolutely ingenuous, she produced a little bag and gazed at herself in a little mirror, and patted her chin with a little puff, and then smiled happily at Henry. Yes, and Henry approved. He was forced to approve, forced to admit the artificial and decadent but indubitable charm of paint and powder. The contrast between Cosette's lips and her brilliant teeth was utterly bewitching.

She was not beautiful. In facial looks, she was simply not in the same class with Geraldine. And as to intellect, also, Geraldine was an easy first.

But in all other things, in the things that really mattered (such was the dim thought at the back

of Henry's mind), she was to Geraldine what
Geraldine was to Aunt Annie. Her gown was a
miracle, her hat was another, and her coiffure
a third. And when she removed a glove—her
rings, and her finger-nails! And the glimpses of
her shoes! She was so *finished*. And in the way
of being frankly feminine, Geraldine might go to
school to her. Geraldine had brains and did not
hide them; Geraldine used the weapon of seriousness. But Cosette knew better than that. Cosette
could surround you with a something, an emana-
tion of all the woman in her, that was more
efficient to enchant than the brains of a Georges
Sand could have been.

And Paris, or that part of the city which con-
stitutes Paris for the average healthy Englishman,
was an open book to this woman of twenty-four.
Nothing was hid from her. Nothing startled her,
nothing seemed unusual to her. Nothing shocked
her except Henry's ignorance of all the most
interesting things in the world.

"Well, what do you think of a French 'revue,'
my son?" asked Tom when he returned with
Loulou.

"Don't know," said Henry, with his gibus tipped
a little backward. "Haven't seen it. We've been
talking. The music's a fearful din." He felt
nearly as Parisian as Tom looked.

"*Tiens!*" Cosette twittered to Loulou, making
a gesture towards Henry's ears. "*Regarde-moi
ces oreilles. Sont jolies. Pas?*"

And she brought her teeth together with a click
that seemed to render somewhat doubtful Tom's
assurance that she would not eat Henry.

Soon afterwards Tom and Henry left the
auditorium, and Henry parted from Cosette with

mingled sensations of regret and relief. He might never see her again. Geraldine . . .

But Tom did not emerge from the outer precincts of the vast music-hall without several more conversations with fellows-well-met, and when he and Henry reached the pavement Cosette and Loulou happened to be just getting into a cab. Tom did not see them, but Henry and Cosette caught sight of each other. She beckoned to him.

"You come and take lunch with me to-morrow? *Hein?*" she almost whispered in that ear of his.

"*Avec plaisir,*" said Henry. He had studied French regularly for six years at school.

"Rue de Bruxelles, No. 3," she instructed him. "Noon."

"I know it!" he exclaimed delightedly. He had, in fact, passed through the street during the day.

No one had ever told him before that his ears were pretty.

When, after parleying nervously with the concierge, he arrived at the second-floor of No. 3, Rue de Bruxelles, he heard violent high sounds of altercation through the door at which he was about to ring, and then the door opened, and a young woman, flushed and weeping, was sped out on to the landing, Cosette herself being the exterminator.

"Ah, *mon ami!*" said Cosette, seeing him. "Enter then."

She charmed him inwards and shut the door, breathing quickly.

"It is my *domestique*, my servant, who steals me," she explained. "Come and sit down in the salon. I will tell you."

The salon was a little room about eight feet by ten, silkily furnished. Besides being the salon, it was clearly also the *salle à manger,* and when one person had sat down therein it was full. Cosette took Henry's hat and coat and umbrella and pressed him into a chair by the shoulders, and then gave him the full history of her unparalleled difficulties with the exterminated servant. She looked quite a different Cosette now from the Cosette of the previous evening. Her black hair was loose; her face pale, and her lips also a little pale; and she was draped from neck to feet in a crimson peignoir, very fluffy.

"And now I must buy the lunch," she said. "I must go myself. Excuse me."

She disappeared into the adjoining room, the bedroom, and Henry could hear the *fracas* of silk and stuff. "What do you eat for lunch?" she cried out.

"Anything," Henry called in reply.

"Oh! *Que les hommes sont bêtes!*" she murmured, her voice seemingly lost in the folds of a dress. "One must choose. Say."

"Whatever you like," said Henry.

"Rumsteak? Say."

"Oh yes," said Henry.

She reappeared in a plain black frock, with a reticule in her hand, and at the same moment a fox-terrier wandered in from somewhere.

"*Mimisse!*" she cried in ecstasy, snatching up the animal and kissing it. "You want to go with your mamma? Yess. What do you think of my fox? She is real English. *Elle est si gentille avec sa mère! Ma Mimisse! Ma petite fille!* My little girl! *Dites, mon ami,*"—she abandoned the dog—"have you some money for our lunch? Five francs?"

"That enough?" Henry asked, handing her the piece.

"Thank you," she said. "*Viens, Mimisse.*"

"You haven't put your hat on," Henry informed her.

"*Mais, mon pauvre ami*, is it that you take me for a duchess? I come from the *ouvriers*, me, the working peoples. I avow it. Never can I do my shops in a hat. I should blush."

And with a tremendous flutter, scamper, and chatter, Cosette and her *fox* departed, leaving Henry solitary to guard the flat.

He laughed to himself, at himself. "Well," he murmured, looking down into the court, "I suppose——"

Cosette came back with a tin of sardines, a piece of steak, some French beans, two cakes of the kind called "nuns," a bunch of grapes, and a segment of Brie cheese. She put on an apron, and went into the kitchenlet, and began to cook, giving Henry instructions the while how to lay the table and where to find the things. Then she brought him the coffee-mill full of coffee, and told him to grind it.

The lunch seemed to be ready in about three minutes, and it was merely perfection. Such steak, such masterly handling of green vegetables, and such "nuns"! And the wine!

There were three at table, Mimisse being the third. Mimisse partook of everything except wine.

"You see I am a woman *pot-au-feu*," said Cosette, not without satisfaction, in response to his praises of the meal. He did not exactly know what a woman *pot-au-feu* might be, but he agreed enthusiastically that she was that sort of woman.

At the stage of coffee—Mimisse had a piece of
sugar steeped in coffee—she produced cigarettes,
and made him light his cigarette at hers, and put
her elbows on the table and looked at his ears.
She was still wearing the apron, which appeared to
Henry to be an apron of ineffable grace.

"So you are *fiancé, mon petit*? Eh?" she said.

"Who told you?" Henry asked quickly.
"Tom?"

She nodded; then sighed. He was instructed
to describe Geraldine in detail. Cosette sighed
once more.

"Why do you sigh?" he demanded.

"Who knows?" she answered. "*Dites!* English
ladies are cold? Like that?" She affected the
supercilious gestures of Englishwomen whom she
had seen in the streets and elsewhere. "No?"

"Perhaps," Henry said.

"Frenchwomen are better? Yes? *Dites-moi
franchement.* You think?"

"In some ways," Henry agreed.

"You like Frenchwomen more than those cold
Englishwomen who have no *chic*?"

"When I'm in Paris I do," said Henry.

"*Ah! Comme tous les Anglais!*"

She rose, and just grazed his ear with her little
finger. "*Va!*" she said.

He felt that she was beyond anything in his
previous experience.

A little later she told him she had to go to the
Scala to sign her contract, and she issued an order
that he was to take Mimisse out for a little exercise,
and return for her in half an hour, when she would
be dressed. So Henry went forth with Mimisse at
the end of a strap.

In the Boulevard de Clichy who should accost

him but Tom, whom he had left asleep as usual ⸱
the hotel!

"What dog is that?" Tom asked.

"Cosette's," said Henry, unsuccessfully trying ⸱
assume a demeanour at once natural and tranquil.

"My young friend," said Tom, "I perceive tha
it will be necessary to look after you. I was ju
going to my studio, but I will accompany you ⸱
your divagations."

They returned to the Rue de Bruxelles togethe
Cosette was dressed in all her afternoon splendou
for the undoing of theatrical managers. The rô
of woman *pot-au-feu* was finished for that day.

"I'm off to Monte Carlo to-morrow," said To
to her. "I'm going to paint a portrait there. An
Henry will come with me."

"To Monte Carlo?" Henry gasped.

"To Monte Carlo."

"But——"

"Do you suppose I'm going to leave you here?
Tom inquired. "And you can't return to Londo
yet."

"No," said Cosette thoughtfully, "not London."

They left her in the Boulevard de Strasbourg
and then Tom suggested a visit to the Luxembour
Gallery. It was true: a life-sized statue of Sapph
signed "Dolbiac," did in fact occupy a prominen
place in the sculpture room. Henry was impressed
so also was Tom, who explained to his young cousi
all the beauties of the work.

"What else is there to see here?" Henry asked
when the stream of explanations had slackened.

"Oh, there's nothing much else," said Tom
dejectedly.

They came away. This was the beginning and

e end of Henry's studies in the monuments of
ris.

At the hotel he found opportunity to be alone.
He wished to know exactly where he stood,
d which way he was looking. It was certain
at the day had been unlike any other day in his
reer.

"I suppose that's what they call Bohemia," he
claimed wistfully, solitary in his bedroom.

And then later:

"Jove! I've never written to Geraldine to-day!"

CHAPTER XXV

THE RAKE'S PROGRESS

"*FAITES vos jeux, messieurs*," said the chie croupier of the table.

Henry's fingers touched a solitary five franc piece in his pocket, large, massive, seductive.

Yes, he was at Monte Carlo. He could scarcel believe it, but it was so. Tom had brought him The curious thing about Tom was that, though he lied frequently and casually, just as some men hitc their collars, his wildest statements had a way o being truthful. Thus, a work of his had in fac been purchased by the French Government an placed on exhibition in the Luxembourg. An thus he had in fact come to Monte Carlo to pair a portrait—the portrait of a Sicilian Countess, h said, and Henry believed, without actually havin seen the alleged Countess—at a high price. Ther were more complexities in Tom's character tha Henry could unravel. Henry had paid the entir bill at the Grand Hotel, had lent Tom a sovereig another sovereign, and a five-pound note, and woul certainly have been mulcted in Tom's fare on th expensive *train de luxe* had he not sagaciousl demanded money from Tom before entering th ticket-office. Without being told, Henry kne that money lent to Tom was money dropped dow grating in the street. During the long journey ithwards Tom had confessed, with a fine apprecia-n of the fun, that he lived in Paris until his :ditors made Paris disagreeable, and then went ;ewhere, Rome or London, until other creditors ide Rome or London disagreeable, and then he turned to Paris.

Henry had received this remark in silence.

As the train neared Monte Carlo—the hour was eate and matutinal—Henry had observed Tom ring at the scenery through the window, his ffee untasted, and tears in his rapt eyes. "What's ?" Henry had innocently inquired. Tom turned him fiercely. "Silly ass!" Tom growled with thing contempt. "Can't you feel how beautiful all is?"

And this remark, too, Henry had received in ence.

"Do you reckon yourself a great artist?" Tom d asked, and Henry had laughed. "No, I'm t joking," Tom had insisted. "Do you honestly :kon yourself a great artist? I reckon myself e. There's candour for you. Now tell me, nkly." There was a wonderful and rare charm Tom's manner as he uttered these words. "I n't know," Henry had replied. "Yes, you do," m had insisted. "Speak the truth. I won't it go any farther. Do you think yourself as g as George Eliot, for example?" Henry had sitated, forced into sincerity by Tom's persuasive d serious tone. "It's not a fair question," Henry d said at length. Whereupon Tom, without the ist warning, had burst into loud laughter: "My ld buccaneer, you take the cake. You always l. You always will. There is something about u that is colossal, immense, and magnificent."

And this third remark also Henry had receiv
in silence.

It was their second day at Monte Carlo, a
Tom, after getting Henry's card of admission
him, had left him in the gaming rooms, and go
off to the alleged Countess. The hour was on
half-past eleven, and none of the roulette tabl
was crowded; two of the trente-et-quarante tabl
had not even begun to operate. For some minut
Henry watched a roulette table, fascinated by tl
munificent style of the croupiers in throwing fiv
franc pieces, louis, and bank-notes about the gre
cloth, and the neat twist of the thumb and fing
with which the chief croupier spun the ball. The
were thirty or forty persons round the table,
solemn and intent, and most of them noting tl
sequence of winning numbers on little car
"What fools!" thought Henry. "They know tl
Casino people make a profit of two thousand a da
They know the chances are mathematically again
them. And yet they expect to win!"

It was just at this point in his meditations up
the spectacle of human foolishness that he felt tl
five-franc piece in his pocket. An idea crossed l
mind that he would stake it, merely in order
be able to say that he had gambled at Monte Car
Absurd! How much more effective to assert th
he had visited the tables and not gambled! .
And then he knew that something within hi
more powerful than his common sense would for
him to stake that five-franc piece. He glanc
furtively at the crowd to see whether anyone w
observing him. No. Well, it having been decid
to bet, the next question was, how to bet? No
Henry had read a magazine article concerning tl
tables at Monte Carlo, and, being of a mathematic

ırn, had clearly grasped the principles of the game.
Ie said to himself, with his characteristic caution:
I'll wait till red wins four times running, and then
ll stake on the black."

(" But surely," remarked the logical superior per-
ɒn in him, " you don't mean to argue that a spin of
ıe ball is affected by the spins that have preceded
? You don't mean to argue that, because red
ins four times, or forty times, running, black is
ıy the more likely to win at the next spin?"
You shut up!" retorted the human side of him
ɒssly. " I know all about that.")

At last, after a considerable period of waiting,
d won four times in succession. Henry felt hot
ıd excited. He pulled the great coin out of his
ɔcket and dropped it in again, and then the
ɔupier spun the ball and exhorted the company
veral times to make their games, and precisely
the croupier was saying sternly, "*Rien ne va
us,*" Henry took the coin again, and with a
emendous effort of will, leaning over an old man
ated in front of him, pitched it into the meadow
evoted to black stakes. He blushed; his hair
ıgled at the root; he was convinced that every-
ɒdy round the table was looking at him with
rdonic amusement.

" *Quatre, noir, pair, et manque,*" cried the croupier.
Black had won.

Henry's heart was beating like a hammer.
ven now he was afraid lest one of the scoundrels
ho, according to the magazine article, infested the
oms, might lean over his shoulder and snatch his
wful gains. He kept an eye lifting. The
ɔupier threw a five-franc piece to join his own,
ıd Henry, with elaborate calmness, picked both
eces up. His temperature fell; he breathed

7

more easily. "It's nothing, after all," he though
"Of course, on that system I'm bound to win."

Soon afterwards the old man in front of hi
grunted and left, and Henry slipped into th
vacant chair. In half an hour he had mad
twenty francs; his demeanour had hardened; h
felt as though he had frequented Monte Car
steadily for years; and what he did not kno
about the art and craft of roulette was apocryphal.

"Place this for me," said a feminine voice.

He turned swiftly. It was Cosette's voic
There she stood, exquisitely and miraculous
dressed, behind his chair, holding a note of th
Bank of France in her gloved hand!

"When did you come?" he asked loudly, in h
extreme astonishment.

"Pstt!" she smilingly admonished him f
breaking the rule of the saloons. "Place this f
me."

It was a note for a thousand francs.

"This?" he said.

"Yes."

"But where?"

"Choose," she whispered. "You are luck
You will bring happiness."

He did not know what he was doing, so mad
whirled his brain, and, as the black enclosure ha
pened to be nearest to him, he dropped the no
there. The croupier at the end of the tab
manœuvred it with his rake, and called out to th
centre: "Billet de mille francs." Then, when
was too late, Henry recollected that black h
already turned up three times together. But in
moment black had won.

"I can quite understand the fascination th
game has for people," Henry thought.

" Leave them there," said Cosette, pointing to
he two notes for a thousand francs each. " I like
o follow the run."

Black won again.

" Leave them there," said Cosette, pointing to
he four notes for a thousand francs each. " I did
ay you would bring happiness." They smiled at
ach other happily.

Black won again.

Cosette repeated her orders. Such a method of
laying was entirely contrary to Henry's expert
pinion. Nevertheless, black, in defiance of rules,
ontinued to win. When sixteen thousand francs
f paper lay before Henry, the croupier addressed
im sharply, and he gathered, with Cosette's
ssistance, that the maximum stake was twelve
nousand francs.

" Put four thousand on the odd numbers," said
osette. " Eh ? You think ? "

" No," said Henry. " Evens."

And the number four turned up again.

At a stroke he had won sixteen thousand francs,
x hundred and forty pounds, for Cosette, and the
otal gains were one thousand two hundred and
rty pounds.

The spectators were at last interested in Henry's
lay. It was no longer an illusion on his part that
eople stared at him.

" Say a number," whispered Cosette. " Shut the
yes and say a number."

" Twenty-four," said Henry. She had told him
was her age.

" *Bien !* *Voilà huit louis !* " she exclaimed, open-
g her purse of netted gold ; and he took the
ght coins and put them on number twenty-four.
ght notes for a thousand francs each remained

on the even numbers.   The other notes were i
Henry's hip-pocket, a crushed mass.

Twenty-four won.   It was nothing but blac
that morning.   "*Mais c'est épatant!*" murmure
several onlookers anxiously.

A croupier counted out innumerable notes, an
sundry noble and glorious gold *plaques* of a hundre
francs each.   Henry could not check the total
but he knew vaguely that another three hundre
pounds or so had accrued to him, on behalf c
Cosette.

" I fancy red now," he said, sighing.

And feeling a terrible habitué, he said to th
croupier in French : " *Maximum.   Rouge.*"

" *Maximum.   Rouge,*" repeated the croupier.

Instantly the red enclosure was covered with th
stakes of a quantity of persons who had deter
mined to partake of Henry's luck.

And red won ; it was the number fourteen.

Henry was so absorbed that he did not observ
a colloquy between two of the croupiers at th
middle of the table.   The bank was broken, an
every soul in every room knew it in the fraction c
a second.

"Come," said Cosette, as soon as Henry ha
received the winnings.   "Come," she repeate
pulling his sleeve nervously.

"I've broken the bank at Monte Carlo!" h
thought as they hurried out of the luxurious hall
"I've broken the bank at Monte Carlo!   I'v
broken the bank at Monte Carlo!"

If he had succeeded to the imperial throne c
China, he would have felt much the same as h
felt then.

Quite by chance he remembered the magazin
article, and a statement therein that prudent peopl

when they had won a large sum, drove straight
to Smith's Bank and banked it *coram publico,* so
that scoundrels might be aware that assault with
violence in the night hours would be futile.

"If we lunch?" Cosette suggested, while Henry
was getting his hat.

"No, not yet," he said importantly.

At Smith's Bank he found that he had sixty-
three thousand francs of hers.

"You dear," she murmured in ecstasy, and
actually pressed a light kiss on his ear in the
presence of the bank clerk! "You let me keep
the three thousand?" she pleaded, like a charming
child.

So he let her keep the three thousand. The
sixty thousand was banked in her name.

"You offer me a lunch?" she chirruped
deliciously, in the street. "I gave you a lunch.
You give me one. It is why I am come to
Monte Carlo, for that lunch."

They lunched at the Hôtel de Paris.

He was intoxicated that afternoon, though not
with the Heidsieck they had consumed. They
sat out on the terrace. It was December, but
like an English June. And the pride of life, and
the beauty of the world and of women and of the
costumes of women, informed and uplifted his soul.
He thought neither of the past nor of the future,
but simply and intensely of the present. He
would not even ask himself why, really, Cosette
had come to Monte Carlo. She said she had
come with Loulou, because they both wanted to
come; and Loulou was in bed with *migraine*;
but as for Cosette, she never had the *migraine,*
she was never ill. And then the sun touched the

Italian hills, and the sea slept, and . . . and . . . what a planet, this earth! He could almost understand why Tom had wept between Cannes and Nice.

It was arranged that the four should dine together that evening, if Loulou had improved and Tom was discoverable. Henry promised to discover him. Cosette announced that she must visit Loulou, and they parted for a few brief hours.

"*Mon petit!*" she threw after him.

To see that girl tripping along the terrace in the sunset was a sight!

Henry went to the Hôtel des Anglais, but Tom had not been seen there. He strolled back to the Casino gardens. The gardeners were drawing suspended sheets over priceless blossoms. When that operation was finished, he yawned, and decided that he might as well go into the Casino for half an hour, just to watch the play.

The atmosphere of the gay but unventilated rooms was heavy and noxious.

He chose a different table to watch, a table far from the scene of his early triumph. In a few minutes he said that he might as well play, to pass the time. So he began to play, feeling like a giant among pigmies. He lost two hundred francs in five spins.

"Steady, my friend!" he enjoined himself.

Now, two hundred francs should be the merest trifle to a man who has won sixty-three thousand francs. Henry, however, had not won sixty-three thousand francs. On the other hand, it was precisely Henry who had paid sixty-five francs for lunch for two that day, and Henry who had lent Tom a hundred and seventy-five francs, and Henry

ho had paid Tom's hotel bill in Paris, and Henry
ho had left England with just fifty-five pounds—
sum which he had imagined to be royally ample
r his needs on the Continent.

He considered the situation.

He had his return-ticket from Monte Carlo to
aris, and his return-ticket from Paris to London.
le probably owed fifty francs at the hotel, and he
ossessed a note for a hundred francs, two notes
r fifty francs, some French gold and silver, and
me English silver.

Continuing to play upon his faultless system, he
st another fifty francs.

"I can ask her to lend me something. I won all
at lot for her," he said.

"You know perfectly well you can't ask her to
nd you something," said an abstract reasoning
ower within him. "It's just because you won all
at lot for her that you can't. You'd be afraid
st she should think you were sponging on her.
an you imagine yourself asking her?"

"Well, I can ask Tom," he said.

"Tom!" exclaimed the abstract reasoning power.

"I can wire to Snyder," he said.

"That would look a bit thick," replied the ab-
ract reasoning power, "telegraphing for money—
om Monte Carlo."

Henry took the note for a hundred francs and
it it on red, and went icy cold in the feet and
nds, and swore a horrid oath.

Black won.

He had sworn, and he was a man of his word.
e walked straight out of the Casino; but un-
rtainly, feebly, as a man who has received a
aggering blow between the eyes, as a man who
s been pitched into a mountain-pool in January,

as a somnambulist who has wakened to find himse
on the edge of a precipice.

He paid his bill at the hotel, and asked the tim
of the next train to Paris. There was no ne
train to Paris that night, but there was a train t
Marseilles. He took it. Had it been a train on
to Nice, or to the Plutonian realms, he would hav
taken it. He said no good-byes. He left n
messages, no explanations. He went. On th
next afternoon but one he arrived at Victoria wit
fivepence in his pocket. Twopence he paid to d
posit his luggage in the cloakroom, and threepenc
for the Underground fare to Charing Cross. Fro
Charing Cross he walked up to Kenilworth Mansio
and got a sovereign from Mark Snyder. Coutts'
where Mark financed himself, was closed, and
sovereign was all that Mark had.

Henry was thankful that the news had not ye
reached London—at any rate, it had not reache
Mark Snyder. It was certain to do so, howeve
Henry had read in that morning's Paris edition
the *New York Herald* : " Mr. Henry S. Knight, th
famous young English novelist, broke the bank a
Monte Carlo the other day. He was understoo
to be playing in conjunction with Mademoisel
Cosette, the well-known Parisian *divette*, who
also on a visit to Monte Carlo. I am told tha
the pair have netted over a hundred and six
thousand francs."

He reflected upon Cosette, and he reflected up
Geraldine. It was like returning to two lumps of sug
in one's tea after having got accustomed to three

He was very proud of himself for having so rut
lessly abandoned Monte Carlo, Cosette, Loulo
Tom, and the whole apparatus. And he had th
right to be.

CHAPTER XXVI

THE NEW LIFE

THEY were nervous, both of them. Although they had been legally and publicly married and their situation was in every way regular, although the new flat in Ashley Gardens was spacious, spotless, and luxurious to an extraordinary degree, although they had a sum of nearly seven thousand pounds at the bank, although their consciences were clear and their persons ornamental, Henry and Geraldine were decidedly nervous as they sat in their drawing-room awaiting the arrival of Mrs. Knight and Aunt Annie, who had accepted an invitation to afternoon tea and dinner.

It was the third day after the conclusion of their mysterious honeymoon.

" Have one, dearest ? " said Geraldine, determined to be gay, holding up a morsel which she took from a coloured box by her side. And Henry took it with his teeth from between her charming fingers. " Lovely, aren't they ? " she mumbled, munching another morsel herself, and he mumbled that they were.

She was certainly charming, if English. Thoughts of Cosette, which used to flit through his brain with a surprising effect that can only be likened to an effect of flamingoes sweeping across an English

meadow, had now almost entirely ceased to disturb
him.   He had but to imagine what Geraldine's
attitude towards Cosette would have been had
the two met, in order to perceive the over
powering balance of advantages in Geraldine's
favour.

Much had happened since Cosette.

As a consequence of natural reaction, he had at
once settled down to be extremely serious, and to
take himself seriously.   He had been assisted in
the endeavour by the publication of an article in
a monthly review, entitled "The Art of Henry
Shakspere Knight."   The article explained to him
how wonderful he was, and he was ingenuously
and sincerely thankful for the revelation.   It also,
incidentally, showed him that "Henry Shakspere
Knight" was a better signature for his books than
"Henry S. Knight," and he decided to adopt it
in his next work.   Further, it had enormously
quickened in him the sense of his mission in the
world, of his duty to his colossal public, and his
potentiality for good.

He put aside a book which he had already
haltingly commenced, and began a new one, in
which a victim to the passion for gambling was
redeemed by the love of a pure young girl.   It
contained dramatic scenes in Paris, in the *train de
luxe,* and in Monte Carlo.   One of the most striking
scenes was a harmony of moonlight and love on
board a yacht in the Mediterranean, in which she,
Veronica prevailed upon Hubert to submerge an
ill-gotten gain of six hundred and sixty-three
thousand francs, although the renunciation would
leave Hubert penniless.   Geraldine watched the
progress of this book with absolute satisfaction
She had no fault to find with it.   She gazed at

Henry with large admiring eyes as he read aloud to her chapter after chapter.

"What do you think I'm going to call it?" he demanded of her once, gleefully.

"I don't know," she said.

"*Red and Black*," he told her. "Isn't that a fine title?"

"Yes," she said. "But it's been used before;" and she gave him particulars of Stendhal's novel, of which he had never heard.

"Oh, well!" he exclaimed, somewhat dashed. "As Stendhal was a Frenchman, and his book doesn't deal with gambling at all, I think I may stick to my title. I thought of it myself, you know."

"Oh yes, dearest. I *know* you did," Geraldine said eagerly.

"You think I'd better alter it?"

Geraldine glanced at the floor. "You see," she murmured, "Stendhal was a really great writer."

He started, shocked. She had spoken in such a way that he could not be sure whether she meant, "Stendhal was a really *great* writer," or, "*Stendhal* was a *really* great writer." If the former, he did not mind, much. But if the latter—well, he thought uncomfortably of what Tom had said to him in the rain. And he perceived again, and more clearly than ever before, that there was something in Geraldine which baffled him—something which he could not penetrate, and never would penetrate.

"Suppose I call it *Black and Red*? Will that do?" he asked forlornly.

"It would do," she answered; "but it doesn't sound so well."

"I've got it!" he cried exultantly. "I've got it! *The Plague-Spot*. Monte Carlo the plague-spot of Europe, you know."

"Spendid!" she said with enthusiasm. "You are always magnificent at titles."

And it was universally admitted that he was.

The book had been triumphantly finished, and the manuscript delivered to Macalistairs via Mark Snyder, and the huge cheque received under cover of a letter full of compliments on Henry's achievement. Macalistairs announced that their *Magazine* would shortly contain the opening chapters of Mr. Henry Shakspere Knight's great romance *The Plague-Spot*, which would run for one year and which combined a tremendous indictment of certain phases of modern life with an original love-story by turns idyllic and dramatic. *Gordon's Monthly* was serializing the novel in America. About this time, an interview with Henry, suggested by Sir Hugh Macalistair himself, appeared in an important daily paper. "It is quite true," said Henry in the interview, "that I went to Monte Carlo to obtain first-hand material for my book. The stories of my breaking the bank there, however, are wildly exaggerated. Of course, I played a little, in order to be able to put myself in the place of my hero. I should explain that I was in Monte Carlo with my cousin, Mr. Dolbiac, the well-known sculptor and painter, who was painting portraits there. Mr. Dolbiac is very much at home in Parisian artistic society, and he happened to introduce me to a famous French lady singer who was in Monte Carlo at the time. This lady and I found ourselves playing at the same table. From time to time I put down her stake for her; that was all. She certainly had an extraordinary run of luck, but the bank was actually broken at last by the united bets of a number of people. That is the whole story, and I'm afraid it is much less exciting and picturesque than the rumours which have been flying about. I have never seen the lady since that day."

Then his marriage had filled the air.

At an early stage in the preparations for that event his mother and Aunt Annie became passive —ceased all activity. Perfect peace was maintained, but they withdrew. Fundamentally and absolutely, Geraldine's ideas were not theirs, and Geraldine did as she liked with Henry. Geraldine and Henry interrogated Mark Snyder as to the future. "Shall we be justified in living at the rate of two thousand a year?" they asked him. "Yes," he said, "and four times that!" He had just perused *The Plague-Spot* in manuscript. "Let's make it three thousand, then," said Geraldine to Henry. And she had planned the establishment of their home on that scale. Henry did not tell the ladies at Dawes Road that the rent of the flat was three hundred a year, and that the furniture had cost over a thousand, and that he was going to give Geraldine two hundred a year for dress. He feared apoplexy in his mother, and a nervous crisis in Aunt Annie.

The marriage took place in a church. It was not this that secretly pained Mrs. Knight and Aunt Annie; all good Wesleyan Methodists marry themselves in church. What secretly pained them was the fact that Henry would not divulge, even to his own mother, the locality of the honeymoon. He did say that Geraldine had been bent upon Paris, and that he had completely barred Paris ("Quite right," Aunt Annie remarked), but he would say no more. And so after the ceremony the self-conscious pair had disappeared for a fort-night into the unknown and the unknowable.

And now they had reappeared out of the unknown and the unknowable, and, with the help of four servants, meant to sustain life in Mrs. Knight and Aunt Annie for a period of some five hours.

They heard a ring in the distance of the flat.

"Prepare to receive cavalry," said Geraldine, sitting erect in her blue dress on the green settee in the middle of the immense drawing-room.

Then, seeing Henry's face, she jumped up, crossed over to her husband, and gave him a smacking kiss between the eyes. "Dearest, I didn't mean it!" she whispered enchantingly. He smiled. She flew back to her seat just as the door opened.

"Mr. Doxey," said a new parlourmaid, intensely white and black, and intensely aware of the eminence of her young employers. And little Doxey of the P.A. came in, rather shabby and insinuating as usual, and obviously impressed by the magnificence of his surroundings.

"My good Doxey," exclaimed the chatelaine. "How delicious of you to have found us out so soon!"

"How d'you do, Doxey?" said Henry, rising.

"Awfully good of you to see me!" began Doxey, depositing his well-preserved hat on a chair. "Hope I don't interrupt." He smiled. "Can't stop a minute. Got a most infernal bazaar on at the Cecil. Look here, old man," he addressed Henry: "I've been reading your *Love in Babylon* again, and I fancied I could make a little curtain-raiser out of it—out of the picture incident, you know. I mentioned the idea to Pilgrim, of the Prince's Theatre, and he's fearfully struck on it."

"You mean, you think he is," Geraldine put in.

"Well, he is," Doxey pursued, after a brief pause. "I'm sure he is. I've sketched out a bit of a scenario. Now, if you'd give permission and go shares, I'd do it, old chap."

"A play, eh?" was all that Henry said.

Doxey nodded. "There's nothing like the theatre, you know."

"What do you mean—there's nothing like the theatre?"

"For money, old chap. Not short pieces, of course, but long ones; only, short ones lead to long ones."

"I tell you what you'd better do," said Henry, when they had discussed the matter. "You'd better write the thing, and I'll have a look at it, and then decide."

"Very well, if you like," said Doxey slowly. "What about shares?"

"If it comes to anything, I don't mind halving it," Henry replied.

"I see," said Doxey. "Of course, I've had some little experience of the stage," he added.

His name was one of those names which appear from time to time in the theatrical gossip of the newspapers as having adapted, or as being about to adapt, something or other for the stage which was not meant for the stage. It had never, however, appeared on the playbills of the theatres; except once, when, at a benefit matinée, the great John Pilgrim, whom to mention is to worship, had recited verses specially composed for the occasion by Alfred Doxey.

"And the signature, dear?" Geraldine glanced up at her husband, offering him a suggestion humbly, as a wife should in the presence of third parties.

"Oh!" said Henry. "Of course, Mr. Doxey's name must go with mine, as one of the authors of the piece. Certainly."

"Dearest," Geraldine murmured when Doxey had gone, "you are perfect. You don't really need an agent."

He laughed. "There's rather too much 'old chap' about Doxey," he said. "Who's Doxey?"

"He's quite harmless, the little creature," said Geraldine good-naturedly.

They sat silent for a time.

"Miles Robinson makes fifteen thousand a year out of plays," Geraldine murmured reflectively.

"Does he?" Henry murmured reflectively.

The cavalry arrived, in full panoply of war.

"I am thankful Sarah stays with us," said Mrs. Knight. "Servants are so much more difficult to get now than they were in my time."

Tea was nearly over; the cake-stand in four storeys had been depleted from attic to basement, and, after admiring the daintiness and taste displayed throughout Mrs. Henry's drawing-room, the ladies from Dawes Road had reached the most fascinating of all topics.

"When you keep several," said Geraldine, "they are not so hard to get. It's loneliness they object to."

"How many shall you have, dear?" Aunt Annie asked.

"Forty," said Henry, looking up from a paper.

"Don't be silly, dearest!" Geraldine protested. (She seemed so young and interesting and bright and precious, and so competent, as she sat there, behind the teapot, between her mature visitors in their black and their grey: this was what Henry thought.) "No, Aunt Annie; I have four at present."

"Four!" repeated Aunt Annie, aghast. "But ——"

"But, my dear!" exclaimed Mrs. Knight. "Surely——"

Geraldine glanced with respectful interest at Mrs. Knight.

"Surely you'll find it a great trial to manage them all?" said Aunt Annie.

"No," said Geraldine. "At least, I hope not. I never allow myself to be bothered by servants. I just tell them what they are to do. If they do it, well and good. If they don't, they must leave. I give an hour a day to domestic affairs. My time is too occupied to give more.

"She likes to spend her time going up and down in the lift," Henry explained.

Geraldine put her hand over her husband's mouth and silenced him. It was a pretty spectacle, and reconciled the visitors to much.

Aunt Annie examined Henry's face. "Are you quite well, Henry?" she inquired.

"I'm all right," he said, yawning. "But I want a little exercise. I haven't been out much to-day. I think I'll go for a short walk."

"Yes, do, dearest."

"Do, my dear."

As he approached the door, having kissed his wife, his mother, without looking at him, remarked in a peculiarly dry tone, which she employed only at the rarest intervals: "You haven't told me anything about your honeymoon yet, Henry."

"You forget, sister," said Aunt Annie stiffly, "it's a secret."

"Not now—not now!" cried Geraldine brightly. "Well, we'll tell you. Where do you think we drove after leaving you? To the Savoy Hotel."

"But why?" asked Mrs. Knight ingenuously.

"We spent our honeymoon there, right in the middle of London. We pretended we were strangers to London, and we saw all the sights that Londoners never do see. Wasn't it a good idea?"

"I—I don't know," said Mrs. Knight.

"It seems rather queer — for a honeymoon," Aunt Annie observed.

"Oh, but it was splendid!" continued Geraldine. "We went to the theatre or the opera every night, and lived on the fat of the land in the best hotel in Europe, and saw everything—even the Tower and the Mint and the Thames Tunnel and the Tate Gallery. We enjoyed every moment."

"And think of the saving in fares!" Henry put in, swinging the door to and fro.

"Yes, there was that, certainly," Aunt Annie agreed.

"And we went everywhere that omnibuses go," Henry proceeded. "Once even we got as far as the Salisbury, Fulham."

"Well, dear." Mrs. Knight said sharply, "I do think you might have popped in."

"But, mamma," Geraldine tried to explain, "that would have spoilt it."

"Spoilt what?" asked Mrs. Knight. "The Salisbury isn't three minutes off our house. I do think you might have popped in. There I was—and me thinking you were gone abroad!"

"See you later," said Henry, and disappeared.

"He doesn't look quite well, does he, Annie?" said Mrs. Knight.

"I know how it used to be," Aunt Annie said. "Whenever he began to make little jokes, we knew he was in for a bilious attack."

"My dear people," Geraldine endeavoured to cheer them, "I assure you he's perfectly well—perfectly."

"I've decided not to go out, after all," said Henry, returning surprisingly to the room. "I don't feel like it." And he settled into an ear-flap chair that had cost sixteen pounds ten.

"Have one?" said Geraldine, offering him the coloured box from which she had just helped herself.

"No, thanks," said he, shutting his eyes.

"I beg your pardon, I'm sure;" Geraldine turned to her visitors and extended the box. "Won't you have a *marron glacé*?"

And the visitors gazed at each other in startled, affrighted silence.

"Has Henry eaten some?" Mrs. Knight asked, shaken.

"He had one or two before tea," Geraldine answered. "Why?"

"I *knew* he was going to be ill!" said Aunt Annie.

"But he's been eating *marrons glacés* every day for a fortnight. Haven't you, sweetest?" said Geraldine.

"I can believe it," Aunt Annie murmured, "from his face."

"Oh dear! Women! Women!" Henry whispered facetiously.

"He's only saving his appetite for dinner," said Geraldine, with intrepid calm.

"My dear girl," Mrs. Knight observed, again in that peculiar dry tone, "if I know anything about your husband, and I've had him under my care for between twenty and thirty years, he will eat nothing more to-day."

"Now, mater," said Henry, "don't get excited. By the way, we haven't told you that I'm going to write a play."

"A play, Henry?"

"Yes. So you'll have to begin going to theatres in your old age, after all."

There was a pause.

"Shan't you?" Henry persisted.

"I don't know, dear. What place of worship are you attending?"

There was another pause.

"St. Philip's, Regent Street, I think we shall choose," said Geraldine.

"But surely that's a *church*?"

"Yes," said Geraldine. "It is a very good one. I have belonged to the Church of England all my life."

"Not High, I hope," said Aunt Annie.

"Certainly, High."

The beneficent Providence which always watched over Henry, watched over him then. A gong resounded through the flat, and stopped the conversation. Geraldine put her lips together.

"There's the dressing-bell, dearest," said she, controlling herself.

"I won't dress to-night," Henry replied feebly. "I'm not equal to it. You go. I'll stop with mother and auntie."

"Don't you fret yourself, mater," he said as soon as the chatelaine had left them. "Sir George has gone to live at Redhill, and given up his pew at Great Queen Street. I shall return to the old place and take it."

"I am very glad," said Mrs. Knight. "Very glad."

"And Geraldine?" Aunt Annie asked.

"Leave me to look after the little girl," said Henry. He then dozed for a few moments.

The dinner, with the Arctic lamps dotted about the table, and two servants to wait, began in the most stately and effective fashion imaginable. But it had got no further than the host's first spoonful of *soupe aux moules*, when the host rose abruptly, and without a word departed from the room.

The sisters nodded to each other with the cheerful gloom of prophetesses who find themselves in the midst of a disaster which they have predicted.

"You poor, foolish boy!" exclaimed Geraldine, running after Henry. She was adorably attired in white.

.   .   .   .   .   .

The clash of creeds was stilled in the darkened and sumptuous chamber, as the three women bent with murmurous affection over the bed on which lay, swathed in a redolent apparatus of eau-de-Cologne and fine linen, their hope and the hope of English literature. Towards midnight, when the agony had somewhat abated, Mrs. Knight and Aunt Annie reluctantly retired in a coupé which Geraldine had ordered for them by telephone.

And in the early June dawn Henry awoke, refreshed and renewed, full of that languid but genuine interest in mortal things which is at once the compensation and the sole charm of a dyspepsy. By reaching out an arm he could just touch the hand of his wife as she slept in her twin couch. He touched it; she awoke, and they exchanged the morning smile.

"I'm glad that's over," he said.

But whether he meant the *marrons glacés* or the first visit of his beloved elders to the glorious flat cannot be decided.

Certain it is, however, that deep in the minds of both the spouses was the idea that the new life, the new heaven on the new earth, had now fairly begun.

CHAPTER XXVII

HE IS NOT NERVOUS

"YES," said Henry with judicial calm, after he had read Mr. Doxey's stage version of *Love in Babylon*, "it makes a nice little piece."

"I'm glad you like it, old chap," said Doxey. "I thought you would."

They were in Henry's study, seated almost side by side at Henry's great American roll-top desk.

"You've got it a bit hard in places," Henry pursued. "But I'll soon put that right."

"Can you do it to-day?" asked the adapter.

"Why?"

"Because I know old Johnny Pilgrim wants to shove a new curtain-raiser into the bill at once. If I could take him this to-morrow——"

"I'll post it to you to-night," said Henry. "But I shall want to see Mr. Pilgrim myself before anything is definitely arranged."

"Oh, of course," Mr. Doxey agreed. "Of course. I'll tell him."

Henry softened the rigour of his collaborator's pen in something like half an hour. The perusal of this trifling essay in the dramatic form (it certainly did not exceed four thousand words, and could be played in twenty-five minutes) filled his mind with a fresh set of ideas. He suspected

that he could write for the stage rather better
than Mr. Doxey, and he saw, with the eye of
faith, new plumes waving in his cap. He was
aware, because he had read it in the papers, that
the English drama needed immediate assistance,
and he determined to render that assistance.
The first instalment of *The Plague-Spot* had just
come out in the July number of *Macalistair's
Magazine,* and the extraordinary warmth of its
reception had done nothing to impair Henry's
belief in his gift for pleasing the public. Hence
be stretched out a hand to the West End stage
with a magnanimous gesture of rescuing the fallen.

And yet, curiously enough, when he entered
the stage-door of Prince's Theatre one afternoon,
to see John Pilgrim, he was as meek as if the
world had never heard of him.

He informed the doorkeeper that he had an
appointment with Mr. Pilgrim, whereupon the
doorkeeper looked him over, took a pull at a glass
of rum-and-milk, and said he would presently
inquire whether Mr. Pilgrim could see anyone.
The passage from the portals of the theatre to
Mr. Pilgrim's private room occupied exactly a
quarter of an hour.

Then, upon beholding the figure of John
Pilgrim, he seemed suddenly to perceive what
fame and celebrity and renown really were. Here
was the man whose figure and voice were known
to every theatre-goer in England and America,
and to every idler who had once glanced at a
photograph-window; the man who for five-and-
twenty years had stilled unruly crowds by a gesture,
conquered the most beautiful women with a single
smile, died for the fatherland, and lived for love,

before a nightly audience of two thousand persons; who existed absolutely in the eye of the public, and who long ago had formed a settled, honest, serious conviction that he was the most interesting and remarkable phenomenon in the world. In the ingenuous mind of Mr. Pilgrim the universe was the frame, and John Pilgrim was the picture: his countless admirers had forced him to think so.

Mr. Pilgrim greeted Henry as though in a dream.

"What name?" he whispered, glancing round, apparently not quite sure whether they were alone and unobserved.

He seemed to be trying to awake from his dream, to recall the mundane and the actual, without success.

He said, still whispering, that the little play pleased him.

"Let me see," he reflected. "Didn't Doxey say that you had written other things?"

"Several books," Henry informed him.

"Books? Ah!" Mr. Pilgrim had the air of trying to imagine what sort of things books were. "That's very interesting. Novels?"

"Yes," said Henry.

Mr. Pilgrim, opening his magnificent chest and passing a hand through his brown hair, grew impressively humble. "You must excuse my ignorance," he explained. "I am afraid I'm not quite abreast of modern literature. "I never read." And he repeated firmly: "I never read. Not even the newspapers. What time have I for reading?" he whispered sadly. "In my brougham, I snatch a glance at the contents-bill of the evening papers. No more."

Henry had the idea that even to be ignored

by John Pilgrim was more flattering than to be admired by the rest of mankind.

Mr. Pilgrim rose and walked several times across the room; then addressed Henry mysteriously and imposingly:

" I've got the finest theatre in London."

" Yes ? " said Henry.

" In the world," Mr. Pilgrim corrected himself.

Then he walked again, and again stopped.

" I'll produce your piece," he whispered. " Yes, I'll produce it."

He spoke as if saying also: " You will have a difficulty in crediting this extraordinary and generous decision: nevertheless you must endeavour to do so."

Henry thanked him lamely.

" Of course I shan't play in it myself," added Mr. Pilgrim, laughing as one laughs at a fantastic conceit.

" No, naturally not," said Henry.

" Nor will Jane," said Mr. Pilgrim.

Jane Map was Mr. Pilgrim's leading lady, for the time being.

" And about terms, young man ? " Mr. Pilgrim demanded, folding his arms. " What is your notion of terms ? "

Now, Henry had taken the precaution of seeking advice concerning fair terms.

" One pound a performance is my notion," he answered.

" I never give more than ten shillings a night for a curtain-raiser," said Mr. Pilgrim ultimatively. " Never. I can't afford to."

" I'm afraid that settles it, then, Mr. Pilgrim," said Henry.

" You'll take ten shillings ? "

"I'll take a pound. I can't take less. I'm like you, I can't afford to."

John Pilgrim showed a faint interest in Henry's singular—indeed, incredible—attitude.

"You don't mean to say," he mournfully murmured, "that you'll miss the chance of having your play produced in my theatre for the sake of half a sovereign?"

Before Henry could reply to this grieved question, Jane Map burst into the room. She was twenty-five, tall, dark, and arresting. John Pilgrim had found her somewhere.

"Jane," said Mr. Pilgrim sadly, "this is Mr. Knight."

"Not the author of *The Plague-Spot*?" asked Jane Map, clasping her jewelled fingers.

"*Are* you the author of *The Plague-Spot*?" Mr. Pilgrim whispered—"whatever *The Plague-Spot* is."

The next moment Jane Map was shaking hands effusively with Henry. "I just adore you!" she told him. "And your *Love in Babylon*—oh, Mr. Knight, how *do* you think of such beautiful stories?"

John Pilgrim sank into a chair and closed his eyes.

"Oh, you must take it! you must take it!" cried Jane to John, as soon as she learnt that a piece based on *Love in Babylon* was under discussion. "I shall play Enid Anstruther myself. Don't you see me in it, Mr. Knight?"

"Mr. Knight's terms are twice mine," John Pilgrim intoned, without opening his eyes. "He wants a pound a night."

"He must have it," said Jane Map. "If I'm in the piece——"

" But, Jane——"

" I insist!" said Jane, with fire.

" Very well, Mr. Knight," John Pilgrim continued to intone, his eyes still shut, his legs stretched out, his feet resting perpendicularly on the heels " Jane insists. You understand—Jane insists. Take your pound. I call the first rehearsal for Monday."

Thenceforward Henry lived largely in the world of the theatre, a pariah's life, the life almost of a poor relation. Doxey appeared to enjoy the existence; it was Doxey's brief hour of bliss. But Henry, spoilt by editors, publishers, and the reading public, could not easily reconcile himself to the classical position of an author in the world of the theatre. It hurt him to encounter the prevalent opinion that, just as you cannot have a dog without a tail or a stump, so you cannot have a play without an author. The actors and actresses were the play, and when they were pleased with themselves the author was expected to fulfil his sole function of wagging.

Even Jane Map, Henry's confessed adorer, was the victim, Henry thought, of a highly-distorted sense of perspective. The principal comfort which he derived from Jane Map was that she ignored Doxey entirely.

The preliminary rehearsals were desolating. Henry went away from the first one convinced that the piece would have to be rewritten from end to end. No performer could make anything of his own part, and yet each was sure that all the other parts were effective in the highest degree.

At the fourth rehearsal John Pilgrim came down

o direct. He sat in the dim stalls by Henry's
ide, and Henry could hear him murmuring softly
nd endlessly :

> "Punch, brothers, punch with care—
>   Punch in the presence of the passenjare ! "

The scene was imagined to represent a studio,
nd Jane Map, as Enid Anstruther, was posing on
he model's throne.

"Jane," Mr. Pilgrim hissed out, "you pose for all
the world like an artist's model ! "

"Well," Jane retorted. "I am an artist's
model."

"No, you aren't," said John. "You're an actress
on my stage, and you must pose like one."

Whereupon Mr. Pilgrim ascended to the stage
and began to arrange Jane's limbs. By accident
Jane's delightful elbow came into contact with
John Pilgrim's eye. The company was horror-
struck as Mr. Pilgrim lowered his head and pressed
a handkerchief to that eye.

"Jane, Jane ! " he complained in his hoarse and
conspiratorial whisper, "I've been teaching you the
elements of your art for two years, and all you have
achieved is to poke your elbow in my eye. The
rehearsal is stopped."

And everybody went home.

Such is a specimen of the incidents which were
continually happening.

However, as the first night approached, the condition of affairs improved a little, and Henry saw
with satisfaction that the resemblance of Prince's
Theatre to a lunatic asylum was more superficial
than real. Also, the tone of the newspapers in
referring to the imminent production convinced
even John Pilgrim that Henry was perhaps not

quite an ordinary author. John Pilgrim cancelled a proof of a poster which he had already passed, and ordered a double-crown, thus:

LOVE IN BABYLON.

A PLAY IN ONE ACT, FOUNDED ON
HENRY SHAKSPERE KNIGHT'S FAMOUS NOVEL.

BY

HENRY SHAKSPERE KNIGHT AND ALFRED DOXEY.

ENID ANSTRUTHER—MISS JANE MAP.

Geraldine met Jane, and asked her to tea at the flat. And Geraldine hired a brougham at thirty pounds a month. From that day Henry's reception at the theatre was all that he could have desired, and more than any mere author had the right to expect. At the final rehearsals, in the absence of John Pilgrim, his word was law. It was whispered in the green-room that he earned ten thousand a year by writing things called novels. "Well, dear old pal," said one old actor to another old actor, "it takes all sorts to make a world. But ten thousand! Johnny himself don't make more than that, though he spends more."

The mischief was that Henry's digestion, what with the irregular hours and the irregular drinks, went all to pieces.

"You don't *look* nervous, Harry," said Geraldine when he came into the drawing-room before dinner on the evening of the production.

"Nervous?" said Henry. "Of course I'm not."

"Then, why have you forgotten to brush your hair, dearest?" she asked.

He glanced in a mirror. Yes, he had certainly forgotten to brush his hair.

"Sheer coincidence," he said, and ate a hearty meal.

Geraldine drove to the theatre. She was to meet there Mrs. Knight and Aunt Annie, in whose breasts pride and curiosity had won a tardy victory over the habits of a lifetime; they had a stage-box. Henry remarked that it was a warm night and that he preferred to walk; he would see them afterwards.

No one could have been more surprised than Henry, when he arrived at Prince's Theatre, to discover that he was incapable of entering that edifice. He honestly and physically tried to go in by the stage-door, but he could not, and, instead of turning within, he kept a straight course along the footpath. It was as though an invisible barrier had been raised to prevent his ingress.

"Never mind!" he said. "I'll walk to the Circus and back again, and then I'll go in."

He walked to the Circus and back again, and once more failed to get himself inside Prince's Theatre.

"This is the most curious thing that ever happened to me," he thought, as he stood for the second time in Piccadilly Circus. "Why the devil can't I go into that theatre? I'm not nervous. I'm not a bit nervous." It was so curious that he felt an impulse to confide to someone how curious it was.

Then he went into the Criterion Bar and sat down. The clock showed seventeen minutes to nine. His piece was advertised to start at eight-thirty precisely. The Criterion Bar is never empty,

but it has its moments of lassitude, and seventee
minutes to nine is one of them. After an interv.
a waiter slackly approached him.

"Brandy-and-soda!" Henry ordered, well knowin
that brandy-and-soda never suited him.

He glanced away from the clock, repeated "Punch
brothers, punch with care," twenty times, recite
"God save the Queen," took six small sips at th
brandy-and-soda, and then looked at the clock
again, and it was only fourteen minutes to nine. H
had guessed it might be fourteen minutes to ten.

He caught the eye of a barmaid, and she seeme
to be saying to him sternly: "If you think you ca
occupy this place all night on a ninepenny drink
you are mistaken. Either you ought to orde
another or hook it." He braved it for several mor
ages, then paid, and went; and still it was only te
minutes to nine. All mundane phenomena wer
inexplicably contorted that night. As he was pass
ing the end of the short street which contains th
stage-door of Prince's Theatre, a man, standing a
the door on the lookout, hailed him loudly. H
hesitated, and the man—it was the doorkeeper—
flew forward and seized him and dragged him in.

"Drink this, Mr. Knight," commanded the doorkeeper.

"I'm all right," said Henry. "What's up?"

"Yes, I know you're all right. Drink it."

And he drank a whisky-and-soda.

"Come upstairs," said the doorkeeper. "You'll
be wanted, Mr. Knight."

As he approached the wings of the stage, under
the traction of the breathless doorkeeper, he was
conscious of the falling of the curtain, and of the
noisiest noise beyond the curtain that he had ever
heard.

"Here, Mr. Knight, drink this," said someone in his ear. "Keep steady. It's nothing."

And he drank a glass of port.

His overcoat was jerked off by a mysterious agency.

The noise continued to be terrible: it rose and fell like the sea.

Then he was aware of Jane Map rushing towards him and of Jane Map kissing him rapturously on the mouth. "Come *on*," cried Jane Map, and pulled him by the hand, helter-skelter, until they came in front of a blaze of light and the noise crashed at his ears.

"I've been through this before somewhere," he thought, while Jane Map wrung his hand. "Was it in a previous existence? No. The Alhambra!" What made him remember the Alhambra was the figure of little Doxey sheepishly joining himself and Jane. Doxey, with a disastrous lack of foresight, had been in the opposite wing, and had had to run round the stage in order to come before the curtain. Doxey's share in the triumph was decidedly less than half. . . .

"No," Henry said later, with splendid calm, when Geraldine, Jane, Doxey, and himself were drinking champagne in Jane's Empire dressing-room, "it wasn't nervousness. I don't quite know what it was."

He gathered that the success had been indescribable.

Jane radiated bliss.

"I tell you what, old man," said Doxey; "we must adapt *The Plague-Spot*, eh?"

"We'll see about that," said Henry.

Two days afterwards Henry arose from a bed of
8

pain, and was able to consume a little tea and dry toast. Geraldine regaled his spiritual man with the press notices, which were tremendous. But more tremendous than the press notices was John Pilgrim's decision to put *Love in Babylon* after the main piece in the bill of Prince's Theatre. *Love in Babylon* was to begin at the honourable hour of ten-forty in future, for the benefit of the stalls and the dress-circle.

"Have you thought about Mr. Doxey's suggestion?" Geraldine asked him.

"Yes," said Henry; "but I don't quite see the point of it."

"Don't see the point of it, sweetheart?" she protested, stroking his dressing-gown. "But it would be bound to be a frightful success, after this."

"I know," said Henry. "But why drag in Doxey? I can write the next play myself."

She kissed him.

CHAPTER XXVIII

HE SHORTENS HIS NAME

ONE day Geraldine needed a doctor. Henry was startled, frightened, almost shocked. But when the doctor, having seen Geraldine, came into the study to chat with Geraldine's husband, Henry put on a calm demeanour, said he had been expecting the doctor's news, said also that he saw no cause for anxiety or excitement, and generally gave the doctor to understand that he was in no way disturbed by the work of Nature to secure a continuance of the British Empire. The conversation shifted to Henry's self, and soon Henry was engaged in a detailed description of his symptoms.

" Purely nervous," remarked the doctor—" purely nervous."

" You think so ? "

" I am sure of it."

" Then, of course, there is no cure for it. I must put up with it."

" Pardon me," said the doctor, " there is an absolutely certain cure for nervous dyspepsia—at any rate, in such a case as yours."

" What is it ? "

" Go without breakfast."

" But I don't eat too much, doctor," Henry said plaintively.

"Yes, you do," said the doctor. "We all do."

"And I'm always hungry at meal-times. If a meal is late it makes me quite ill."

"You'll feel somewhat uncomfortable for a few days," the doctor blandly continued. "But in a month you'll be cured."

"You say that professionally?"

"I guarantee it."

The doctor shook hands, departed, and then returned. "And eat rather less lunch than usual," said he. "Mind that."

Within three days Henry was informing his friends: "I never have any breakfast. No, none. Two meals a day." It was astonishing how frequently the talk approached the great food topic. He never sought an opportunity to discuss the various methods and processes of sustaining life, yet, somehow, he seemed to be always discussing them. Some of his acquaintances annoyed him excessively—for example, Doxey.

"That won't last long, old chap," said Doxey, who had called about finance. "I've known other men try that. Give me the good old English breakfast. Nothing like making a good start."

"Ass!" thought Henry, and determined once again, and more decisively, that Doxey should pass out of his life.

His preoccupation with this matter had the happy effect of preventing him from worrying too much about the perils which lay before Geraldine. Discovering the existence of an Anti-Breakfast League, he joined it, and in less than a week every newspaper in the land announced that the ranks of the Anti-Breakfasters had secured a notable recruit in the person of Mr. Henry Shakspere

Knight. It was widely felt that the Anti-Breakfast Movement had come to stay.

Still, he was profoundly interested in Geraldine, too. And between his solicitude for her and his scientific curiosity concerning the secret recesses of himself the flat soon overflowed with medical literature.

The entire world of the theatre woke up suddenly and simultaneously to the colossal fact of Henry's genius. One day they had never thought of him; the next day they could think of nothing else. Every West End manager, except two, wrote to him to express pleasure at the prospect of producing a play by him; the exceptional two telegraphed. Henry, however, had decided upon his arrangements. He had grasped the important truth that there was only one John Pilgrim in the world.

He threw the twenty-five chapters of *The Plague-Spot* into a scheme of four acts, and began to write a drama without the aid of Mr. Alfred Doxey. It travelled fast, did the drama; and the author himself was astonished at the ease with which he put it together out of little pieces of the novel. The scene of the third act was laid in the gaming-saloons of Monte Carlo; the scene of the fourth disclosed the deck of a luxurious private yacht at sea under a full Mediterranean moon. Such flights of imagination had hitherto been unknown in the serious drama of London. When Henry, after three months' labour, showed the play to John Pilgrim, John Pilgrim said:

"This is the play I have waited twenty years for!"

"You think it will do, then?" said Henry.

"It will enable me," observed John Pilgrim, "to show the British public what acting is."

Henry insisted on an agreement which gave him ten per cent. of the gross receipts. Soon after the news of the signed contract had reached the press, Mr. Louis Lewis, the English agent of Lionel Belmont, of the United States Theatrical Trust, came unostentatiously round to Ashley Gardens, and obtained the American rights on the same terms.

Then Pilgrim said that he must run through the manuscript with Henry, and teach him those things about the theatre which he did not know. Henry arrived at Prince's at eleven o'clock, by appointment; Mr. Pilgrim came at a quarter to twelve.

"You have the sense *du théâtre,* my friend," said Pilgrim, turning over the leaves of the manuscript. "That precious and incommunicable gift—you have it. But you are too fond of explanations. Now, the public won't stand explanations. No long speeches. And so whenever I glance through a play I can tell instantly whether it is an acting play. If I see a lot of speeches over four lines long, I say, Dull! Useless! Won't do! For instance, here. That speech of Veronica's while she's at the piano. Dull! I see it. I feel it. It must go! The last two lines must go!"

So saying, he obliterated the last two lines with a large and imperial blue pencil.

"But it's impossible," Henry protested. "You've not read them."

"I don't need to read them," said John Pilgrim. "I know they won't do. I know the public won't have them. It must be give and take—give and take between the characters. The ball must be kept in the air. Ah! The theatre!" He paused, and gave Henry a piercing glance. "Do you know how I came to be *du théâtre*—of the theatre, young man?" he demanded. "No? I will tell you. My father was an old fox-hunting squire in the Quorn country. One of the best English families, the Pilgrims, related to the Earls of Waverley. Poor, unfortunately. My eldest brother was brought up to inherit the paternal mortgages. My second brother went into the Army. And they wanted me to go into the Church. I refused. 'Well,' said my old father, 'damn it, Jack! if you won't go to heaven, you may as well ride straight to hell. Go on the stage.' And I did, sir. I did. Idea for a book there, isn't there?"

The blue-pencilling of the play proceeded. But whenever John Pilgrim came to a long speech by Hubert, the part which he destined for himself, he hesitated to shorten it. "It's too long! It's too long!" he whispered. "I feel it's too long. But, somehow, that seems to me essential to the action. I must try to carry it off as best I can."

At the end of the second act Henry suggested an interval for lunch, but John Pilgrim, opening Act III. accidentally, and pouncing on a line with his blue pencil, exclaimed with profound interest:

"Ah! I remember noting this when I read it. You've got Hubert saying here: 'I know I'm a silly fool.' Now, I don't think that's quite in the part. You must understand that when I study a character I become that character. Perhaps it would not be too much to say that I know more about that character than the author does. I merge myself into the character with an intense effort. Now, I can't see Hubert saying 'I know I'm a silly fool.' Of course I've no objection whatever to the words, but it seemed to me—you understand what I mean? Shall we strike that out?"

A little farther on Henry had given Veronica a little epigram: "When a man has to stand on his dignity, you may be sure his moral stature is very small."

"That's more like the sort of thing that Hubert would say," John Pilgrim whispered. "Women never say those things. It's not true to nature. But it seems to fit in exactly with the character of Hubert. Shall we—transfer——?" His pencil waved in the air. . . .

"Heavenly powers!" Mr. Pilgrim hoarsely murmured, as they attained the curtain of Act III., "it's four o'clock. And I had an appointment for lunch at two. But I never think of food when I am working. Never!"

Henry, however, had not broken his fast since the previous evening.

The third and the greatest crisis in the unparalleled popularity of Henry Shakspere Knight began to prepare itself. The rumour of its coming was heard afar off, and every literary genius in England and America who was earning less than ten thousand pounds a year ground his teeth and clenched his hands in impotent wrath. The boom and resounding of *The Plague-Spot* would have been deafening and immense in any case; but Henry had an idea, and executed it, which multiplied the advertisement tenfold. It was one of those ideas, at once quite simple and utterly original, which only occur to the favourites of the gods.

The serial publication of *The Plague-Spot* finished in June, and it had been settled that the book should be issued simultaneously in England and America in August. Now, that summer John Pilgrim was illuminating the provinces, and he had fixed a definite date, namely, the tenth of October, for the reopening of Prince's Theatre with the dramatic version of *The Plague-Spot*. Henry's idea was merely to postpone publication of the book until the production of the play. Mark Snyder admitted himself struck by the beauty of this scheme, and he made a special journey to America in connection with it, a journey which cost over a hundred pounds. The result was an arrangement under which the book was to be issued in London and New York, and the play to be produced by John Pilgrim at Prince's Theatre, London, and by Lionel Belmont at the Madison Square Theatre, New York, simultaneously on one golden date.

The splendour of the conception appealed to all that was fundamental in the Anglo-Saxon race.

John Pilgrim was a finished master of advertisement, but if any man in the wide world could give him lessons in the craft, that man was Lionel Belmont. Macalistairs, too, in their stately, royal way, knew how to impress facts upon the public.

Add to these things that Geraldine bore twins, boys.

No earthly power could have kept those twins out of the papers, and accordingly they had their share in the prodigious, unsurpassed and unforgetable publicity which their father enjoyed without any apparent direct effort of his own.

He had declined to be interviewed ; but one day, late in September, his good-nature forced him to yield to the pressure of a journalist. That journalist was Alfred Doxey, who had married on the success of *Love in Babylon,* and was already in financial difficulties. He said he could get twenty-five pounds for an interview with Henry, and Henry gave him an interview. The interview accomplished,

8*

he asked Henry whether he cared to acquire for cash his, Doxey's, share of the amateur rights of *Love in Babylon*. Doxey demanded fifty pounds, and Henry amiably wrote out the cheque on the spot and received Doxey's lavish gratitude. *Love in Babylon* is played on the average a hundred and fifty times a year by the amateur dramatic societies of Great Britain and Ireland, and for each performance Henry touches a guinea. The piece had run for two hundred nights at Prince's, so that the authors got a hundred pounds each from John Pilgrim.

On the morning of the tenth of October Henry strolled incognito round London. Every bookseller's shop displayed piles upon piles of *The Plague-Spot*. Every newspaper had a long review of it. The *Whitehall Gazette* was satirical as usual, but most people felt that it was the *Whitehall Gazette*, and not Henry, that thereby looked ridiculous. Nearly every other omnibus carried the legend of *The Plague-Spot*; every hoarding had it. At noon Henry passed by Prince's Theatre. Two small crowds had already taken up positions in front of the entrances to the pit and the gallery; and several women, seated on camp-stools, were diligently reading the book in order the better to appreciate the play.

Twelve hours later John Pilgrim was thanking his kind patrons for a success unique even in his rich and gorgeous annals. He stated that he should cable the verdict of London to the Madison Square Theatre, New York, where the representation of the noble work of art which he had had the honour of interpreting to them was about to begin.

" It was a lucky day for you when you met me,

young man," he whispered grandiosely and mysteriously, yet genially, to Henry.

On the façade of Prince's there still blazed the fiery sign, which an excited electrician had forgotten to extinguish:

THE PLAGUE-SPOT.

SHAKSPERE KNIGHT.

CHAPTER XXIX

THE PRESIDENT

PRINCE'S THEATRE, when it was full, held
three hundred and forty pounds' worth of solid
interest in the British drama. Of *The Plague-
Spot* six evening and two morning performances
were given every week for nearly a year, and
Henry's tenth averaged more than two hundred
pounds a week. His receipts from Lionel Belmont's
various theatres averaged rather more. The book
had a circulation of a hundred and twenty thousand
in England, and two hundred thousand in America,
and on every copy Henry got one shilling and
sixpence. The magnificent and disconcerting
total of his income from the *The Plague-Spot* within
the first year, excluding the eight thousand pounds
which he had received in advance from Macalistairs,
was thirty-eight thousand pounds. I say disconcerting because it emphatically did disconcert
Henry. He could not cope with it. He was like
a child who has turned on a tap and can't turn it
off again, and finds the water covering the floor
and rising, rising, over its little shoe-tops. Not
even with the help of Sir George could he quite
successfully cope with this deluge of money which
threatened to drown him each week. Sir George,
accustomed to keep his nerve in such crises, bored

one hole in the floor and called it India Three per
Cents., bored a second and called it Freehold
Mortgages, bored a third and called it Great
Northern Preference, and so on; but, still, Henry
was never free from danger. And the worst of it
was that, long before *The Plague-Spot* had exhausted
its geyser-like activity of throwing up money,
Henry had finished another book and another
play. Fortunately, Geraldine was ever by his side
to play the wife's part.

From this point his artistic history becomes
monotonous. It is the history of his investments
alone which might perchance interest the public.

Of course, it was absolutely necessary to abandon
the flat in Ashley Gardens. A man burdened with
an income of forty thousand a year, and never
secure against a sudden rise of it to fifty, sixty, or
even seventy thousand, cannot possibly live in a
flat in Ashley Gardens. Henry exists in a superb
mansion in Cumberland Place. He also possesses
a vast country-house at Hindhead, Surrey. He
employs a secretary, though he prefers to dictate
his work into a phonograph. His wife employs
a secretary, whose chief duty is, apparently,
to see to the flowers. The twins have each a
nurse, and each a perambulator; but when they
are good they are permitted to crowd themselves
into one perambulator, as a special treat. In the
newspapers they are invariably referred to as
Mr. Shakspere Knight's "pretty children" or
Mrs. Shakspere Knight's "charming twins."
Geraldine, who has abandoned the pen, is un-
disputed ruler of the material side of Henry's
life. The dinners and the receptions at Cumberland Place are her dinners and receptions. Henry
has no trouble; he does what he is told, and

does it neatly. Only once did he indicate to her, in his mild, calm way, that he could draw a line when he chose. He chose to draw the line when Geraldine spoke of engaging a butler, and perhaps footmen.

" I couldn't stand a butler," said Henry.

" But, dearest, a great house like this——"

" I couldn't stand a butler," said Henry.

" As you wish, dearest, of course."

He would not have minded the butler, perhaps, had not his mother and Aunt Annie been in the habit of coming up to Cumberland Place for tea.

Upon the whole the newspapers and periodicals were very kind to Henry, and even the rudest organs were deeply interested in him. Each morning his secretary opened an enormous packet of press-cuttings. In a good average year he was referred to in print as a genius about a thousand times, and as a charlatan about twenty times. He was not thin-skinned ; and he certainly was good-tempered and forgiving ; and he could make allowances for jealousy and envy. Nevertheless, now and then, some casual mention of him, or some omission of his name from a list of names, would sting him into momentary bitterness.

He endeavoured to enforce his old rule against interviews. But he could not. The power of public opinion was too strong, especially the power of American public opinion. As for photographs, they increased. He was photographed alone, with Geraldine, with the twins, and with Geraldine and the twins. It had to be. For permission to reproduce the most pleasing groups, Messrs. Antonio, the eminent firm in Regent Street, charged weekly papers a fee of two guineas.

"And this is fame!" he sometimes said to himself. And he decided that, though fame was pleasant in many ways, it did not exactly coincide with his early vision of it. He felt himself to be so singularly unchangeable! It was always the same he! And he could only wear one suit of clothes at a time, after all; and in the matter of eating, he ate less, much less, than in the era of Dawes Road. He persisted in his scheme of two meals a day, for it had fulfilled the doctor's prediction. He was no longer dyspeptic. That fact alone contributed much to his happiness.

Yes, he was happy, because he had a good digestion and a kind heart. The sole shadow on his career was a spasmodic tendency to be bored. "I miss the daily journey on the Underground," he once said to his wife. "I always feel that I ought to be going to the office in the morning." "You dear thing!" Geraldine caressed him with her voice. "Fancy anyone with a gift like yours going to an office!"

Ah, that gift! That gift utterly puzzled him. "I just sit down and write," he thought. "And there it is! They go mad over it!"

At Dawes Road they worshipped him, but they worshipped the twins more. Occasionally the twins, in state, visited Dawes Road, where Henry's mother was a little stouter and Aunt Annie a little thinner and a little primmer, but where nothing else was changed. Henry would have allowed his mother fifty pounds a week or so without an instant's hesitation, but she would not accept a penny over three pounds; she said she did not want to be bothered.

One day Henry read in the *Times* that the

French Government had made Tom a Chevalier of the Legion of Honour, and that Tom had been elected President of the newly-formed Cosmopolitan Art Society, which was to hold exhibitions both in London and Paris. And the *Times* seemed to assume that in these transactions the honour was the French Government's and the Cosmopolitan Art Society's.

Frankly, Henry could not understand it. Tom did not even pay his creditors.

"Well, of course," said Geraldine, " everybody knows that Tom *is* a genius."

This speech slightly disturbed Henry. And the thought floated again vaguely through his mind that there was something about Geraldine which baffled him. "But, then," he argued, "I expect all women are like that."

A few days later his secretary brought him a letter.

"I say, Geraldine," he cried, genuinely moved, on reading it. "What do you think? The Anti-Breakfast League want me to be the President of the League."

"And shall you accept?" she asked.

"Oh, certainly!" said Henry. "And I shall suggest that it's called the National Anti-Breakfast League in future."

"That will be much better, dearest," Geraldine smiled.

PRINTED BY MORRISON AND GIBB LTD., EDINBURGH

A FEW OF
MESSRS. METHUEN'S
PUBLICATIONS

Allcroft (A. Hadrian). DOWNLAND PATHWAYS. With an Introduction by E. V. LUCAS. Illustrated. Crown 8vo. 7s. 6d. net.

Archer (D.). CORSICA : THE SCENTED ISLE. Illustrated. Demy 8vo. 10s. 6d. net.

Armstrong (Warwick W.). THE ART OF CRICKET. *Third Edition.* Illustrated. Crown 8vo, 3s. net.

Bain (F. W.)—
IN THE GREAT GOD'S HAIR (*Seventh Edition*); A DRAUGHT OF THE BLUE (*Seventh Edition*); AN INCARNATION OF THE SNOW (*Fourth Edition*); A MINE OF FAULTS (*Fifth Edition*); A DIGIT OF THE MOON (*Fourteenth Edition*); THE LIVERY OF EVE (*Third Edition*); A HEIFER OF THE DAWN (*Twelfth Edition*); AN ESSENCE OF THE DUSK (*Fifth Edition*); THE DESCENT OF THE SUN (*Ninth Edition*); THE ASHES OF A GOD (*Third Edition*); BUBBLES OF THE FOAM (*Third Edition*); A SYRUP OF THE BEES (*Second Edition*); THE SUBSTANCE OF A DREAM (*Second Edition*). Fcap. 8vo, 5s. net each. AN ECHO OF THE SPHERES. Wide Demy 8vo, 10s. 6d. net.

Baker (C. H. Collins). CROME. Illustrated. Quarto, £5, 5s. net.

Bell (Aubrey F. G.). A PILGRIM IN SPAIN. Illustrated. Demy 8vo. 12s. 6d. net.

Belloc (H.)—
MARIE ANTOINETTE. Illustrated. *Fifth Edition.* Demy 8vo. 18s. net. PARIS. Illustrated. *Fifth Edition.* Crown 8vo, 8s. 6d. net. THE PYRENEES. *A New Edition.* Crown 8vo, 8s. 6d. net. HILLS AND THE SEA. *Thirteenth Edition.* Fcap. 8vo, 6s. net. Also Fcap. 8vo, 2s. net. ON NOTHING. *Fourth Edition.* Fcap. 8vo, 6s. net; also Fcap. 8vo, 2s. net. ON EVERYTHING. *Fourth Edition.* Fcap. 8vo, 6s. net; also Fcap. 8vo, 2s. net. ON SOMETHING. *Third Edition.* Fcap. 8vo, 6s. net; also Fcap. 8vo, 2s. net. FIRST AND LAST. *Second Edition.* Fcap. 8vo, 6s. net. THIS AND THAT AND THE OTHER. *Second Edition.* Fcap. 8vo, 6s. net. ON. Fcap. 8vo, 6s. net. ON ANYTHING. Fcap. 8vo, 6s. net.

Butler (Kathleen T.). A HISTORY OF FRENCH LITERATURE. Two Vols. Each Cr. 8vo. 10s. 6d. net.

Campbell (Olwen Ward). SHELLEY AND THE UNROMANTICS. Illustrated. *Second Edition.* Demy 8vo. 16s. net.

Chandler (Arthur), D.D., late Lord Bishop of Bloemfontein.
ARA CŒLI : An Essay in Mystical Theology. *Eighth Edition.* 5s. net. FAITH AND EXPERIENCE. *Third Edition.* 5s. net. THE CULT OF THE PASSING MOMENT. *Fifth Edition.* 6s. net. THE ENGLISH CHURCH AND RE-UNION. 5s. net. SCALA MUNDI. 4s. 6d. net.

Chesterton (G. K.)—
THE BALLAD OF THE WHITE HORSE. *Sixth Edition.* 6s. net. ALL THINGS CONSIDERED. *Fourteenth Edition.* 6s. net; also Fcap. 8vo, 2s. net. TREMENDOUS TRIFLES. *Sixth Edition.* 6s. net; also Fcap. 8vo, 2s. net. ALARMS AND DISCURSIONS. *Second Edition.* 6s. net. A MISCELLANY OF MEN. *Third Edition.* 6s. net. THE USES OF DIVERSITY. *Third Edition.* 6s. net. WINE, WATER, AND SONG. *Thirteenth Edition.* 1s. 6d. net. FANCIES VERSUS FADS. 6s. net. CHARLES DICKENS. *Thirteenth Edition.* 3s. 6d. net.

Clutton-Brock (A.)—
THOUGHTS ON THE WAR, 1s. 6d. net ; WHAT IS THE KINGDOM OF HEAVEN ? 5s. net ; ESSAYS ON ART, 5s. net ; ESSAYS ON BOOKS, 6s. net ; MORE ESSAYS ON BOOKS, 6s. net ; SHAKESPEARE'S HAMLET, 5s. net. SHELLEY : THE MAN AND THE POET, 7s. 6d. net.

Conrad (Joseph). THE MIRROR OF THE SEA : MEMORIES AND IMPRESSIONS. *Fourth Edition.* Fcap. 8vo, 6s. net. Also, in a uniform edition. Fcap. 8vo. 3s. 6d. net.

Dark (Sidney) and Grey (Rowland). W. S. GILBERT : HIS LIFE AND LETTERS. Illustrated. *Second Edition.* Demy 8vo, 15s. net.

Dickinson (G. Lowes). THE GREEK VIEW OF LIFE. *Fifteenth Edition.* Crown 8vo, 5s. net.

Dolls' House (The Queen's). THE BOOK OF THE QUEEN'S DOLLS' HOUSE. Vol. I. THE QUEEN'S DOLLS' HOUSE. Edited by A. C. BENSON, C.V.O., and SIR LAWRENCE WEAVER, K.B.E. Vol. II. THE QUEEN'S DOLLS' HOUSE LIBRARY. Edited by E. V. LUCAS. Illustrated. Crown 4to. £6, 6s. net.

EVERYBODY'S BOOK OF THE QUEEN'S DOLLS' HOUSE. Illustrated. *Second Edition.* Crown 4to. 5s. net.

Drever (James). THE PSYCHOLOGY OF EVERYDAY LIFE. *Fourth Edition.* Crown 8vo, 6s. net.

THE PSYCHOLOGY OF INDUSTRY. Crown 8vo, 5s. net.

Einstein (A.). RELATIVITY : THE SPECIAL AND THE GENERAL THEORY. *Seventh Edition.* Crown 8vo, 5s. net.

SIDELIGHTS ON RELATIVITY. Crown 8vo, 3s. 6d. net.

THE MEANING OF RELATIVITY. Crown 8vo, 5s. net.

Other Books on the Einstein Theory

THE PRINCIPLE OF RELATIVITY. By ALBERT EINSTEIN, H. A. LORENTZ, H. MINKOWSKI, and H. WEYL. With Notes by A. SOMMERFELD. Demy 8vo, 12s. 6d. net.

EINSTEIN'S THEORY OF RELATIVITY. By MAX BORN. Demy 8vo. 12s. net.

THE FOUNDATIONS OF EINSTEIN'S THEORY OF GRAVITATION. By ERWIN FREUNDLICH. Crown 8vo. 6s. net.
Write for Complete List.

Evans (Lady). LUSTRE POTTERY. With 24 Plates. Royal Quarto, £2, 12s. 6d. net.

" Evoe " (E. V. Knox)—
PARODIES REGAINED. Fcap. 8vo, 5s. net. THESE LIBERTIES. Fcap. 8vo, 4s. 6d. net. FICTION AS SHE IS WROTE. FANCY NOW ! Each Fcap. 8vo, 6s. net.

Fitzgerald (Edward). THE RUBÁIYÁT OF OMAR KHAYYÁM. An edition illustrated by EDMUND J. SULLIVAN. Wide Crown 8vo, 10s. 6d. net.

Fyleman (Rose)—
FAIRIES AND CHIMNEYS. *Eighteenth Edition.* Fcap. 8vo, 3s. 6d. net. THE FAIRY GREEN. *Tenth Edition.* Fcap. 8vo, 3s. 6d. net. THE FAIRY FLUTE. *Eighth Edition.* Fcap. 8vo, 3s. 6d. net. THE RAINBOW CAT AND OTHER STORIES. *Second Edition.* Fcap. 8vo, 3s. 6d.

net. A SMALL CRUSE. *Fcap.* 8vo, 4s. 6d. net. FORTY GOOD-NIGHT TALES. *Fourth Edition.* Fcap. 8vo, 3s. 6d. net. THE ROSE FYLEMAN FAIRY BOOK. Illustrated. Crown 4to. 10s. 6d. net. EIGHT LITTLE PLAYS FOR CHILDREN. Fcap. 8vo. 3s. 6d. net.

Geering (Thomas). OUR SUSSEX PARISH. With an Introduction and a Biographical Chapter by ARTHUR BECKETT. Illustrated. Crown 8vo. 8s. 6d. net.

Gibbins (H. de B.). THE INDUSTRIAL HISTORY OF ENGLAND. With 5 Maps and a Plan. *Twenty-seventh Edition.* Crown 8vo, 5s.

Gibbon (Edward). THE DECLINE AND FALL OF THE ROMAN EMPIRE. Edited, with Notes, Appendices, and Maps, by J. B. BURY. Illustrated. Seven Volumes. Demy 8vo, each 12s. 6d. net. Also, unillustrated. Seven Volumes. Crown 8vo, each 7s. 6d. net.

Glover (T. R.)—
THE CONFLICT OF RELIGIONS IN THE EARLY ROMAN EMPIRE. *Tenth Edition.* Demy 8vo, 10s. 6d. net. POETS AND PURITANS. *Third Edition.* Demy 8vo, 10s. 6d. net. VIRGIL. *Fifth Edition.* Demy 8vo, 10s. 6d. net. FROM PERICLES TO PHILIP. *Third Edition.* Demy 8vo, 10s. 6d. net.

Graham (Harry). THE WORLD WE LAUGH IN: MORE DEPORTMENTAL DITTIES. Illustrated by "FISH," *Second Edition.* Fcap. 8vo, 5s. net.

Grahame (Kenneth), Author of "The Golden Age." THE WIND IN THE WILLOWS. With a Frontispiece by GRAHAM ROBERTSON. *Fourteenth Edition.* Crown 8vo, 7s. 6d. net. *Illustrated Edition.* With drawings in colour and line, by NANCY BARNHART. Small 4to, 10s. 6d. net.

Hadfield (J. A.). PSYCHOLOGY AND MORALS: An Analysis of Character. *Fourth Edition.* Crown 8vo, 6s. net.

Hall (H. R.). THE ANCIENT HISTORY OF THE NEAR EAST FROM THE EARLIEST TIMES TO THE BATTLE OF SALAMIS. Illustrated. *Sixth Edition, Revised.* Demy 8vo, £1, 1s. net.

Holdsworth (W. S.). A HISTORY OF ENGLISH LAW. Seven volumes. Demy 8vo. Each £1, 5s. net.

Hoppé (E. O.). IN GIPSY CAMP AND ROYAL PALACE: WANDERINGS IN RUMANIA. With a Preface by the QUEEN OF RUMANIA. Illustrated. Demy 8vo. 15s. net.

Hutton (Edward)—
THE CITIES OF UMBRIA (*Sixth Edition*); THE CITIES OF LOMBARDY; THE CITIES OF ROMAGNA AND THE MARCHES; SIENA AND SOUTHERN TUSCANY (*Third Edition*); VENICE AND VENETIA (*Second Edition*); THE CITIES OF SPAIN (*Fifth Edition*); NAPLES AND SOUTHERN ITALY (*Second Edition*). Illustrated. Crown 8vo. Each 8s. 6d. net. COUNTRY WALKS ABOUT FLORENCE (*Third Edition*). Fcap. 8vo, 7s. 6d. net. ROME (*Fifth Edition*). FLORENCE AND NORTHERN TUSCANY, WITH GENOA (*Fourth Edition*). Each 7s. 6d. net.

Inge (W. R.). CHRISTIAN MYSTICISM. (The Bampton Lectures for 1899.) *Fifth Edition.* Crown 8vo, 7s. 6d. net.

Jenks (E.). A SHORT HISTORY OF ENGLISH LAW. *Third Edition, Revised.* Demy 8vo, 12s. 6d. net.

Jones (M. E. Monckton). ANCIENT EGYPT FROM THE RECORDS. Illustrated. Crown 8vo. 7s. 6d. net.

Julian (Lady), Anchoress at Norwich, A.D. 1373. REVELATIONS OF DIVINE LOVE. A Version from the MS. in the British Museum. Edited by GRACE WARRACK. *Eighth Edition.* Crown 8vo, 5s. net.

Kidd (Benjamin)—

THE SCIENCE OF POWER. *Ninth Edition.* Crown 8vo, 7s. 6d. net.
SOCIAL EVOLUTION. A New Edition. Demy 8vo, 8s. 6d. net. A
PHILOSOPHER WITH NATURE. *Second Edition.* Crown 8vo, 6s. net.

Kipling (Rudyard). BARRACK-ROOM BALLADS.
233rd Thousand. Fifty-fifth Edition. Crown 8vo, 7s. 6d. net. Also
Fcap. 8vo, 6s. net ; leather, 7s. 6d. net. Also a Service Edition. Two
volumes. Square Fcap. 8vo. Each 3s. net.

THE SEVEN SEAS. *172nd Thousand. Thirty-fourth
Edition.* Crown 8vo, 7s. 6d. net. Also Fcap. 8vo, 6s. net ; leather,
7s. 6d. net. Also a Service Edition. Two Volumes. Square Fcap.
8vo. Each 3s. net.

THE FIVE NATIONS. *138th Thousand. Twenty-second
Edition.* Crown 8vo, 7s. 6d. net. Also Fcap. 8vo, 6s. net ; leather,
7s. 6d. net. Also a Service Edition. Two volumes. Square Fcap. 8vo.
Each 3s. net.

DEPARTMENTAL DITTIES. *111th Thousand. Thirty-
seventh Edition.* Crown 8vo, 7s. 6d. net. Also Fcap. 8vo, 6s. net ;
leather, 7s. 6d. net. Also a Service Edition. Two volumes. Square
Fcap. 8vo. Each 3s. net.

THE YEARS BETWEEN. *95th Thousand.* Crown 8vo,
7s. 6d. net. Also Fcap. 8vo, 6s. net ; leather, 7s. 6d. net. Also a
Service Edition. Two volumes. Square Fcap. 8vo. Each 3s. net.

TWENTY POEMS FROM RUDYARD KIPLING.
403rd Thousand. Fcap. 8vo, 1s. net.

A KIPLING ANTHOLOGY—VERSE Selected from
the Poetry of RUDYARD KIPLING. *Third Edition.* Fcap. 8vo, 6s.
net. Leather, 7s. 6d. net.

Lamb (Charles and Mary). THE COMPLETE WORKS.
Edited by E. V. LUCAS. A New and Revised Edition in six volumes.
With Frontispiece. Fcap. 8vo. Each 6s. net.
The Volumes are :—

   I. MISCELLANEOUS PROSE.   II. ELIA AND THE LAST ESSAYS
OF ELIA.   III. BOOKS FOR CHILDREN.   IV. PLAYS AND POEMS.
v. and VI. LETTERS.

Lankester (Sir Ray)—

SCIENCE FROM AN EASY CHAIR. First Series. Illustrated. *Fifteenth
Edition.* Crown 8vo, 7s. 6d. net. Also Fcap. 8vo, 2s. net. SCIENCE
FROM AN EASY CHAIR. Second Series. Illustrated. *Third Edition.*
Crown 8vo, 7s. 6d. net. Also as MORE SCIENCE FROM AN EASY CHAIR.
Fcap. 8vo, 2s. net. DIVERSIONS OF A NATURALIST. Illustrated.
Third Edition. Crown 8vo, 7s. 6d. net. SECRETS OF EARTH AND SEA.
Illustrated. *Second Edition.* Crown 8vo, 8s. 6d. net. GREAT AND
SMALL THINGS. Illustrated. Crown 8vo, 7s. 6d. net.

Lodge (Sir Oliver)—

MAN AND THE UNIVERSE, Crown 8vo, 7s. 6d. net ; also Fcap. 8vo,
2s. net ; THE SURVIVAL OF MAN ; A Study in Unrecognized Human
Faculty, Crown 8vo, 7s. 6d. net ; also Fcap. 8vo, 2s. net ; REASON
AND BELIEF, 2s. net ; THE SUBSTANCE OF FAITH, 2s. net ; RAYMOND
REVISED, 6s. net.

Lucas (E. V.)—

THE LIFE OF CHARLES LAMB, two volumes, Fcap. 8vo, 21s. net ;
EDWIN AUSTIN ABBEY, R.A., 2 vols., £6, 6s. net ; VERMEER OF DELFT,
Fcap. 4to, 10s. 6d. net. A WANDERER IN HOLLAND, 10s. 6d. net ; A
WANDERER IN LONDON, 10s. 6d. net ; LONDON REVISITED, 10s. 6d. net ;
A WANDERER IN PARIS, 10s. 6d. net ; A WANDERER IN FLORENCE,
10s. 6d. net ; A WANDERER IN VENICE, 10s. 6d. net ; A WANDERER
AMONG PICTURES : A Guide to the Great Galleries of Europe, 8s. 6d.

net ; The Open Road : A Little Book for Wayfarers, Fcap. 8vo, 6s. net ; also an edition illustrated by Claude A. Shepperson, 10s. 6d. net ; also an edition on India Paper, Leather, 7s. 6d. net ; The Friendly Town : A Little Book for the Urbane, 6s. net ; Fireside and Sunshine, 6s. net ; Character and Comedy, 6s. net ; The Gentlest Art : A Choice of Letters by Entertaining Hands, 6s. 6d. net ; The Second Post, 6s. net ; Her Infinite Variety : A Feminine Portrait Gallery, 6s. net ; Good Company : A Rally of Men, 6s. net ; One Day and Another, 6s. net ; Old Lamps for New, 6s. net ; Loiterer's Harvest, 6s. net ; Cloud and Silver, 6s. net ; A Boswell of Baghdad and other Essays, 6s. net ; 'Twixt Eagle and Dove, 6s. net ; The Phantom Journal, and Other Essays and Diversions, 6s. net ; Giving and Receiving, 6s. net ; Luck of the Year, 6s. net ; Encounters and Diversions, 6s. net ; Specially Selected : A Choice of Essays, illustrated by G. L. Stampa, 7s. 6d. net ; Urbanities, illustrated by G. L. Stampa, 7s. 6d. net ; You Know What People Are, illustrated by George Morrow, 5s. net ; The Same Star : A Comedy in three Acts, 3s. 6d. net ; The British School : An Anecdotal Guide to the British Painters and Paintings in the National Gallery, 6s. net ; Little Books on the Great Masters, 5s. net each ; Roving East and Roving West, 5s. net.   See also Dolls' House (The Queen's).

Lynd (Robert). THE BLUE LION. Fcap. 8vo, 6s. net.
THE PEAL OF BELLS. Fcap. 8vo, 6s. net.

McDougall (William)—
An Introduction to Social Psychology. *Eighteenth Edition.* Cr. 8vo, 8s. 6d. net ; Body and Mind : A History and a Defence of Animism, with Diagrams, *Sixth Edition*, Demy 8vo, 12s. 6d. net ; An Outline of Psychology, Demy 8vo, 12s. net ; National Welfare and National Decay, with Illustrations. Crown 8vo, 6s. net. Ethics and Some Modern World Problems, 7s. 6d. net.

Maeterlinck (Maurice)—
The Blue Bird : A Fairy Play in Six Acts, 6s. net and 2s. 6d. net ; The Betrothal, Fcap., 6s. net, paper 3s. 6d. net ; Mary Magdalene, 5s. net and 2s. net ; Death, 3s. 6d. net ; Our Eternity, 6s. net ; The Unknown Guest, 6s. net ; The Wrack of the Storm, 6s. net ; The Miracle of Saint Anthony : A Play in One Act, 3s. 6d. net ; The Burgomaster of Stilemonde : A Play in Three Acts, 5s. net ; Mountain Paths, 6s. net ; Tyltyl, Told for Children (illustrated), 21s. net. (The above books are Translated by A. Teixeira de Mattos.) Poems, 5s. net (Done into English by Bernard Miall) ; The Cloud that Lifted and The Power of the Dead : Two Plays, Translated by F. M. Atkinson, 7s. 6d. net ; The Great Secret (Translated by Bernard Miall), 7s. 6d. net.

Marriott (Sir J. A. R.). ECONOMICS AND ETHICS. Demy 8vo, 10s. 6d. net.

Methuen (Sir A.). AN ANTHOLOGY OF MODERN VERSE. With Introduction by Robert Lynd. 82nd Thousand. *Eighteenth Edition.* Fcap. 8vo, 6s. net. Thin paper, leather, 7s. 6d. net.
SHAKESPEARE TO HARDY : An Anthology of English Lyrics. *Third Edition.* Fcap. 8vo, 6s. net. Leather, 7s. 6d. net.

Milne (A. A.)—
Not that it Matters. *Fourth Edition.* Fcap. 8vo, 3s. 6d. net. If I May. *Fifth Edition.* Fcap. 8vo, 3s. 6d. net. When we were Very Young. With decorations by Ernest H. Shepard. *Second Edition.* Crown 8vo, 7s. 6d. net.

Oman (Sir Charles). A HISTORY OF THE ART OF WAR IN THE MIDDLE AGES, A.D. 378–1485. *Second Edition, Revised and Enlarged.* Two Volumes. Illustrated. Demy 8vo, £1, 16s. net.

Oxenham (John). Eight Volumes of Poems. Small Pott 8vo, 1s. 3d. net each volume.
BEES IN AMBER. 2s. net. ALL'S WELL; THE KING'S HIGH WAY; THE VISION SPLENDID; THE FIERY CROSS; HEARTS COURAGEOUS; HIGH ALTARS; ALL CLEAR!

Perry (W. J.)—
THE CHILDREN OF THE SUN. With Maps, Demy 8vo, 18s. net; THE ORIGIN OF MAGIC AND RELIGION, Crown 8vo, 6s. net; THE GROWTH OF CIVILIZATION. With Maps, Crown 8vo, 6s. net.

Petrie (Sir Flinders). A HISTORY OF EGYPT. Illustrated. Six Volumes. Crown 8vo, each 9s. net.
I. FROM THE IST TO XVITH DYNASTY. *Eleventh Edition* (12s. net). II. THE XVIITH AND XVIIITH DYNASTIES. *Seventh Edition Revised.* III. XIXTH TO XXXTH DYNASTIES. *Second Edition.* IV. EGYPT UNDER THE PTOLEMAIC DYNASTY. J. P. MAHAFFY. *Second Edition.* V. EGYPT UNDER ROMAN RULE. J. G. MILNE. *Third Edition, Revised* (12s. net). VI. EGYPT IN THE MIDDLE AGES. STANLEY LANE-POOLE. *Second Edition* (10s. net).

Pollitt (Arthur W.). THE ENJOYMENT OF MUSIC. Crown 8vo, 5s. net.

Ponsonby (Arthur). ENGLISH DIARIES. Demy 8vo, 21s. net.

Smith (C. Fox)—
SAILOR TOWN DAYS, Illustrated, *Second Edition*, Crown 8vo, 6s. net; SHIP ALLEY: MORE SAILOR TOWN DAYS, Illustrated, Crown 8vo, 6s. net; SEA SONGS AND BALLADS, 1917–1922, Illustrated, *Second Edition*, Crown 8vo, 6s. net; A BOOK OF FAMOUS SHIPS, Illustrated, Crown 8vo, 6s. net. THE RETURN OF THE "CUTTY SARK." Illustrated. Fcap. 4to, 3s. 6d. net.

Stevenson (R. L.). THE LETTERS OF ROBERT LOUIS STEVENSON TO HIS FAMILY AND FRIENDS. Selected and Edited by SIR SIDNEY COLVIN. Four Volumes. *Fifth Edition.* Fcap. 8vo, 6s. net each.

Tatchell (Frank). THE HAPPY TRAVELLER: A BOOK FOR POOR MEN. *Fourth Edition.* Crown 8vo, 7s. 6d. net.

Thomson (J. Arthur). WHAT IS MAN? *Second Edition.* Crown 8vo, 6s. 6d. net.

SCIENCE AND RELIGION. *Crown 8vo.* 7s. 6d. net.

Tilden (W. T.)—
THE ART OF LAWN TENNIS. Illustrated. *Sixth Edition.* Crown 8vo, 6s. net. LAWN TENNIS FOR YOUNG PLAYERS; LAWN TENNIS FOR CLUB PLAYERS; LAWN TENNIS FOR MATCH PLAYERS. Each Fcap. 8vo, 2s. 6d. net. SINGLES AND DOUBLES. Illustrated. *Second Edition.* Crown 8vo, 6s. net. THE COMMON SENSE OF LAWN TENNIS. Illustrated. Crown 8vo. 5s. net.

Tileston (Mary W.). DAILY STRENGTH FOR DAILY NEEDS. *Twenty-ninth Edition.* Medium 16mo, 3s. 6d. net.

Underhill (Evelyn). MYSTICISM. A Study in the Nature and Development of Man's Spiritual Consciousness. *Tenth Edition.* Demy 8vo, 15s. net.

THE LIFE OF THE SPIRIT AND THE LIFE OF TO-DAY. *Fourth Edition.* Crown 8vo, 7s. 6d. net.

Vardon (Harry). HOW TO PLAY GOLF. Illustrated. *Eighteenth Edition.* Crown 8vo, 5s. net.

Waterhouse (Elizabeth). A LITTLE BOOK OF LIFE
AND DEATH. Selected and Arranged. *Twenty-second Edition.*
Small Pott 8vo, cloth, 2s. 6d. net ; paper, 1s. 6d. net.

Wilde (Oscar). THE WORKS OF OSCAR WILDE.
Sixteen Volumes. Fcap. 8vo, each 6s. 6d. net. Some also Fcap.
8vo, 2s. net.

    I. LORD ARTHUR SAVILE'S CRIME AND THE PORTRAIT OF MR.
W. H. II. THE DUCHESS OF PADUA. III. POEMS. IV. LADY
WINDERMERE'S FAN. V. A WOMAN OF NO IMPORTANCE. VI.
AN IDEAL HUSBAND. VII. THE IMPORTANCE OF BEING EARNEST.
VIII. A HOUSE OF POMEGRANATES. IX. INTENTIONS. X. DE
PROFUNDIS AND PRISON LETTERS. XI. ESSAYS. XII. SALOME,
A FLORENTINE TRAGEDY, AND LA SAINTE COURTISANE. XIII. A
CRITIC IN PALL MALL. XIV. SELECTED PROSE OF OSCAR WILDE.
XV. ART AND DECORATION. XVI. FOR LOVE OF THE KING : A
Burmese Masque (5s. net).

A HOUSE OF POMEGRANATES. Illustrated. Crown
4to, 21s. net.

Wilding (Anthony F.), Lawn Tennis Champion 1910–1911.
ON THE COURT AND OFF. Illustrated. *Eighth Edition.*
Crown 8vo, 7s. 6d. net.

Young (E. Hilton). BY SEA AND LAND. Illustrated.
Crown 8vo. 10s. 6d. net.

The Antiquary's Books

Illustrated. Demy 8vo, 10s. 6d. net each volume

ANCIENT PAINTED GLASS IN ENGLAND ; ARCHÆOLOGY AND FALSE ANTI-
QUITIES ; THE BELLS OF ENGLAND ; THE BRASSES OF ENGLAND ;
CHURCHWARDENS' ACCOUNTS ; THE DOMESDAY INQUEST ; THE
CASTLES AND WALLED TOWNS OF ENGLAND ; ENGLISH CHURCH
FURNITURE ; ENGLISH MONASTIC LIFE ; ENGLISH SEALS ; FOLK-LORE
AS AN HISTORICAL SCIENCE ; THE GILDS AND COMPANIES OF LONDON ;
THE HERMITS AND ANCHORITES OF ENGLAND ; THE MANOR AND
MANORIAL RECORDS ; THE MEDIÆVAL HOSPITALS OF ENGLAND ;
OLD ENGLISH INSTRUMENTS OF MUSIC ; OLD ENGLISH LIBRARIES ;
OLD SERVICE BOOKS OF THE ENGLISH CHURCH ; PARISH LIFE IN
MEDIÆVAL ENGLAND ; THE PARISH REGISTERS OF ENGLAND ;
REMAINS OF THE PREHISTORIC AGE IN ENGLAND ; THE ROMAN ERA
IN BRITAIN ; ROMANO-BRITISH BUILDINGS AND EARTHWORKS ; THE
ROYAL FORESTS OF ENGLAND ; THE SCHOOLS OF MEDIÆVAL ENG-
LAND ; SHRINES OF BRITISH SAINTS.

The Arden Shakespeare

Demy 8vo, 6s. net each volume

An edition of Shakespeare in Single Plays. Edited with
a full Introduction, Textual Notes, and a Commentary at
the foot of the page. The edition is now complete in
thirty-nine volumes.

Classics of Art

Edited by Dr. J. H. W. LAING

Illustrated. Wide Royal 8vo, from 15s. net to £3, 3s. net.

THE ART OF THE GREEKS ; THE ART OF THE ROMANS ; CHARDIN ;
DONATELLO ; FLORENTINE SCULPTORS ; GEORGE ROMNEY ; GHIRLANDAIO ;
LAWRENCE ; MICHELANGELO ; RAPHAEL ; REMBRANDT'S PAINTINGS ;
RUBENS ; SANDRO BOTTICELLI ; TINTORETTO ; TITIAN ; TURNER'S
SKETCHES AND DRAWINGS ; VELAZQUEZ.

The " Complete " Series
Illustrated.   Demy 8vo, from 5s. net to 18s. net.

THE COMPLETE AIRMAN ; THE COMPLETE AMATEUR BOXER ; THE
COMPLETE ATHLETIC TRAINER ; THE COMPLETE BILLIARD PLAYER ;
THE COMPLETE COOK ; THE COMPLETE FOXHUNTER ; THE COMPLETE
GOLFER ; THE COMPLETE HOCKEY PLAYER ; THE COMPLETE HORSEMAN ;
THE COMPLETE JUJITSUAN (Crown 8vo) ; THE COMPLETE LAWN TENNIS
PLAYER ; THE COMPLETE MOTORIST ; THE COMPLETE MOUNTAINEER ;
THE COMPLETE OARSMAN ; THE COMPLETE PHOTOGRAPHER ; THE
COMPLETE RUGBY FOOTBALLER ; THE COMPLETE SHOT ; THE COMPLETE
SWIMMER ; THE COMPLETE YACHTSMAN.

The Connoisseur's Library
Illustrated.   Wide Royal 8vo, 31s. 6d. net.

ENGLISH COLOURED BOOKS ; ETCHINGS ; EUROPEAN ENAMELS ; FINE
BOOKS ; GLASS ; GOLDSMITHS' AND SILVERSMITHS' WORK ; ILLU-
MINATED MANUSCRIPTS ; IVORIES ; JEWELLERY ; MEZZOTINTS ; MINIA-
TURES ; PORCELAIN ; SEALS ; WOOD SCULPTURE.

Eight Books by R. S. Surtees
With the original Illustrations in Colour by J. LEECH and others.
Fcap. 8vo, 6s. net and 7s. 6d. net.

ASK MAMMA ; HANDLEY CROSS ; HAWBUCK GRANGE ; HILLINGDON HALL ;
JORROCKS'S JAUNTS AND JOLLITIES ; MR. SPONGE'S SPORTING TOUR ;
MR. FACEY ROMFORD'S HOUNDS ; PLAIN OR RINGLETS ?

Plays
Fcap. 8vo, 3s. 6d. net.

KISMET ; MILESTONES ; AN IDEAL HUSBAND ; THE WARE CASE ;
GENERAL POST ; THE GREAT ADVENTURE ; THE HONEYMOON ;
ACROSS THE BORDER (Crown 8vo) ; THE SAME STAR.

Fiction

Novels by RICHARD BAGOT, H. C. BAILEY, ARNOLD BENNETT, G. A.
BIRMINGHAM, MARJORIE BOWEN, EDGAR RICE BURROUGHS, G. K. CHES-
TERTON, JOSEPH CONRAD, DOROTHY CONYERS, MARIE CORELLI, BEATRICE
HARRADEN, R. S. HICHENS, ANTHONY HOPE, W. W. JACOBS, E. V. LUCAS,
STEPHEN McKENNA, LUCAS MALET, A. E. W. MASON, W. B. MAXWELL,
ARTHUR MORRISON, JOHN OXENHAM, SIR GILBERT PARKER, ALICE PERRIN,
EDEN PHILLPOTTS, RICHARD PRYCE, " Q.," W. PETT RIDGE, H. G. WELLS,
C. N. and A. M. WILLIAMSON, and P. G. WODEHOUSE.

A Complete List can be obtained on application.

Methuen's Half-Crown and Two Shilling Series

These are series of copyright books—fiction and general literature—
which have been such a popular success. If you obtain lists of them
you will see that they contain more books by distinguished writers than
any other series. You will find the volumes at all booksellers and on all
railway bookstalls.